SECRETS IN STONES

SECRETS IN STONES

Anna Shone

St. Martin's Press ≈ New York

Library of Congress Cataloging-in-Publication Data

Shone, Anna.
Secrets in stones / by Anna Shone.
p.   cm.
ISBN 0-312-14043-6 (hardcover)
1. France, Southern—Antiquities—Collection and
preservation—Fiction.   2. Private investigators—
France, Southern—Fiction.   3. Archaeologists—
France, Southern—Fiction.   I. Title.
PR9105.9.S55S43   1996
823'.914—dc20   95-26251   CIP

First published in Great Britain by
Constable & Company Ltd

First U.S. Edition: May 1996

10   9   8   7   6   5   4   3   2   1

1

Sir Hilary Compton skipped nimbly down the sweeping staircase of his Gloucestershire mansion with a sprightliness surprising for a man of his sixty-seven years and portliness of build.

He snatched his morning *Times* in mid-flight as it descended from the letter box to the marble floor of the spacious hallway. He tucked the journal under his arm and, for decency's sake, closed the last button on his knee-length dressing-gown. He had just showered and was wearing nothing beneath the heavy velour robe. Sir Hilary's great pleasure, now in his semi-retirement, was to enjoy a leisurely breakfast, his head buried in his beloved *Times*, his large, still energetic body constricted only by the soft fabric of his dressing-gown.

His life was now, thankfully, free of pressing timetables, lectures, research schedules, appointments in foreign capitals, TV deadlines and press conferences. He did not miss the demands on his time – it was wonderful to have time to oneself – but he did occasionally miss the celebrity, seeing his face on television, hearing his voice on the radio, reading quotations from his books in newspapers and magazines.

It was twenty years since he had discovered the now famous Bronze Age rock drawings in the Vallée des Prêtres in the Italian Alps which had made him the most celebrated archaeologist in the world at the time.

The passionate interest that the discovery had aroused in the media had long since died down. He was still, of course, the acknowledged expert on the engravings and was occasionally asked to speak at universities and archaeological seminars but he was no longer, he had reluctantly to admit, the household name he had been twenty years earlier. Perhaps now all that would change.

He entered the dining-room whistling cheerfully. He kissed his wife, Beatrice, breezily on the cheek and took his seat opposite her at the table.

He opened *The Times* at page two and there it was, in large bold capitals: his name, SIR HILARY COMPTON, a photograph of his bearded smiling face alongside.

'It's in, Bea,' he said happily. 'Shall I read it aloud?'

'Why not, dear,' said Beatrice. She smiled rather wistfully at her husband. He was still just a big boy, thrilled at discovery and excited as a small child would be at seeing his name in print.

Sir Hilary coughed and read aloud: '"The archaeologist, Sir Hilary Compton, will fly out this weekend to the Vallée des Prêtres in the Franco-Italian Alps, the site of his historic discovery of Bronze Age rock drawings in 1972. The purpose of his visit will be to authenticate further drawings discovered recently by a young British archaeologist, Oliver Hardcastle. Sir Hilary is the only living archaeologist qualified to judge the authenticity of the new drawings. Sir Hilary, who, during the twenty years since the first engravings were discovered, has not ceased his research into their significance, commented cautiously yesterday on the latest finds:

'"'I am very excited about these finds. Naturally I cannot, at this stage, make any professional comment on them – but I do believe they are going to be of quite astonishing importance and significance. The drawings, I believe, have been hidden for millennia under fallen rock and will therefore be of a clarity and precision never before seen in drawings exposed through the centuries to erosion and pollution. In addition, accompanying the new drawings is a hieroglyphic of a type unknown in Europe. European Bronze Age man had not, as far as we know, reached the intellectual and social sophistication of symbolic writing.

'"'If these inscriptions prove to date from the same period as the other drawings (that is to say, early and middle Bronze Age – 4000 to 2000 BC) then these finds will indeed be spectacular.'"'

The article went on to add that a book elucidating Sir Hilary's current thinking on the significance of the engravings in the Vallée des Prêtres was to be published in two months' time.

'What do you think, dear?' asked Beatrice. 'Do you think they might be genuine?'

'Impossible to say until I see them,' said Sir Hilary, 'but from what I know of the manner of their discovery it would seem highly improbable that they are fakes. The spot where they were found is inaccessible to the ordinary tourist and walker. The slab of rock that had hidden them was, it seems, struck by lightning. Much of the rock in the Vallée des Prêtres contains pockets of iron ore which of course attracts lightning and makes the valley particularly dangerous for walkers in the stormy season. Only an enthusiastic archaeologist such as this young Hardcastle would go out of his way to search for drawings in the inaccessible dangerous parts of the valley.'

'Won't it be dangerous for you then?' asked Beatrice worriedly. 'You'll have to climb up to see the drawings, won't you?'

Sir Hilary smiled at his wife, noting, as he had on several occasions recently, how wan and pale she was becoming with increasing age.

'Beatrice, my dear, you've forgotten that I've scoured every inch of that valley looking for drawings. There is no part that is inaccessible to me.'

'That was twenty years ago,' she said. 'You're no longer a young man, you know.'

For an instant a frown darkened Sir Hilary's features but was quickly chased away by his habitual cheerful smile.

'I may not be a young man,' he said jovially, 'but I'm a fit one – look at me.' He pulled open his bathrobe to expose his powerful, hairy chest and abdomen.

'No surplus fat there,' he boomed, patting his muscular stomach. 'No excess cholesterol in these arteries.' He thumped his chest, making Beatrice wince. 'I'm in perfect health. When was the last time I saw a quack – you tell me that, Bea?'

Beatrice, whose face had reddened slightly at the sight of her husband's nudity, smiled weakly back at him. He was right, of course – she couldn't remember the last time he had visited a doctor. She tore her eyes from the sight of his hairy stomach which he was now scratching exuberantly. She could feel the colour still rising in her cheeks. Beatrice had not yet accustomed herself to the unexpected and almost libertine personal habits that her husband had adopted since his retirement three years earlier from full-time work. She was still highly embarrassed by the increasing pleasure he took from wandering around their bedroom naked. She nursed a nagging anxiety that one day he might take it into his head to wander in an undressed state down to the dining-room for breakfast. She could imagine him laughing aloud and saying that he was free to do as he pleased in his own house – and he would be right, of course – but what on earth would the servants think? They would leave immediately and she would never be able to find replacements.

Beatrice Compton knew her husband well. Sir Hilary had been known and respected throughout the world for his qualities of intractability, single-mindedness and nonconformity to accepted views in the pursuit of his academic career, but such qualities could become transformed into obduracy, egoism and eccentricity in the privacy of the home.

Beatrice had no idea, now, how to express her concern to her husband about his behaviour. She had never in their married life had reason to criticise or contradict him. She had lived under his wing, raising their four sons, and happy to benefit from his financial and social success, but since the children had grown and left home Beatrice had found herself in a limbo world devoid of purpose. She felt sometimes that she was nothing more than a ghost of her former self – a phantom of a human being living in the shadow of her husband's glory and fading slowly away towards the inevitable void of old age and death.

Hilary, on the other hand, had come even more to life since his retirement – taking great pleasure in eating, drinking, walking with the dogs in the countryside and attending concerts. He even watched films and television now that he was working less and had adopted the curious habit on a Saturday afternoon of watching the local football team, Cheltenham Rangers, in their uncomfortable stadium on the outskirts of the town.

Lady Compton had always considered football as the sport of lower class thugs and was rather dubious about Sir Hilary's explanation that this new passion was a means of satisfying an unrealised dream of his childhood to become a football player. His parents too had considered the sport socially unacceptable and had forbidden him to participate in it.

Beatrice Compton had found herself married, unexpectedly, to a football fan – no, more than that, to a football fanatic!

Hilary had become, it seemed to her, more *alive* as he got older, more energetic, more enthusiastic about life – but not, she reflected sometimes with anguish, about *her*. He treated her, as he always had, with the requisite degree of respect and affection that respectable husbands showed their wives but she had never received from him during the long years of their marriage the *passion* that he felt for everything else in his life – no, more than that, the passion that he felt for life itself. Perhaps he considered that she was only half alive – perhaps, she thought bitterly to herself, he was right.

Sir Hilary glanced over at his wife as he turned the pages of his newspaper. He was right, she did look particularly pale this morning – almost like a ghost, as if she were fading away.

He reached over the table and patted her hand affectionately.

'I have an idea, Bea,' he said. 'You can come with me to the valley – see these new engravings. Now, isn't that a splendid idea?'

'What?' she asked incredulously. 'Me? Climb up a mountain?'

'Yes, why not? The mountain air and the exercise will make a new woman of you. What do you say, Bea?' He beamed over at her, his grey eyes sparkling.

'Well,' she said hesitantly, 'if you think I could do it . . .'

Sir Hilary picked up the brass bell that stood on the table to summon the housekeeper. The woman came immediately.

'Get out the spare haversack, Mrs McGhee,' he declared triumphantly, 'and Lady Compton's walking boots. You'll find them at the back of the locker in the lobby. Lady Compton is accompanying me to the Alps.'

Mrs McGhee, a small elderly woman who had been in the Comptons' service for thirty years, stood rooted to the spot, a flush rising from her neck to her temples.

'Well?' said Sir Hilary, looking enquiringly up at her. Then his eyes followed the direction of her gaze, which was fixed with a kind of petrified embarrassment on to his naked torso.

Beatrice gazed stricken at her husband as he closed his robe with a flourish. Then he laughed, a great booming bellow of hilarity, as the horrified housekeeper turned and fled from the room.

2

'Bedad, Mrs Percival, if you could see me tomorrow you wouldn't know me!'

Mrs Percival, a stout, buxom woman in her fifties, raised an eyebrow and cast a quizzical glance over one shoulder at her employer. In that peculiar Irish way of his, Ulysses Finnegan Donaghue, London's most reputed private detective, could be infuriatingly incomprehensible at times.

She turned from the stove and placed two poached eggs on to Donaghue's buttered wholewheat toast.

'And why should that be, Mr Donaghue?' she asked drily.

'Because at this time tomorrow . . .' He glanced at his watch, which read nine thirty, '. . . I'll be fairly skipping up and down mountains . . . nimble as a mountain goat . . . fairly skipping I tell you, bearing stout walking shoes on my feet and a haversack on my back. Now, did you ever see me dressed like that, Mrs Percival?'

'Skipping, my eye!' grumbled Mrs Percival. 'Nimble as a goat! More like crawling up on all fours with that weight you're carrying.' She eyed Donaghue's ample midriff with a ponderous disdain.

'It's not a matter of weight, Mrs Percival,' said Donaghue authoritatively. 'When it comes to climbing mountains it's a question only of stamina.'

He lifted a short stout leg from under the table and, rolling his cotton slacks up to the knee, held out a hairy left calf for his housekeeper's inspection.

'Look at the muscle on that leg, Mrs P,' he said proudly. 'As solid as a rock and bursting with vigour. I have not been walking to work for the past four weeks for nothing. I'm in fine fettle for climbing any number of mountains . . . at least my legs are, and those are the vehicles that will be carrying me up, are they not? You don't need to have bulging biceps and a flat stomach to walk now, do you?'

'Mr Donaghue,' said Mrs Percival, her tone not without a hint of scorn, 'you're not trying to tell me that walking two miles across Hampstead Heath every day is the same thing as climbing them Alps or wherever it is you're going?'

'Walking two miles horizontally and two miles vertically are much the same thing,' countered Donaghue. 'It is only, as I said, a question of stamina. Walking, Mrs P, is the one sport that is not the prerogative of the young. You yourself could climb the Matterhorn if you put your mind to it.'

Mrs Percival tutted irritably at the gross stupidity of Donaghue's suggestion.

'What I don't understand,' she said as she poured coffee into his cup, 'is why you don't climb one of our English mountains instead of risking life and limb flying off to God knows where. There are mountains in Scotland, you know, and in Wales.'

Donaghue declined to point out that Scottish and Welsh mountains were not in fact English. Mrs Percival had never, as far as he had discovered in the long years that he had employed her, resolved her confusion about the terms 'English' and 'British'. As far as Mrs Percival was concerned the one meant the other.

'To my knowledge, Mrs Percival, no mountains in the British Isles bear engravings made by our prehistoric ancestors.'

'Is that why you're going to them Alps, then?' asked Mrs Percival in great surprise. 'To look at drawings on rocks?'

'Absolutely!' replied Donaghue, beaming broadly.

'It takes all sorts,' said Mrs Percival in incredulity. 'Me, I'd rather go to Bingo.'

It takes all sorts, Donaghue agreed silently to himself. He pondered for a moment on the absolute simplicity of Mrs Percival's world view before saying, 'Put an extra cup out, Mrs P. I do believe that's Bridget's 2CV pulling up outside.'

An expression of absolute disapproval crossed Mrs Percival's ruddy face at her employer's words but she set her lips tight and said nothing as the door bell rang and a cheerful girl's voice called out, 'Don't worry, it isn't the milkman for his bill. You can come out of hiding, Mr Donaghue. It's me, Bridget!'

Mrs Percival laid out a second cup and saucer as the door opened to admit Donaghue's quite stunningly beautiful secretary, Bridget, who stood enshrined in the light from the doorway, the vision setting Mrs Percival's lips just a fraction

11

tighter. Mrs Percival didn't approve at all of the idea of her employer going off on a weekend trip with his secretary, a girl half his age and engaged to be married on top of that.

Donaghue gazed admiringly at Bridget, who was wearing her travelling outfit of tight jeans that appeared to have been rolled over her long shapely legs and a cotton T-shirt that revealed her slender arms. Her mass of red corkscrew curls hung over her shoulders and cascaded down her back.

A delightful change, Donaghue mused to himself, after the rather drab suits that Bridget wore to work.

Donaghue, too, had misgivings about going on this trek with his secretary but he had not been able to refuse her when she had implored him to take her along. She just adored walking, she'd said, and was fascinated by cave drawings. Tim, her fiancé, detested mountain trekking so she had little time to indulge in the pastime.

'Look at me,' she had said two days earlier at the office, as she ingenuously lifted her skirt to show her employer the musculature of her legs. 'With legs like that I'm made for walking, wouldn't you agree with that, Mr Donaghue?'

Donaghue, tearing his eyes modestly from the splendour of Bridget's legs, could only agree. He had found himself subsequently with no reason to refuse her request. Fortunately his reputation would be safeguarded by the fact that Bridget was not to be his sole companion on the trip. The idea of the four-day trek to the Italian Alps had been the brainchild of his oldest and closest friend, Clothilde Blanche, whose passion was walking and whose disdain for her friend's largely sedentary lifestyle matched that of Mrs Percival, if not in frequency then certainly in fervour.

'Walking in the Alps will broaden your mind and reduce your midriff,' she had promised when she had insisted that he accompany her. 'Wisdom and unpolluted air – the nectar and ambrosia of middle age.'

Donaghue had been pleased to welcome Bridget along when she had asked. His youthful secretary never reminded him of his advancing age.

Bridget, smiling cheerfully at Mrs Percival, took her seat at the table, the material of her jeans stretching perilously over her

12

rounded bottom. Mrs Percival served the girl coffee, eyeing her warily.

'How's your fiancé, Miss Kilkenny?' she asked somewhat caustically.

'I really don't know, Mrs Percival,' Bridget replied brightly. 'He's crossing the Sahara in a jeep at the moment. I haven't heard from him for three weeks. But I'm not worried – I don't suppose they have post offices in the middle of the Sahara.' Bridget tittered and Donaghue coughed in mild embarrassment. Somewhere, deep down in the detective's unconscious, lurked a secret guilty wish that Bridget's tall architect fiancé, Tim, would one day fail to return from the life-imperilling car rallies that he took part in twice a year and on which Bridget refused to accompany him. Bridget shared with her employer a profound fear of travelling at speed in flimsy-sided vehicles. Like him, she felt a great deal more secure on her own two feet.

It occurred to Donaghue in moments of reverie that despite their difference in age, height and physical attractiveness, he and Bridget might have a great deal in common.

Mrs Percival returned to the cooker which she proceeded to clean with a venomous vigour, her lack of response to Bridget's answer a clear indication of her contempt for the extraordinary indifference with which modern young people related to each other.

'What's that, Bridget?' asked Donaghue as his secretary idly turned the pages of a small booklet that she had taken from her jeans pocket. She held it up for Donaghue to look at.

'It's just a little book I picked up from the local library on the engravings we're going to see. It's a guide to the site and an explanation of the significance of the drawings – by Sir Hilary Compton.'

'Compton?' said Donaghue. 'I do believe I've heard of him. The name rings a bell.'

'"Sir Hilary Compton,"' said Bridget, reading from the booklet, '"the acknowledged expert in the field of European Bronze Age rock drawings, particularly those found in the Vallée des Prêtres in the Franco-Italian Alps."' She handed the booklet over to Donaghue. 'Sir Hilary has spent the last twenty years researching and dating the engravings. He has the archaeological world up in arms at the moment with his current theory that the drawings were not made for magical and religious purposes as the experts have always believed they were.'

'What does he believe, then?' asked Donaghue.

'He believes that they were in all probability the graffiti of the day with no more significance than the graffiti we see on city walls today. His ideas have caused a great deal of controversy but the problem might soon be resolved. Satellite photos have revealed more drawings beneath layers of oxide and lichen. At the same time a young British archaeologist has recently discovered drawings in a part of the valley were nobody expected to find them – so these discoveries should shed some light on the question of the origin of the engravings.'

Donaghue, who had not bothered to research the site he was going to visit (knowing full well that his friend Clothilde would have done so on his behalf), looked with unabashed admiration at his secretary.

'Have you always been interested in rock drawings?' he asked a little sheepishly. He had generally assumed that Bridget spent her time outside hours of work gyrating her hips in discos or lounging in the passenger seat of her fiancé, Tim's, sports car.

Bridget's almond-shaped green eyes widened with enthusiasm. 'I just love everything that's old,' she said fervently. 'I suppose it's because I'm young. The more ancient it is the more it fascinates me.'

She smiled at Donaghue, a gay ingenuous smile that lit up her freckled face. Donaghue's eyes misted over. Did that mean – could it possibly be that Bridget might some day become fascinated by him?

He quickly pulled himself together, smiling at her in his habitual avuncular manner. He stood up, running his fingers through his mass of unruly hair in an attempt at reducing it to some semblance of order.

'Drink up, Bridget,' he said. 'We'll have to get going – it's a long way to Gatwick in that 2CV of yours. And God help us if we miss our rendezvous with Clothilde. The Bard, with great compassion, once said that the quality of mercy was not strained . . .' Donaghue's leathery monkey-like features creased into a boyish grin, '. . . but when it comes to punctuality the quality of Clothilde's mercy can be put severely to the test.'

14

3

Dr Clothilde Blanche, retired plastic surgeon, inveterate walker and lifelong friend of Ulysses F. Donaghue, packed her rucksack with the efficiency and competence of the practised trekker: change of underwear, light sweater, rubberised cape, torch, Swiss army knife, first-aid kit, boiled sweets, water gourd and change of shoes – no need for tents and sleeping bags as they would be sleeping in a refuge, a kind of primitive hostel in the valley itself which provided dormitory beds, washing facilities and two good meals.

For this trip to the Vallée des Prêtres she had invested in a rigid back support for her rucksack, which after several years of wear and tear was beginning to droop. She had ensured that the metal support was plastic-covered – the valley was notorious for its late summer storms which could appear quite literally out of a clear blue sky, taking the unfortunate walker by surprise with their power and savagery.

This weekend cloudless skies and sunshine had been promised but Clothilde was going to take no chances with a metal back support. She must remember, before they set off walking, to check Donaghue's young secretary for metal hair-pins and buckles. Girls of that age liked to glitter: Clothilde could not for the life of her imagine why. She had, in the course of her walking life, seen dozens of such young girls traipsing around mountains scintillating like Christmas trees with their dangling ear-rings and jangling bracelets. In the Vallée des Prêtres, caught in one of its legendary storms, a girl jingling with metal jewellery would be a sitting target for the lightning that was, when viewed from the safety of a rubberised body cape, quite awesome in its power and beauty.

She glanced at her watch – four fifteen. She had arranged to meet Donaghue and his secretary here at the village inn where they would spend the night before setting off early the following morning for the three-hour climb up the valley.

Donaghue had obstinately refused her offer to meet him at the airport at Nice and had insisted that Bridget drive them in a hired 2CV. It would take them, she calculated, at the snail's speed that Bridget drove, three hours to cover the seventy-kilometre journey. She, Clothilde, would have got them here in twenty minutes. Clothilde tutted irritably. Donaghue, formidably intelligent though he was, was handicapped by an utterly irrational fear of speed which he had evidently imparted to his secretary – or perhaps, Clothilde reflected, such a fear was a national characteristic of the Irish. The two were of the same eccentric race, after all.

Clothilde had never been able to convince her friend Donaghue that speed was time and time was life. Donaghue's argument that speed could curtail life was, she considered, shortsighted: anything, particularly the habit of sitting safely and securely on one's backside for most of one's life, could curtail life – as Clothilde frequently reminded Donaghue when criticising him for his sedentary lifestyle.

She glanced at her watch again. The plane had arrived at two fifteen. They were not likely to arrive before five. She had time to study her literature on the engravings of the Vallée des Prêtres.

She opened the guidebook she had bought in the village newsagent's. The booklet, with an introduction written by the engravings expert, Sir Hilary Compton, had been translated into French. She had bought an English language version for Donaghue.

4

A new black XJS pulled up beside the mountain lake that marked the start of the walk up to the Vallée des Prêtres. A young man climbed out, pulling his lightweight rucksack from the passenger seat, then locked the car, glancing at his reflection in the Jaguar's glossy side door. There was no doubt about it – he looked pretty good in shorts and walking boots. The long trek up and down from the site had hardened the muscles of his thighs so that when contracted they were as hard as the rocks he was going to pore over for the next few days.

Oliver Hardcastle had remained at the site since his discovery a week before of the sensational new Bronze Age engravings and had made a point of walking up and down the 1500-metre ascent each day for the firmness it afforded his abdomen and thighs.

Having adjusted his rucksack he stretched, arching his back, and breathed in the pure morning air. He leaned over the wall that bordered the lake and gazed appreciatively at the glassy green surface of the water.

A smile played on his lips, lending to his bronzed, handsome face the insouciant expression of a child at play. His cap of fair hair, ruffled by the morning breeze, fell back into its carefully coiffured order.

Oliver Hardcastle was, and he knew it, an extraordinarily good-looking man. He was also at the prime of his life – thirty years of age and already known and respected in his profession. His discovery of the new drawings would, once they were authenticated, give him, overnight, the celebrity of Sir Hilary Compton himself. He might even receive a knighthood – and all that at thirty years of age! He smiled again. Everything – this beautiful lake, these magnificent mountains, the bright morning sunshine, his memories of the night before – all conspired to make him feel on top of the world.

He felt his body suffused by a sudden overwhelming sensation of power, of his own charismatic force. He was at his peak of strength and beauty; his career would soon reach its pinnacle; his power over women was absolute.

The woman he had spent the night with at the nearby Italian town of Ventimiglia had been powerless to resist him – as they all were, from the plainest to the most beautiful. What had she said her name was? Marie Pierre, Marie Claire . . . Marie something or other. She had been French and reasonably good-looking – no, give her credit, she'd been quite beautiful – but mediocre in bed. But then Oliver Hardcastle had yet to meet a woman whom he considered his equal in sexual competence and technique. Perhaps he should, from time to time, seduce an older, more mature woman – they would probably be less inhibited. But on the other hand, he reflected, an older woman might be domineering, she might want to control him. The smile disappeared from his boyish face. Oliver Hardcastle didn't like the idea of anyone, man or woman, attempting to control him.

Still, he thought cheerfully as he turned his head at the sound of a passing car, an older woman might make an interesting challenge.

The car flashed past at phenomenal speed, a long low blur of brilliant red, then screeched to a halt fifty metres or so further up the narrow road. The driver reversed the sleek Italian two-seater with quite astonishing speed and accuracy to within a centimetre of the wall that bordered the lake, and stepped out of the car.

An older woman, he noted with some amusement as she leaned over the driver's seat to pick up her walking equipment. But when she stood up and turned in his direction to scan the road, he saw with some disappointment that she was quite disconcertingly ugly – the ugliest woman in fact that he had ever seen.

He realised with embarrassment that she was nodding at him in polite acknowledgement of his sole presence on the road and he smiled respectfully back. She stepped forward and he was struck by the awful thought that she might be coming over to speak to him.

To his relief the attention of both was diverted by the approach of a third car – this time a rather shabby 2CV that struggled slowly up the slight inclination that led to the lake.

Oliver leaned back against the wall and watched the progress of the ridiculous car with feigned interest – anything to avoid eye contact with the old crow in the Ferrari. In his experience single women walkers, particularly ugly ones, always wanted to *talk*.

As the car approached him his interest suddenly became real. His head jerked forward involuntarily. The girl driving the car! He had never in his life seen a girl as beautiful as this one. His brain registered somewhere on the periphery of his conscious-ness that she was in the company of a man but dismissed the perception as irrelevant: the man was obviously her father or uncle.

His head swivelled to the right as the 2CV struggled on up to the Ferrari and parked in front of it.

In great fascination Oliver watched the occupants gather their equipment together and climb out of the car. For a few seconds he lost all of his habitual self-possession and leaned forward, craning his neck, to gaze at the girl; she had stood up to her full extraordinary height and appeared even more magnificent standing than she had when sitting at the wheel of her nonsensical car.

The short, rather unkempt little man at her side was evidently not the girl's father nor in any way related to her. Two such opposing physical types could not possibly have come from the same genetic stock.

He watched with interest as the ugly woman from the Ferrari approached the couple, then, with their rucksacks secured, the three moved towards him to take the mountain path that led up to the site of the engravings.

He gazed with fascination at the curious trio as they approached him. All three nodded, smiling at him as they passed, but his gaze was fixed avidly on the figure of the girl. Her mass of copper curls glinted in the morning sunshine beneath the peaked cap that restrained them, and her long legs in their green cotton shorts were the most beautiful he had seen on any woman before.

'Interesting,' he murmured to himself as they took the path and disappeared from sight around the first bend. He leaned back against the wall, giving them a few minutes' head start, then set off up the track behind them.

Clothilde Blanche, a veteran walker, liked to start a long steep ascent at a brisk pace. The first half-hour, she knew, was always the most difficult but once one got into one's stride the climbing became effortless. So she set off up the path to the Vallée des Prêtres at a fairly rapid pace. Bridget, on her long legs, strode easily alongside her but Donaghue, whose short legs had not (as his housekeeper Mrs Percival had so rightly pointed out) become accustomed, by his daily trek across Hampstead Heath, to walking upwards, lagged, puffing heavily, behind the two women.

'As you insist on smoking your foul-smelling cigars,' Clothilde called to him over her shoulder, 'then you have to take the consequences. How can you expect lungs poisoned by tobacco fumes to perform their function of providing oxygen to the muscles? It's like putting the contents of your dustbin into your petrol tank and expecting the car to go!'

19

She slowed her pace to allow Donaghue to catch up with her.

'Look at you, Ulysses,' she chided. 'You're huffing and puffing like a steam engine and you haven't even warmed up yet. You're not getting enough oxygen in those nicotine-lined bronchia of yours. On top of that the air is rarefied at this altitude and will be even rarer when we reach the top. So you've got to learn to breathe correctly.'

She pulled him to a halt and placed her coarse mottled hand on his solid rounded chest.

'Now breathe in deeply,' she commanded, 'and then let your breath out sharply – blow it out as if you're blowing out a candle.'

Donaghue reluctantly obeyed her instructions, casting an anxious eye behind him in case the young man who'd been standing at the lakeside should appear suddenly around the bend in the path.

'That's right,' said Clothilde. 'Now inhale and expire regularly like that. Concentrate on your breathing and forget the ache in your legs. You'll find that after a few minutes the oxygen will actually reach your muscles and your legs will carry you onwards and upwards as if they didn't even belong to you . . . like that!'

She gazed admiringly as the young man from the road below strode past them on his tanned muscular legs with a facility that made Donaghue wince with embarrassment at his breathless state and Bridget gape with incredulity.

The young man bade them good morning as he passed and continued nonchalantly on up the path as if he were walking along a flat suburban street.

'Now there's a fit young man,' said Clothilde admiringly.

'And incredibly good-looking,' added Bridget. 'English as well.'

'Yes,' said Clothilde. 'He has that indefinable allure of class that only fair-haired Anglo-Saxons possess.'

'Obviously a brain surgeon and Nobel prize-winner as well,' Donaghue muttered dourly and the two women looked at him in surprise.

Clothilde took Donaghue's arm and pulled him along beside her.

'Ulysses Donaghue,' she said, her face creasing, in imitation of a concertina, into one of her rare smiles, 'I do believe you're jealous.'

Donaghue spluttered. 'Jealous? Me? There's not a jealous bone in my body – and never has been.'

'Nor in mine,' said Bridget brightly. 'I refuse absolutely to demean myself to jealousy. As far as I'm concerned it's a negative state that only ever damages the person in it. I don't see any point in indulging in something that will cause me harm.'

'Unlike Ulysses here,' said Clothilde drily, 'who smokes, damaging his physical health, and now manifests envy of the young and fit thereby impairing his emotional equilibrium.'

Donaghue smiled wanly at Clothilde.

'"Speak of me as I am,"' he said, '"of one that loved not wisely but too well – of one not easily jealous but, being wrought, perplex'd in the extreme" . . . Othello,' he added by way of an explanation, 'after he had murdered his wife.'

'Oh, how I cried when I saw that scene,' exclaimed Bridget. 'What a marvellous play it was.'

'Are you fond of the Bard then, Bridget?' asked Donaghue in surprise.

'I only like his plays about love and passion,' she said. 'I'm not too keen on the ones about the power of kings – the Henrys and all that. I have to admit that they make me fall asleep.'

Donaghue regarded Bridget curiously. There really was more to his secretary than had ever met his eye in the three years that she had worked for him.

He walked thoughtfully a few paces behind the two women, making sure that his breathing was deep and regular enough to satisfy Dr Blanche's requirements.

Was it possible, he asked himself, that Clothilde was right? Was he, without realising it, jealous of the young? He had never consciously felt such a sentiment before – and if so, why? He found himself staring at Bridget's slender back and long shapely legs. Was it perhaps because of his new-found admiration for his secretary? He dismissed the notion as absurd.

I am, he said to himself, repeating the words of the Moor, one not easily jealous but being wrought, perplex'd in the extreme.

That's it, he told himself, it's perplexed that I am, not jealous at all, merely perplexed. He concentrated on his breathing as

Clothilde had instructed him and put all foolish notions of envy out of his mind.

Oliver Hardcastle, striding effortlessly up the path, found it difficult to put from his mind the vision of the red-haired girl with the beautiful slanted eyes and shapely legs. She was obviously British – they had been speaking English together – but he found it difficult to even hazard a guess as to what a superb girl like that was doing with the odd older couple who accompanied her.

Lost in his reverie he almost collided, on turning a sharp bend, with a young couple who had stopped to take photos of the spectacular view of the valley below.

Muttering an apology, he continued hurriedly on his way, spotting, to his annoyance, another figure which was plodding with great difficulty up the steep incline before him. He loped along and overtook the walker, who proved to be an overweight young man and quite obviously American from his sandy crew-cut, checked shirt and jeans that fitted badly over the rump.

Hardcastle bounced ahead until he had covered a sufficient distance to make it impossible for those behind to overtake him then slowed his pace, his tanned face darkened by a frown. He had not expected quite so many tourists at this time of the year. In fact he had counted on there being none at all. Few walkers came to the Vallée des Prêtres after the first week of August. The unexpected and ferocious storms for which the valley was notorious, particularly in autumn, daunted even the most intrepid trekkers. It was really quite irritating having all these walkers around – he'd been hoping for a quiet four days in the company of Sir Hilary Compton and one or two fellow archaeologists. Of course, one of the people he had passed could have been a journalist – perhaps the one with the camera. It wouldn't have been so bad, he thought, if they'd all been women – like the redhead. Now that, perhaps, he wouldn't have minded at all.

Jim Baxter placed his camera carefully back into its bag and frowned crossly at the departing back of the hasty maniac who'd just almost knocked him over the precipitous edge of the path.

'Bloody idiot,' he muttered as he carefully snapped shut the clasp of his camera case. 'Some people think they own the whole bloody world!'

The girl beside him looked anxiously from one to the other. Meryss Jones, an archaeology student from Cardiff, had met Jim at the bottom of the path and had gratefully accepted his invitation to accompany him up to the valley.

With his straggly, rather outdated beard and rimless spectacles, Jim was not what Meryss could have called an attractive young man – but then she was no beauty herself. A persistent acne – due, she knew, to an indulgence for jam doughnuts that she was powerless to control – marred what might have been a pale but pleasing English complexion. The lankness of her hair she had attempted to redeem with a home perm that had resulted in an uncontrollable frizz. The close set of her eyes was unredeemable, as was the abnormal width of her hips and the thickness of her ankles. Her eyes were, fortunately, shortsighted, so she was able to conceal them with her glasses – but her other major imperfections were undisguisable.

Meryss had occasionally indulged in dreams of a surgical remodelling of her entire physical structure, but had accepted stoically that such fantasies could be realised only by superstars of the screen and not by a penniless twenty-one-year-old student of archaeology. She was grateful therefore for any attention she received from a member of the opposite sex.

She glanced from the fleeting vision of the Superwalker's legs to Jim, whose pale hairy calves were visible beneath baggy knee-length colonial shorts. There was no comparison, of course – but then, she corrected herself, one shouldn't compare. She glanced at her companion's morose profile as they resumed their ascent. He would, she decided, look a lot better without the beard.

'Are the public really interested in archaeological finds?' she asked conversationally. 'I wouldn't have thought it was exactly headline news.'

Baxter smiled grimly. 'It wouldn't ever get into the tabloids,' he said. 'Can you imagine your average tabloid reader poring over a speech by Sir Hilary Compton? But it can make page two in the more serious papers. Sensational finds can become nine-day wonders and hit the headlines, like the drawings in this valley when they were first discovered twenty years ago.'

'I take it yours is a serious newspaper then,' said Meryss.

'You don't imagine that I'd work for anything else, do you?' said Baxter indignantly.

Meryss thought but didn't say that she couldn't imagine him working for anything other than a very serious, very sober English newspaper.

'Do you think these finds will receive the same attention as the originals?' she asked.

'It's possible,' said Jim cautiously. 'One never knows. My newspaper is certainly interested in them. And you . . .?' he asked, turning to speak to her. He stopped in mid-sentence, finding himself blinking rapidly as her eye caught his and a thought, an extraordinary wild and crazy thought, flashed through his mind, startling him with its indecency. He could, if he wanted to, grab this girl and kiss her right there and then on the mountain path – no one in the world would see . . .

Meryss was looking at him curiously.

'And I . . .?' she queried, noting as she spoke how much nicer he looked when his perpetual frown was replaced, as it was now, by an expression of ingenuous surprise.

The frown returned as rapidly as it had disappeared and he turned his head quickly to address his boots as he spoke.

'I . . . I just wanted to know if you have any opinion on the finds – as a student in the field, I mean. Do you think it's possible that they could be fakes, for instance?'

'I think it highly unlikely, now that the site is protected, that anyone could make fake engravings and not be seen doing it. The sites of the drawings are only accessible through guided visits and are regularly patrolled for vandals in the summer season. Personally I'm very excited about them, which is why I've come. I'm intrigued by the fact that there are hieroglyphics with these drawings. I have a personal theory that European Bronze Age man did write but considered that communication by language was inferior to, less efficient than, communication through art. I'm not so sure that they weren't right. No matter how refined our language becomes we still have difficulty making ourselves mutually understood. I am also intrigued by Sir Hilary Compton's latest ideas on the significance of the drawings – that they might be nothing more than graffiti. I take it you've read up a bit on that?'

'A bit,' said Baxter dourly.

'Don't you find it all terribly exciting?' said Meryss, whose grey eyes behind her spectacles had lit up.

Jim, who found it scarcely credible that anyone, two or three millennia hence, might find excitement in reading the reports he made for his sober journal, found equally little excitement in regarding what he considered the banal communications of primitive man. So, primitive man believed that the bull who pulled his wooden plough was a demi-god – nowadays half the populations of so-called advanced civilisations believed that the people they saw in soap operas on the TV were real! As far as Baxter was concerned the human race had made little intellectual progress since the Bronze Age.

He didn't say as much to Meryss, who was evidently extremely enthusiastic about her chosen field of study.

Admirable, he thought, looking at her gloomily. An admirable optimism – an admirable girl all round.

'I can see you're not particularly enthusiastic about this assignment,' said Meryss.

'You can say that again,' said Jim. 'I'm an investigative journalist, not a specialist in ancient history. I'm only doing this job as a replacement for a colleague.' He turned to look at her, a curious gleam glittering in his eye. 'My mission', he said fiercely, 'is to weed out all the corrupt and rotten maggots that infest the power structure, not to spend my valuable time listening to over-glamourised eggheads like that Hardcastle . . .' He indicated with a furious nod of his head the empty path ahead, '. . . waffling on about what primitive man thought about his bull and its power of fertility. I am concerned about the present, about the living, not the past and all its millions of dead and departed.'

Meryss looked at Jim, surprised by the tone of anger in his voice.

'You're very bitter about something, aren't you, Jim?' she said softly.

'Bitter?' he said, his face reddening. 'Of course I'm bitter. You've only got to open your eyes and look around you. You'd have to be deaf, dumb and blind to live in this corrupt and rotten world and not be bitter!'

'Me,' said Meryss cheerfully, 'I'd rather turn a blind eye to

25

what I don't like to see – pretend that it doesn't exist. That way I can get on happily with my own life.'

'We are opposite, then,' said Baxter glumly. 'We see life from entirely opposing points of view.'

And opposites, thought Meryss happily, often attract.

Herman Browning, panting heavily from the strain of carrying his heavy bulk up the steep path, glanced humorously at the departing back of the man who had overtaken him. He had recognised him as the English archaeologist Oliver Hardcastle, who had discovered the new drawings in the valley.

Arrogant British, Browning thought – hadn't even had the decency to stop and say hello. Probably thought he'd taken Compton's place already at the top of their professional ladder, and the drawings hadn't even been authenticated yet. But Oliver Hardcastle might find himself brought down a peg or two in the very near future. He, Herman Browning, had a trick or two up his sleeve. He had a shrewd idea about the origin of these new drawings. He hadn't been given a chair at one of America's most prestigious universities at the age of thirty for nothing. He had spent the last five years researching the language of Bronze Age man and was confident that he knew more than anyone else, even Hilary Compton himself, about the communication skills of primitive man. Wouldn't the Big Guys be in for a shock when an unknown college professor pipped them at their intellectual post?

Browning's bland baby face broke into a smile – Hardcastle had his mug in all the papers because he'd stumbled over a few broken rocks and because he looked like a goddamned film star! It was not beyond the bounds of imagination that Hardcastle had faked the drawings himself and hacked out a few meaningless hieroglyphics to add to the sensationalism of the find. Compton, for all his age and repute, would not be qualified to analyse the hieroglyphics. Only he, Browning, was qualified to do that.

The climbing path was getting steeper as it neared the top. He panted, his breath coming in irregular spasms. Goddamn it – he should have cut down on the pepperoni sandwiches and pistachio ice-cream that had been his staple diet during the long years of his research. But a few treks up and down this mountain, he thought, grinning at the idea, and he'd be as fit and trim as that goddamned arrogant bum Hardcastle.

5

Michou Santinelli, the proprietress of the valley's refuge, hummed happily to herself as she dusted and tidied the English archaeologist's room. The archaeologists were housed in a well-appointed lodge that stood at a right angle to the main refuge building so that the whole structure formed an L shape.

The lodge comprised four double bedrooms and a small common room. It was reserved exclusively for the archaeologists and anthropologists who came to study the rock drawings in the valley. The main two-storeyed refuge building contained communal dormitories on the first floor and a dining-room, common room and showers on the ground floor. The archaeologists ate with the tourists and guides in the refuge dining-room. It was not possible in such a remote spot to provide a special cuisine for the more honoured guests.

During the busy months of June and July Michou and her husband Mario employed students from the nearby university of Nice to carry out the menial tasks of cleaning and washing up – but the season was now over and for this unexpected weekend Michou had to do all the tiresome chores herself. Still, there were some compensations . . . She had looked forward this morning to coming into the English archaeologist's room. Michou had fallen in love with the handsome Oliver Hardcastle as soon as she had seen him when he had arrived a week before.

She glanced at herself in his wardrobe mirror and preened. She was still, at forty, an attractive woman, if a little top heavy – but then few men minded that. Her Mario certainly didn't. She was sure the Englishman would be no exception. It was rare to have such a good-looking man at the refuge; walkers tended to be a dreary lot on the whole. And this weekend, to make up for the extra work, there were two extremely attractive men at the refuge. The Italian archaeologist – or was he an anthropologist? –

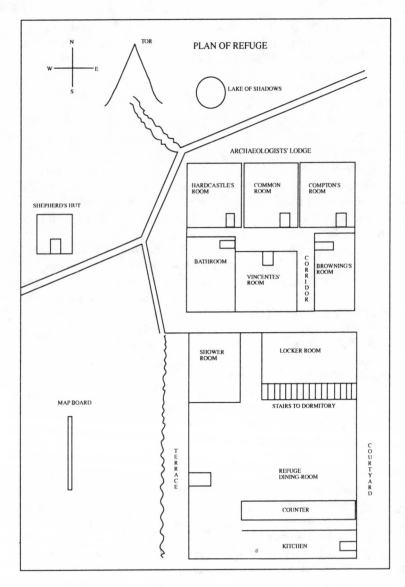

PLAN OF REFUGE

Dr Vincente was certainly as good-looking as the Englishman but he was Italian, and Michou knew Italian men well. After all, she had been married to one for twenty years. She loved her Mario, there was no doubt about that, but if she had the choice over again she'd go for the northern type – she'd heard they were more reasonable and not nearly as jealous as the Mediterranean males.

She dusted the shelves and restacked a pile of tools that lay on the floor in an untidy heap. They had some peculiar-looking implements, those researchers, she thought to herself as she placed a rectangular object that was unrecognisable to her next to a set of magnifyng glasses. She quickly straightened the bed cover then picked up the pillow on which Oliver Hardcastle had lain his handsome head and, hugging it to her ample bosom, waltzed it around the room.

The door to the room opened and Michou found herself gazing in great embarrassment at the Englishman, who stood smiling at her in the doorway.

'*Excusez moi, excusez moi*,' she mumbled, her broad face turning crimson. 'I was feeling happy this morning – I wanted to dance.'

An older woman, Hardcastle mused to himself, and a not altogether unattractive one – a Frenchwoman at that. He was well aware that Frenchwomen were far less inhibited sexually than their English counterparts.

She quickly replaced the pillow, patting it into shape, and edged her way past him through the doorway. He remained where he was, one arm resting nonchalantly against the door jamb.

'Would that I were the pillow,' he whispered in French as she squeezed past him under his outstretched arm. He stood smiling reflectively in the doorway as she ran from the room. He could seduce her whenever he wished. He might do so if he had the time. Then the smile vanished as he noticed the newly tidied shelves in his room. The damned woman had messed with his tools. He'd have to tell her – nicely, of course – that she wasn't under any circumstances to touch his belongings.

From the refuge dining-room a tenor voice sang out in imitation of Luciano Pavarotti. The voice, which was very slightly off key, belonged to Mario Santinelli, husband of Michou and keeper of the refuge. As he sang out each stanza the couple's parrot, Petrocelli, which was standing on its perch at the end of the counter, repeated the song with the exact deflection from key as its master. Had Mario sung in tune Petrocelli would have done so too. Petrocelli was a master of imitation among parrots.

The door which led to the outside terrace had been flung open as the midday temperatures were high, and Mario's voice soared out into the pure cloudless sky of the valley beyond. When the sun shone as it did today and no storms lurked on the horizon, Mario loved the Vallée des Prêtres. In the sunshine the austerity of the peaks that ringed the valley and the aridity of its treeless rocks took on a light, almost serene aspect in astonishing contrast to the dark and oppressive gloom that enveloped it during its notorious storms. But today the weather was wonderful, and when the weather was wonderful Mario felt wonderful. And when Mario felt wonderful he had to sing. So he sang out joyfully as he worked.

He was preparing a simple lunch of bread, cheese and cold meats. His apron was dusted with the flour of the freshly baked bread, as was his bushy moustache. Under his apron he wore a sleeveless T-shirt which revealed powerful shoulders and biceps. Mario weight-trained every day, even during the two months they spent in the refuge; he was approaching that age when body weight started to change location and Mario wasn't going to end up with spindly legs and a paunch if he could help it. He wasn't going to lose his strength either. As far as he was concerned, a man should remain strong even in old age – it was only a question of training and discipline.

He hummed the melody of an Italian love song as he laid out the buffet lunch on the counter that separated the kitchen from the dining-room. The walkers who had reserved beds would arrive by midday. It took just under three hours to walk up from the lake and they would all welcome a meal, no matter how simple it was, when they arrived.

Mario had been as surprised as his wife, Michou, at the number of reservations they had received for this weekend. He had expected only archaeologists and anthropologists but in addition there were half a dozen tourists – unusual so late in the season. They had obviously heard the weather forecast, which had promised clear skies, and taken a chance – but weather forecasts, as Mario knew only too well, didn't apply to the Vallée des Prêtres. Mario and Michou had run the refuge for twenty years, since the year Sir Hilary had discovered the drawings and the valley had become a major tourist attraction. They knew well how unpredictable the weather in the Vallée des Prêtres could become.

He looked up from his preparations as the door from the hallway opened to admit the dark Italian anthropologist, Dr Emilio Vincente, followed by his small vivacious wife, Maria. The two bade him good morning in their native Italian, their greeting repeated instantly by the parrot, then took their habitual seats in the corner of the room.

Mario, his balding head tilted to one side, smiled graciously at the attractive Signora Vincente then, with an operatic flourish of one muscular arm, he returned his attention to the cutting of cheese.

In their corner Dr Vincente, smiling at something his wife had said, lifted his head as the hallway door opened again to admit twin girls bearing identical manes of long blonde hair and wearing identical baggy sweatshirts and knee-length cycle shorts. The only visible difference between the two was the thick-lensed spectacles worn by one. These were the French students, Ninette and Nanette Fèvre, who had arrived the night before and, so it seemed to Dr Vincente, spent almost all of their time giggling in that silly way that girls of that age did, at everybody and everything.

The two girls glanced over at the Italian and succumbed to a fit of giggles as they slumped into the bench seat by the window, their laughter becoming uncontrollably hysterical as the parrot imitated them, giggling as they had done from its perch at the end of the counter.

The light from the terrace was blocked suddenly by the figure of a tall, lean young woman who entered the dining-room and, without looking at the other guests, made straight for the counter. She was called, as Vincente had learned from Mario, Laura Hutchinson, a polyglot guide who would accompany the tourists and experts to the somewhat dangerous and inaccessible site of the new drawings.

Emilio Vincente regarded the guide, as he had each time he saw her, with interest. His wife watched him, an amused smile playing on her lips.

'She's what one might call an interesting woman, isn't she, Emilio? Too lean to be sensuous or even beautiful – but interesting, don't you think?'

31

'There's something about her,' murmured Emilio. 'A kind of animal restlessness – the way her eyes dart as if she's on alert. You're right. She's very interesting.'

Maria smiled, a brilliant flashing smile that revealed perfect white teeth, then the smile vanished and the small symmetrical features creased into a grimace.

'Damnit,' she said. 'I thought I felt my heels chafing yesterday. I do believe I have a blister.'

She lifted a slender arm and clicked her fingers to summon Mario, who came immediately, dusting his large hands on his apron as he weaved through the wooden dining-tables.

'Would you have such a thing as a plaster?' she asked sweetly. 'I believe I have blisters on my heels.'

'Certainly,' said Mario. 'I have some in the first-aid box. I'll bring them immediately.'

'Immediately,' repeated Petrocelli shrilly and the blonde twins burst once again into a fit of uncontrollable giggles.

As he rushed back to the kitchen Mario almost collided with the guide, who was standing at the counter obviously waiting to order a drink. He apologised stonily. Mario did not like the guide – too tall and thin for his liking and aloof and haughty, the kind of woman who looked down on Italians, particularly a man like him whom she would consider nothing more than a barkeeper.

'I'll be with you in a minute,' he said gruffly as he scrabbled about in the first-aid box.

'In-a-minute!' repeated the parrot.

Laura Hutchinson leaned over the counter, turning her back to the people in the dining-room. She regarded the parrot absently. She had no desire to socialise at the moment. Her fine-sculpted features were set into an expression which could have been interpreted as anxiety but was, in fact, one of profound concentration. She had a lot on her mind. She would concentrate on her work and not get involved in the social chit-chat that people seemed to expect as part of the guide's services. She drummed her long fingers on the counter as she waited for the refuge keeper to serve her.

Herman Browning was the last of the walkers to reach the plateau at the top of the mountain that descended irregularly

32

into the Vallée des Prêtres. He had had to stop and get his breath at regular intervals as the approach to the summit steepened and had been overtaken on the path, first by a rather dour English couple who had managed a mumbled good morning, and then by a rather more cheerful trio who had passed him at a surprisingly rapid pace considering that the two older ones, if not exactly old age pensioners, were definitely past the prime of their lives.

He had then been forced to one side of the track by a four-wheel drive jeep carrying in its back seat Sir Hilary Compton and a pale-faced woman that Herman supposed was his wife. He had thought, when he'd heard the thrum of the engine, that they might offer him a lift, but the jeep had trundled on. Sir Hilary had not so much as turned his head to look at him!

Well, Browning reassured himself, Sir Hilary High Hat Compton would know who Herman Browning was soon enough.

'Do you think we should have offered that young man a lift?' Beatrice Compton asked worriedly of her husband. 'He looked as though he was on his last legs.'

'Do him the world of good,' said Sir Hilary. 'An overweight lump like that.' Then he added grumpily, 'He's doing what we should have done. Walking would have been far healthier than rattling up the way we are in this bone-shaker. I have the feeling that every one of my vital organs has been displaced five centimetres.'

'I'm sorry, dear,' said Beatrice, 'but I simply don't feel confident enough to tackle a three-hour ascent just yet. I'll have enough exercise up in the valley. It's all up and down as far as I remember.'

Sir Hilary shook his leonine head resignedly as the jeep passed two more walkers, forcing them to the side of the path. Rounding a bend, they passed a further three. He glanced curiously at the trio as the jeep overtook them.

'Now there's a couple not far off our age,' he declared, 'and they seem to be having no trouble at all. The woman could well be older than you, Beatrice.'

Beatrice looked back mournfully from the open jeep at Cloth-ilde, who was climbing, apparently without any effort at all, up the last steep leg of the ascent. She settled back unhappily into her seat. She had, perhaps, been silly to give in to Hilary's exhortation to join him on this trip. How could she possibly enjoy herself if he was going to complain and criticise her? She gazed absently out at the fabulous unfolding view of distant hills. She scarcely saw them, so wrapped up was she in her thoughts. Hilary had changed, there was no doubt about it – not just in his personal habits but now in his behaviour towards her. She had never known him to criticise her or complain about her. Supposing he was to do so in front of others? That would be dreadful, absolutely intolerable.

She glanced over at his powerful profile. His attention was riveted by the beauty of the scenery. He was immersed, the whole of his being absorbed in what he was looking at. He had forgotten her, forgotten his grumpiness of a few moments before. He was like that now – like a child, with the dispassionate ardour of a child for what interested it at the moment.

Beatrice Compton had never really understood her husband, nor attempted to. She had simply loved him and relished his solicitude. That he should criticise her, find her wanting, threw her into panic. She quietened her anxiety with the thought that if he were to behave in a socially unacceptable way, she would simply pack her bag, walk down to the village at the bottom of the mountain (walking down must be easier than walking up) and take a taxi to Nice airport. Nobody could stop her doing that, could they?

6

On their arrival at the top Sir Hilary ushered his wife straight to the archaeologists' lodge to unpack their bags and freshen up before lunch.

While Beatrice was in the bathroom Sir Hilary, whistling cheerfully, changed into his walking outfit. This consisted of brightly coloured tight-fitting leggings and an equally vivid tent-like T-shirt that carried a stylised version of the most common of the rock drawings – a horned bull's head – displayed starkly across the front and back. A picture of him in this striking T-shirt would certainly stand out from a newspaper page.

He admired his reflection in the wardrobe mirror. A satisfactory image, he concluded. He added a final touch of gel to his thick head of greying hair so that the abundant mass stood up stylishly. The whole colourful outfit made him feel young and vital. How pleasant it was, he reflected, to be no longer obliged to dress in drab greys and browns. Age, he decided happily, brought a freedom that he had never had in his youth. He chuckled to himself as the door to their room opened. Boy, was he going to enjoy that freedom!

Beatrice stood in the doorway, her mouth hanging open in astonishment at the psychedelic vision that was her husband.

'Hilary . . .' she gasped, her hand flying to her mouth, 'Hilary, have you gone absolutely mad?'

'Not mad, my dear,' said Sir Hilary. 'Sane.' He chuckled. 'I'm going sane in my old age.' He laughed uproariously. 'Only those who are truly free are truly sane. It's only the mad who are locked up – and most people, Beatrice,' his tone was suddenly grave, 'lock themselves up all their lives. They are the ones who are mad.'

Beatrice looked askance at her husband's altogether indecently tight pants and then at his animated face. It was as if she were looking at a complete stranger.

On the west side of the refuge the guests and walkers were busy bringing out tables and benches from the dining-room and arranging them on the sunny terrace. They had complied with Mario's suggestion that it would be a good idea to enjoy what might well be the last day of sunshine in the valley that year by eating outside.

Clothilde and Bridget, who had arrived at the top half an hour earlier, agreed absolutely with the refuge keeper.

Mario had welcomed Clothilde enthusiastically, remembering her from a previous visit to the valley, and had expressed his pleasure at having Bridget as a guest with marginally greater fervour. He had regarded Donaghue's perspiring face and unkempt hair with what approached disdain, thinking that he'd never seen any human face that resembled that of a monkey as much as this one.

After freshening up in the refuge's primitive shower room, the three had changed out of their walking boots and accepted the refuge keeper's invitation to lunch.

By twelve thirty all the guests and walkers were seated at the wooden tables which had been placed end to end on the terrace. The archaeologists, Sir Hilary, Oliver Hardcastle and Herman Browning, along with the anthropologist, Dr Vincente, sat in the company of their wives at one end; Donaghue, Clothilde and Bridget sat at the other end, with Jim Baxter, Meryss Jones, Laura Hutchinson and the French twins, Ninette and Nanette, in the middle.

As Mario and Michou served the buffet meal a strange dishevelled figure, carrying a lamb, appeared from around one corner of the refuge and grinned blankly at the assembled gathering.

'Ah, Antonio!' called Mario, who ran and ushered the extraordinary creature to the empy seat opposite Laura Hutchinson. The diners gazed curiously at the newcomer, the guide the only one to regard him with indifference. In her years in the Alps Laura Hutchinson had come across dozens of mountain shepherds and most of them resembled this Antonio.

Antonio removed his grubby sweater and, spreading it in a shady corner by the refuge wall, laid the lamb tenderly on to it.

Then he took his seat, his gap-toothed smile still creasing his youthful but weathered face into a rugged landscape that was curiously reminiscent of the rocky valley that stretched out in a craggy vista of greys and greens before the diners. A nest of matted curling hair hung over his eyes and the odour that emanated from his shabby pants and tattered shirt made Hardcastle, who was sitting to his right, thankful that they'd decided to eat outside. Ninette, the twin wearing spectacles, who was sitting on Antonio's left, giggled uncontrollably as the shepherd sat down heavily on the bench, making the small bell that hung around his neck tinkle loudly. Petrocelli the parrot, hearing the sound from inside the refuge, immediately imitated it. The assembled diners laughed aloud and a convivial atmosphere was established at the table.

'Antonio is the local shepherd. He's dumb,' Mario explained.

'He was born without a tongue and has never seen any reason to have one fitted – isn't that so, Antonio?'

Antonio grinned broadly, nodding his matted head.

'He carries the bell so that lost walkers can hear him and find him,' Mario went on. 'Antonio knows every inch of the valley. He's as sure-footed as a goat – isn't that so, Antonio?'

Antonio nodded again, grinning happily.

'So don't worry,' Mario advised his audience. 'If any of you get lost just call his name. He'll hear you. He has the hearing of a bat – isn't that so, Antonio?'

Mario glanced over at the lamb lying on Antonio's sweater.

'Is the lamb injured?' he asked.

The shepherd nodded.

'Antonio is a magician with animals,' Mario informed the assembly. 'He can cure them better than any vet. But if they are beyond help he puts them painlessly out of their misery – stuns them with an electric shock then slits their throats. That's how you do it, isn't it, Antonio?'

Antonio nodded again, then, apparently satisfied with the attention he had received, grabbed the pitcher of wine that Mario had placed on the table and poured himself a full glass.

The parrot in the bar, evidently fond of the sound, imitated the tinkling of Antonio's bell once again and the guests, smiling broadly, attacked the buffet meal with relish.

At the archaeologists' end of the table Sir Hilary sat facing Herman Browning, Emilio Vincente sat next to Browning and opposite Sir Hilary's wife. Oliver Hardcastle sat next to Beatrice and opposite Vincente's wife Maria.

Sir Hilary knew Vincente well, having worked with him on the early research into the significance of the valley's drawings. They had ceased working together several years later when Sir Hilary's views became radically different from those of Dr Vincente, whom Sir Hilary considered too classical and conservative in his analysis. Dr Vincente, in turn, considered that Sir Hilary's ideas, plausible though they might be, were not founded on sufficient fact to be credible. The two men, although no longer working together, had nevertheless retained a mutual respect and admiration for each other's work. Compton admired Vincente's thoroughness and Vincente was greatly impressed by Sir Hilary's passion for his subject.

The two wives, Maria and Beatrice, smiled graciously at each other across the table, having met once at a cocktail party during a seminar in Boston.

Hardcastle introduced himself, as did Browning, and Sir Hilary regarded the two with a degree of amusement. The new generation, he thought – and, judging by the firmness of their handshakes, two determined and aggressive young men. Hardcastle's hand had been marginally firmer than Browning's but that could be attributed to his obvious physical superiority.

Sir Hilary regarded Hardcastle with interest. Only an individual with great determination would hack away at broken rock to see what was underneath. Had the young man dislodged every rock he'd come across? Perhaps he'd been searching for the drawings that had shown up on the satellite pictures. But he wouldn't have found these new drawings from photographs such as those. Pictures from space showed engravings hidden by millennia of oxidisation and lichen; they didn't show images hidden by fallen slabs of rock. No, Hardcastle's discovery had been the result of a fanatical determination.

Sir Hilary noted with some amusement that Vincente's wife, Maria, was stealing a sly glance every now and again at the young Englishman. Hardcastle hadn't even noticed – the man was obviously obsessed by his work. Ambition was evidently more important to him than the admiration of women. Yes, Sir Hilary decided, if one word had to be chosen to describe Oliver Hardcastle it would be ambitious.

Sir Hilary looked across at the American, Herman Browning, who was tucking heartily into his cheese and cold meats. An overfed young man, Sir Hilary decided, but very bright. The pale blue eyes in the deceptively youthful freckled face were hard and calculating. It was obvious that Browning, like Hardcastle, was aiming for the top. A professor at thirty and five years' research into the language of primitive man, as Vincente had informed him during the brief conversation they had had before the meal was served.

Sir Hilary leaned forward and addressed the American.

'Might I ask if your lengthy research has borne any fruit?' he asked.

'Sure has,' said Browning through a mouthful of bread and cheese.

'You'll be bringing out a paper on it, I take it?' said Sir Hilary.

'Sure will,' said Browning.

'Are the results sensational?' asked Sir Hilary, a little caustically.

'Sure are,' said Browning.

'I take it from your economy of syntax that you have no wish to reveal them now.'

'Sure don't,' Browning agreed as he filled his mouth with a bite of cheese and ham sandwich. Sir Hilary interpreted the gesture rightly as indicating that the conversation was at an end.

Oliver Hardcastle regarded Browning with amusement. It was obvious that the man had some secret knowledge of primitive man's communication skills that he had no wish to communicate to Sir Hilary Compton. Had the American come to steal the old man's glory? If he had, he was a fool. Compton's glory was established – it couldn't be tarnished as long as he remained alive. Browning must be naïve to think that celebrity was only to do with competence. Competence was secondary – celebrity was only ever to do with *charisma*. And if it came to a choice between himself and Browning he knew who would come out on top. Browning's rating on the charismatic scale was zero, and in any case it was he, Hardcastle, who had discovered the drawings. The glory of this find would go to him. Browning could interpret the hieroglyphics – he would of course enlist his help to do that, although he couldn't now initiate a conversation on the subject after Browning's blatant snub of Compton at the table. He would talk to him privately later. Right now there were other equally interesting matters to consider.

Hardcastle allowed his eyes to wander around the table. He did so discreetly; he did not wish to appear to be staring at the women, but his sharp eyes took them in nevertheless. The fabulous redhead with her ridiculous companions first: number one priority. Next to her, her elderly friend or relative or whoever the old crow was: absolutely out of the question. The French twins: rather young and brainless, but why not? It would be worth a try. The plain girl next to the reporter: not what you could call physically attractive but you never knew with the intellectual type. The guide: now there was an interesting woman. Had he seen her before? Perhaps on another site. Probably voluptuous once but had exercised it all away. Nevertheless, there was something left . . . And up here, at his end of the table, Vincente's wife Maria, luscious Maria. He caught her eye and she looked away. He wondered if she had ever told Vincente. She had said that they were a free-thinking couple and certainly Vincente had shown no sign of hostility towards him. Perhaps once more with Maria.

Then there was the refuge keeper's wife, Michou – a certainty there if he made a play – and, finally, on his right, Sir Hilary Compton's wife.

Hardcastle glanced at Lady Compton's rather constricted profile and mentally shook his head; but then, he thought again, wouldn't it be one in the eye for the old despot, to seduce his wife right here under his nose? That would bring the arrogant old buzzard down a peg or two.

There were nine women at the refuge, six of them pleasing but all of them seduceable. He was here perhaps for five days. An exrtraordinary idea struck him. What a challenge it would be to successfully seduce all nine – even, he thought distastefully, the old dragon with the Ferrari. What an achievement! And why not? He was at the height of his powers. He might never meet such a challenge again.

But it would have to be done discreetly. Hardcastle was experienced enough in the art of seduction to know that the object of his desire must never at any time suspect that there might be another woman in his sights. That was an essential tactic – and it had yet to fail him. It was for that reason that he never flirted in public, only ever in private.

He smiled to himself, feeling the surge of power coursing through his body once again, and, turning to Lady Compton, asked her conversationally if this was her first time in the valley.

Beatrice, overwhelmed by the proximity of the scantily dressed young archaeologist whose tanned thigh was insouciantly pressed against hers on the narrow bench, found herself rendered speechless by the intensity of his clear green eyes and beautiful face as he turned to address her.

'N-no,' she stammered.

She was rescued from her acute embarrassment by Emilio Vincente, who spoke to Hardcastle in perfect though Italian-inflected English.

'Mr Hardcastle,' he said humorously, 'your discovery has been most fortuitous for us the older generation. Interest in primitive man has been ousted recently by a passion for future man – science fiction fantasy has taken over the quest for our origins. Your discovery might well restore primitive man to his rightful place in our scholarship and us old fogies to our former celebrity.' He smiled charmingly. 'It's particularly fortunate for me that you discovered the engravings at this particular moment when I am putting the finishing touches to a book on the social and religious customs of European Bronze Age man.'

Sir Hilary's bushy head lifted itself suddenly from his scrutiny of his plate.

'You're bringing out a book?' he asked sharply.

'Yes,' said Vincente, smiling. 'It will come out in October – a fortunate moment, as I said.'

'But that's extraordinary,' said Sir Hilary. 'I have a book coming out at the same time – the mores of primitive man based on an analysis of the drawings.'

'That's most unfortunate,' said Vincente. 'Two widely divergent views published at the same time.'

'A very unfortunate coincidence,' said Sir Hilary curtly. Then he added, 'But then, these new drawings might throw a completely new light on our theses and our books might both prove outdated before they're even published.'

'That's possible,' mused Vincente. 'If the hieroglyphics are genuine and prove to date from the middle and early Bronze Age then they will be the earliest known hieroglyphics yet discovered – earlier than First Dynasty Egyptian. They will turn on its head all previous teaching about the origins of writing.' He smiled over at Oliver Hardcastle. 'Mr Hardcastle here is the only person who has as yet seen the engravings. Perhaps he could throw some light on the question?'

Hardcastle smiled. 'I am no expert on palaeography nor on hieroglyphics,' he said, 'but from the little I know the symbols I discovered have no relation that I can see to Egyptian hieroglyphics, for instance, or early Chinese. They would, of course, relate to the lives of European man, whose customs were necessarily dictated by a different ecology and climate.' He held out a tanned hand in the direction of the American. 'But Browning here is the man to decide on their authenticity and origins.'

Vincente and Sir Hilary Compton both regarded Browning,

41

who nodded in agreement with Hardcastle, then grinned at all three through a mouthful of semi-masticated bread and cheese.

7

At the end of the table Donaghue was tucking into his meal with relish. The long walk up had left him with that kind of aching hunger that one remembered from childhood when anything – even a piece of dry bread – tasted like ambrosia. As it was, the ewe's cheese that had been served was delicious, as was the dry sausage served with pickled gherkins. The robust Italian wine that accompanied the simple meal left him, when he had finished eating, sated and warmed.

He had spent the meal in quiet contemplation of his fellow diners. He had attempted to converse with the bearded young man sitting next to Bridget, who had informed him in a desultory fashion that he was a journalist there to report on the finds, that he had no personal interest in ancient history and that he only hoped that a storm would not come up and keep them in the godforsaken valley for longer than necessary. The grim-faced young man had then curtailed any further conversation by turning towards his neighbour, who had introduced herself as Meryss Jones, an archaeology student, and devoting all his attention to her.

Donaghue had then attempted to engage in conversation, using his adequate but heavily accented French, with the twin students Ninette and Nanette Fèvre.

'Ulysses Donaghue,' he had said, holding out a stubby hand.

'Ninette,' said the twin wearing glasses.

'Nanette,' giggled the other.

'Fèvre,' they added in unison.

'Archaeology students?' enquired Donaghue.

'No, art,' said the bespectacled Ninette, who appeared very slightly less prone to giggling than her sister.

'I take it that prehistoric art is your speciality then?' Donaghue asked.

The twins looked at each other, then, clapping their hands to their mouths, broke into an uncontrollable burst of merriment.

Donaghue regarded the girls in mystification, wondering what on earth he had said to produce such a reaction.

'As a matter of fact, no,' said Ninette as she removed her metal-framed glasses to wipe the tears of laughter from her eyes. Without her glasses Ninette was, Donaghue noticed, an exact reproduction of her sister. His quick brain took in every aspect of the two faces before him but could find nothing to distinguish them by. Amazing, he thought to himself, amazing . . . it was almost as if they were cloned.

Ninette replaced her round, owl-like glasses and, adopting a serious expression, said, 'We specialise in modern art – commercial art. We want to work with videos, computer graphics, that sort of thing . . . just about as far removed from rock drawings as you can get!'

'I suppose that's true,' murmured Donaghue. 'So, what brought you here then?'

'Oliver Hardcastle,' said Nanette, smiling brightly. 'We saw his picture in the paper . . . he's just gorgeous. We want to use his face for one of our projects. We just had to see him and get a photo of him.' Nanette sighed, her bland face taking on an expression of adoration. Her sister followed suit, the two identical faces gazing at Donaghue in rapture. 'Don't you think he's just gorgeous, Mr Donaghue?' Ninette asked.

Donaghue coughed in slight embarrassment.

'Gorgeous is not the qualification I would use to describe Mr Hardcastle,' he said, 'but then I'm not female and aged seventeen . . . eighteen?' he asked.

'Nineteen,' declared the girls in unison.

Then they had turned their blonde heads to contemplate the object of their adoration at the far end of the table, leaving Donaghue to his solitary scrutiny of the assembled company.

Clothilde and Bridget were engaged in an animated conversation on the merits of constitutional walking which, if he participated in it, would provoke another of Clothilde's lectures on the hazards of smoking. The Welsh student, Meryss Jones, was kept occupied throughout the meal by the sullen Jim Baxter so that no conversation was possible with her, and her neighbour, the guide, Laura Hutchinson, was too far from him to converse with across the table. Laura spent most of the meal in a distracted silence addressing a question in Italian from time to time at the shepherd, Antonio, who sat opposite her and who grinned and nodded in reply.

When the meal was over and the table cleared the guide announced that she would be setting off in thirty minutes' time for the site of the new drawings. She explained that the site was a fifteen-minute walk away and was situated at the top of a particularly steep and inaccessible tor. The walkers were very welcome to accompany the archaeologists but those accustomed only to charted paths should perhaps remain behind.

Jim Baxter tutted in annoyance, grumbling that he was a reporter not a rock climber, but Meryss chided him cheerfully, saying that the challenge would be stimulating and that in any case he had no choice.

'I for one can't wait to get up there,' she said, pulling Jim by the arm. 'Let's go and change into our boots.'

Donaghue, profoundly perturbed by the guide's announcement, expressed his opinion that perhaps he should decline the visit. Clothilde protested vehemently.

'You have just successfully climbed to two thousand metres above sea level,' she exclaimed. 'Do you imagine that you couldn't tackle an ascent marginally steeper than the one we've just come up? If Sir Hilary Compton can do it you certainly can, Ulysses. He's a good fifteen years older than you!'

With Bridget's enthusiastic encouragement added to Clothilde's disparaging confidence, Donaghue finally conceded and agreed to accompany them. They made their way back to the locker room next to the showers to change into their boots.

As they passed the archaeologists' table Maria Vincente let out a small scream.

'How can I go up,' she cried to her husband, 'with my heels in the state they're in? The plasters have come off and the skin will rub against my boots. I want to see the drawings, Emilio,' she wailed. 'What am I going to do?'

'Don't worry, my dear,' Emilio said solicitously. 'We'll find a way of sorting it out.'

He knelt down to take off his wife's slip-on shoes. The plasters

Mario had given her had indeed peeled off, leaving a large raw area of broken blister on each heel.

'Aieee!' commented Hardcastle in commiseration as he leaned over Vincente's shoulder. 'Wait a minute,' he said, 'I have something that might help . . .'

Hardcastle disappeared and returned quickly with a small first-aid box.

'It's a new product,' he explained, bringing out a small tube of ointment. 'You spread it over the wound and it seals like a second skin. It cannot be removed and will be discarded naturally as the new skin grows.'

He took Vincente's place at Maria's feet and, taking one of her feet in his hands, carefully and tenderly spread the gel-like substance over the raw skin. When he had done the same to the other heel, he placed her shoes gently back on to her feet.

'With two pairs of socks,' he said authoritatively, 'you'll be able to wear your boots and you won't feel a thing.'

'Thank you, Mr Hardcastle,' said Maria, gazing up at him in gratitude, the tears of her pain lending an attractive luminosity to her large brown eyes.

'Think nothing of it,' said Hardcastle.

Maria smiled as she dropped her eyes to her feet – a curious smile of complicity that only Donaghue in the entourage had noticed and that only Donaghue understood. Nobody but the stout little detective had noticed that, as Oliver Hardcastle had cupped Signora Vincente's ankle in his hand, one of his fingers had trailed sensuously along the sole of her foot.

The short walk to the tor was relatively flat but strewn with rocks and boulders. As the drawings had been discovered in an unpathed section of the valley the walkers had to negotiate the terrain as they found it. The guide, who had already visited the site with Oliver Hardcastle, warned them to follow her not more than two abreast and not to diverge from the trail she was leading. There were hidden streams and rivulets in the valley, which fed the many lakes and pools and which were often concealed beneath marshy grass. It would be most unpleasant and possibly dangerous, she said, to fall in such a marshy area.

Donaghue, walking with Clothilde at the end of the file, kept his eyes to the ground. Bridget was some way ahead, walking beside Herman Browning. In front of them were Sir Hilary and Maria Vincente, Emilio Vincente with Lady Compton and, heading the procession, Hardcastle and Laura Hutchinson.

Behind Bridget were Jim Baxter and Meryss Jones and directly in front of Donaghue and Clothilde the blonde twins Ninette and Nanette.

The girls were wearing headphones and listening to music from portable disc players. Both Donaghue and Clothilde could hear the music at their distance of a few metres, which meant that it must have been blasting into the girls' ears at a dangerously high level of decibels.

As a result Donaghue felt free to talk to Clothilde without fear of being overheard.

'There are some curious forces at play here among these people,' he said, 'forces of power and jealousy.'

Clothilde looked at her old friend a little quizzically.

'Isn't that statement a trifle melodramatic, Ulysses?' she said. 'Not that I would dream of questioning your judgement on such things – you have been proved correct on so many occasions in the past – but might it not be the ambience of this magnificent but austere valley that brings to mind forces of power? The jealousy, of course, might be a simple reflection of your own inner emotional state.'

Donaghue glanced at Clothilde disparagingly, peeved at her reminder of his remark about Hardcastle earlier in the day.

'I am a great believer in intuition, as you know, Clothilde,' he said, 'and I could feel at the table a force of animosity and dissatisfaction emanating from many of the people there, particularly from those at the other end, from the archaeologists. I could detect, for instance, without having heard what was being said, a great deal of animosity directed towards Sir Hilary Compton.'

'I'm not surprised,' said Clothilde caustically. 'In that ridiculous outfit of his. Good lord – a man of his age got up like an adolescent of fifteen! He seems to have gone completely batty in his old age.'

'Eccentric, I think is what the English call it,' said Donaghue, smiling.

'A convenient euphemism for insanity,' said Clothilde. 'If I were to suddenly appear in psychedelic legwarmers and a matching tube top wouldn't you question the state of my mental well-being?'

Donaghue tried to conjure up the image but the vision refused to linger in his mind.

'Sir Hilary is certainly not the sober academic that I expected,' he agreed. 'His wife appears agitated and distracted. Perhaps her husband is no longer the man she knew.'

'So,' said Clothilde, 'a distinguished academic becomes eccentric in his dress after retirement. One must allow people to change, I suppose – the privilege of age and celebrity.'

'Perhaps he has changed in his thinking also,' said Donaghue. 'I would be interested to talk to him.'

'Ever curious, eh, Ulysses?' said Clothilde, smiling. 'As a matter of fact I wouldn't mind getting a chance to talk to him myself. Perhaps later, after the inspection of the engravings, we could invite him and his wife for a drink after dinner – what do you say?'

'An excellent idea,' said Donaghue. As he spoke he stumbled on a loose rock and Clothilde had to catch his arm to steady him. From then on Donaghue kept his eyes firmly glued to his boots as they made their way along the uneven terrain.

A pleasant chat over a warming cognac (he'd spotted a bottle on the bar's shelves), out on the terrace under a clear canopy of stars. Now that, Donaghue decided, would mark a pleasant end to an interesting and tiring day.

Herman Browning was pleasantly surprised to find himself partnered on the walk by an extremely attractive Irish girl.

'Looks like I'm with you,' she had said brightly as they had formed a file for the trek. 'No one else will have me,' she had added by way of a joke.

Herman had been very happy to have her and had offered her a chewing gum as he'd introduced himself and asked her name and profession.

'Must be fascinating working for a detective,' he said pleasantly. 'Lots of gory murders to solve, I guess.'

'Mr Donaghue does occasionally have to solve a murder,' Bridget replied, 'but a lot of the work can be dreadfully boring –

routine research into fraud, marital infidelity, theft of heirlooms, that sort of thing. It's only very rarely exciting – and in any case,' she added glumly, 'for me it's never exciting. While Mr Donaghue's out there solving the crimes I'm sitting in the office typing and answering the telephone. Your work is far more exciting,' she said fervently. 'This for instance . . .' She waved a long slender arm around at the arid expanse of valley, '. . . is infinitely more exciting than sitting in a boring office.'

Browning smiled. 'An archaeologist's life', he said humorously, 'is probably not so different from a detective's. I spend most of my time sitting at a desk. It's only rarely that I come out into the field, and even more rarely that I come across an exciting find. This one is particularly exciting for me as it relates directly to my field of study – the evolution of written language.'

'Which didn't evolve, I believe, before 3500 BC,' said Bridget. 'Sumerian cuneiform – wasn't that the first form of symbolic writing?'

Browning looked admiringly at the Irish girl.

'You're remarkably well informed for a secretary,' he said, staring at her. Then to Bridget's surprise he suddenly fell, tilting forward and landing in an untidy heap in front of her.

'Oh dear, Mr Browning,' she said worriedly as she helped him up. 'You have to keep your eyes on the path – it's treacherous here.'

'Call me Herman,' he said as she pulled him to his feet.

Sir Hilary, walking along beside Maria Vincente, asked her how her heels were doing.

'Fine,' said Maria. 'That gel Mr Hardcastle put on them is absolutely marvellous – a real second skin. I can't feel a thing.'

She looked slyly up at the imposing, brilliantly coloured figure of Sir Hilary.

'It's such a shame', she said, 'that your book and Emilio's are coming out at the same time. Wouldn't it have been better if you and he had worked together and produced one book between you?'

'Absolutely impossible, Signora Vincente,' said Sir Hilary. 'Our views are too divergent. Your husband is an admirable man but too conservative in my opinion. It's usually the other way round

– the young radical and the old reactionary – but in our case the position is reversed.'

'I suppose at forty-two he is still young,' mused Maria.

'When you're twenty, forty is over the hill,' said Sir Hilary good-humouredly. 'When you're sixty it's the prime of life. Age is relative. You are a young woman – you cannot possibly appreciate that yet.'

'The problem with archaeology,' said Maria, 'is that one must put in a long lifetime of arduous, badly remunerated work before one achieves recognition – a little like the law, I imagine.'

'Because it's a field that requires experience to achieve excellence,' said Sir Hilary. 'This young Hardcastle, for instance, thinks he can achieve fame and fortune overnight because of one chance discovery. I was over forty when I discovered the engravings in the valley and that discovery marked not the end of my career but the beginning of a long period of hard analysis and research. He is one of those ambitious young men who think they can jump to the top of the ladder by putting springs on their feet. It can't be done.'

'And Emilio, what about him?' asked Maria.

'Emilio is like myself,' said Sir Hilary. 'He'll get there in the end through discipline and hard work. But as an anthropologist he'll make no remarkable discoveries to get his name in the papers. He relies on us archaeologists for his raw material.'

By now they had reached the beginning of the steep incline that led to the top of the tor.

Maria turned her head so that Sir Hilary would not see her involuntary wince. She had lied to him when she had said that her heels were fine. They were in fact chafing against the material of the boots – but she wouldn't complain until she was in the company of Oliver Hardcastle. She would ask him to put some more of his gel on her heels. She had enjoyed the feel of his hand on her skin.

8

With much panting, clambering and the occasional slither the last of the stragglers reached the top of the tor. Sir Hilary, Dr Vincente, Hardcastle and Browning were clustered around the two wide slabs of rose-coloured rock that bore the engravings. Laura Hutchinson stood back a little from the group of experts and supervised the approach of the walkers. Finally the whole group was arranged in a semicircle around Sir Hilary and Browning, who were bent over in close inspection of the rock, Sir Hilary paying particular attention to the drawings and Browning to the hieroglyphics.

The drawings were very much in the style of the engravings found ubiquitously in the valley – horned bulls' heads, wedge-shaped daggers, rectangles, and anthropoids formed from a bull's head.

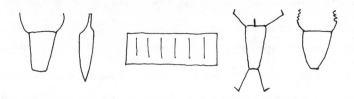

To the right of the drawings was a long inscription carved with great precision into the rock.

Both men took photographs after studying the engravings intently for some time. Browning carefully copied the inscription into a notebook after measuring the distance between the symbols. Sir Hilary made no attempt to copy the drawings – he had seen hundreds of the same type before. But he had never seen with any other drawing an inscription such as this one.

Browning finally stood up to let Sir Hilary peer at the hieroglyphics. The American's face bore an expression of intense gravity.

Jim Baxter took a few shots of Hardcastle standing beside the rock, then in the company of Sir Hilary, and finally of all four experts poring over the engravings.

The photographs taken, Laura Hutchinson pulled Sir Hilary and Browning to one side to ask them a few questions before giving a brief account of the rock's history and significance to the group of walkers.

The experts stood to one side of the rock and engaged in a hushed conversation while Laura Hutchinson ushered the remaining group to inspect the rock.

'It's not possible for me to say at the moment whether the drawings are genuine or not,' she began. 'As many of you will probably already know, some drawings discovered in the valley in recent years have proved to be false, the handiwork of practical jokers, and some of the genuine drawings have, tragically, been irreparably damaged by vandals or people trying to remove them to put on their mantelpieces. As a result the site is now a protected zone and all visits are guided. For this reason it is highly unlikely, in my opinion, that these drawings could have been faked – but it's for the experts to decide on that question and I've no doubt they'll need some time to come to a decision. For the moment we will assume that they are genuine.'

She indicated the simple drawings on the left side of the slab, whose pink oxidised surface was curiously fresh and clear in colour in comparison to that of the rocks surrounding it.

'The surface was hidden for millennia under fallen rock and the drawings are therefore particularly clear and deeply notched.' She indicated a small shape with horns. 'The bull's head shape is common to all Bronze Age cultures and manifests the importance of cattle in the lives of men at that time. The rectangular shape is believed to represent fields. The dagger is self-evident, as is the humanoid form with arms raised. The significance of the drawings is of course open to interpretation, and the interpretations are as varied as the people who make them. Some believe that the bull symbolises fertility and the fear of the storm or of God.

Some see the dagger as not only a weapon but a symbol of male fertility. Interpretation, of course, is a matter of scholarship but is equally a matter of personal conjecture. Sir Hilary Compton, for instance, has recently put forward a theory that the rock drawings are nothing more than the graffiti of the day. That theory, of course, is as valid as any other.'

She indicated the hieroglyphics, apologising for the fact that she was no expert on primitive writing.

'But, having spoken to Mr Browning, our expert in the field, I am qualified to inform you that they appear to be a somewhat advanced form of hieroglyphic – more abstract than the early Egyptian but not quite as sophisticated as Sumerian cuneiform, which is close to alphabetisation. He can see symbols that are common to all early hieroglyphical systems – namely the human-oid figure, the star and the inverted L shape. The human figure is self-evident, the star is often used to represent God and the heavens, and the L shape is common but not always easily deciphered. The diamond shapes, the forked sign and the open square he has never seen before.

'If these drawings prove to date from the early Bronze Age then they could well predate the earliest known hieroglyphics, those of Sumeria and Egypt. If they date from the later Bronze Age they will prove to be the first examples of symbolic writing in Europe. Either way, the find, if proven genuine, will be sensational.

'From their symbolic value and a first inspection of the work-manship, Mr Browning said that he is inclined to believe that they are genuine.'

Laura Hutchinson's rapid and monotone speech came to an end; she left the group to inspect the rock, having instructed them not to touch its surface.

The twins, Ninette and Nanette, having noticed Oliver Hard-castle descending the tor in the company of the Vincentes, set off to follow him down the incline. Laura Hutchinson suggested that they wait, then called the group together. She drew their attention to the splendid view of the valley which spread out in a panorama before them.

'Tomorrow, those of you who wish to may accompany me on a guided visit to some of the sites of the original drawings. There are two principal areas to be visited, one to the north-east and

Your receipt
West Bend Comm Mem. Library

Items that you checked out

Title: Einstein : his life and his universe
ID: 33357003570590
Due: Friday, September 06, 2019

Title: Secrets in stones
ID: 33357001660732
Due: Friday, September 06, 2019

Total items: 2
Account balance: $0.00
8/9/2019 10:19 AM
Ready for pickup: 0
Messages:
Patron status is ok.

Please keep this receipt. To renew call the
library at 262-335-5151 or go online at
www.westbendlibrary.org.

the other to the west. For those who do not wish to take the guided visit I must warn you very strongly not to walk anywhere other than on charted paths. The paths are colour-coded and indicated on the map board outside the refuge. If you decide to leave the paths you do so at your own risk.

'As you can see, the valley is dotted with lakes and pools which are surrounded by areas of marsh. Some of the pools are very dangerous, particularly that one . . .' She indicated a perfectly circular pool of green water directly below the tor and a short distance from the path that led to the north-east site. '. . . that circular pool – it's called the Lake of Shadows – is particularly dangerous. On ground level its precipitous border cannot be seen. Before the zone was restricted several inexperienced walkers were drowned in it. You all passed it on the way up but did any of you see it?'

The assembled walkers shook their heads.

'Those who died quite simply fell into it and were unable to get out. Its vertical sides are so steep that it's impossible to climb out if you fall in.'

The twins gasped in horror, saying '*Mon Dieu!*' in unison. The rest of the group regarded the guide gravely.

'It's for that reason that I insist you stay on the paths, which are all clearly marked.'

With that she wished them a pleasant stay and suggested that those who were not sure of the way down to the refuge should follow her back.

All except Meryss Jones and Jim Baxter accepted the guide's suggestion and followed her down the tor.

Meryss, her eyes glittering with excitement, bent close to inspect the hieroglyphics.

'It's extraordinary,' she said. 'It's almost as if the person who carved these symbols was trying to communicate a message.' She quickly copied the inscription into a notebook.

'Can you imagine maybe three or four thousand years ago someone – a priest or a shepherd or perhaps just someone ordinary like you or me – came up here and carved these symbols in the rock. *There must have been a reason*. Something must have motivated him. Why did he do it? Don't you find that incredibly exciting, Jim?'

Jim looked morosely at Meryss.

'Perhaps he did it out of boredom,' he suggested.

53

Meryss laughed gaily.

'Maybe he did, Jim,' she said. 'But if so, what was he saying in his boredom? That's the question.'

'Some boring litany of how many bulls he had and how big his dagger was – something bloody inane like that,' said Jim. He stood with his arms folded over his narrow chest, regarding the view.

Meryss tutted in mock exasperation and, taking Jim by the arm, led him down the tor in the wake of the other walkers.

Sir Hilary Compton and Herman Browning, having waited for the last tourists to depart, took up position once again before the rock and scrutinised it intently.

9

In the common room of the archaeologists' lodge Michou served the four experts with a tray of aperitifs and mineral water. As soon as she had left the room a lively discussion began. Browning was the first to speak.

'I can't make any judgement on the workmanship of the engravings – I haven't seen sufficient European examples – but from the symbols themselves, the similarity of some of them to known hieroglyphics, I'd say they were genuine. It'll be difficult, of course, to decipher them, having no precedent to go by, but the humanoid, star and L shapes are common to all Bronze Age cultures. The rock, it's obvious to me, had not been exposed to the elements for several millennia.'

'I suppose it's possible that the rock was hidden deliberately,' said Hardcastle. 'Because of the inscription. Perhaps a form of hieroglyphic existed at the time but was forbidden.'

'That is possible,' mused Browning thoughtfully. Then he brought his fist forcefully down upon the table.

'But what an idea!' he exclaimed. 'Imagine that European Bronze Age man was able to write but was forbidden to do so on rocks. Perhaps the priests were only permitted to write on perishable surfaces.' Grinning, he looked over at Sir Hilary. 'That would kinda substantiate your theory, Sir Hilary, wouldn't it?

Writing was sacred and drawing on rocks profane. It would have been no different from today, huh? Don't we write on perishable paper and consider scratching walls as desecration and writing on them as vulgar?'

Sir Hilary looked at Browning reflectively.

'It would indeed,' he said, 'but unfortunately I'm inclined to the opinion that the engravings are fakes.'

Browning looked at Sir Hilary in puzzlement and Oliver Hardcastle's head swivelled violently from the direction of the window, through which he had been watching Maria Vincente as she sat outside leaning against a boulder, tanning her face in the rays of the late afternoon sun.

'Fakes! How can they possibly be fakes?' he asked incredulously. 'I saw them under the splintered rock. I pulled the bloody rocks off them with my own hands.'

'Nevertheless,' said Sir Hilary, 'I have grave doubts as to their authenticity.'

'Can you explain why?' demanded Hardcastle.

'Of course,' said Sir Hilary quietly. 'It's quite simple. All the engravings in the Vallée des Prêtres are notched out of the rock in tiny circular nodules. It's obvious that not all of the drawings were done by the same hand. Some are much finer, more sophisticated than others, but the notching process is always the same. The notchings of these new drawings do not correspond either in size or symmetry to the originals.'

'They could have been done in a different century,' protested Hardcastle. 'Or a different millennium. The tools could have changed.'

'Certainly,' agreed Sir Hilary. 'But that has not been manifested in this valley. Had they appeared elsewhere the same criteria would not apply.'

'But it's simply not possible that they're fakes,' Hardcastle insisted. 'I discovered them myself. I removed the rocks that hid them, for God's sake. Are you saying that somebody faked them and then placed the rocks back on top of them?'

'I'm not saying anything about how it was done. I'm just questioning their authenticity.'

'Who do you think did them then?' asked Hardcastle caustically. 'Some idle football hooligan who just happened to be passing on his way to a match?'

Sir Hilary smiled. 'It's obvious that they weren't done by some passing vandal. One, the valley is scrupulously patrolled in the summer season and two, the drawings are far too well executed to have been done by a tourist.'

Hardcastle's face had paled. 'Are you implying that they were faked by an expert?'

'Nobody else could have done them,' said Sir Hilary.

Hardcastle rose to his feet, his tanned face now pale grey. 'Are you implying that I – ?'

'Calm down, Hardcastle,' said Sir Hilary. 'I have not at any time implied that you faked them – but if they are fakes, they were faked by an expert. That's for sure.'

'Or they weren't faked at all,' spluttered Hardcastle as he sat back into his seat.

Browning regarded the two men with some amusement. 'I for one would very much prefer them to be genuine – then I could devote the next five years to deciphering them and come up with a wholly new slant on the intellectual sophistication of early European man. Maybe he wasn't as simple-minded as we believe he was. Maybe he was even more advanced than the Egyptians, just not concerned about the future as they were. In any case,' he added cheerfully, 'even if they're fakes I'd like to work on the inscription – it intrigues me. Even if it's fake it might have a meaning.' He turned to the Italian.

'What about you, Dr Vincente, what do you think?'

'I'm inclined to go along with you,' said Vincente. 'I'm not qualified either to judge the authenticity or the execution, but it would revolutionise conventional ideas in anthropology if the inscriptions proved to be genuine.'

'So it's all down to Sir Hilary here,' declared Browning. 'Whether he says yea or nay. Our futures, sir, depend on you.'

'Don't worry,' said Sir Hilary jovially. 'I haven't made my mind up yet. I shall make a more thorough inspection of the drawings before making any statements to the press.'

'If they prove to be fakes,' said Vincente, 'I'd be interested to know who's done them.'

'There's a detective at the refuge,' said Browning with a smile. 'Perhaps we could ask him to investigate.'

'A detective?' queried Sir Hilary.

'Yes, the little man that looks like a cross between a baboon and a rhesus monkey. I was talking to his very delightful secretary this afternoon.'

Hardcastle stood up, glaring at Browning.

'I suggest we forget about investigating forgeries until Sir Hilary has made up his mind,' he said stonily. Then he left the room abruptly.

Browning grinned round at Sir Hilary and Dr Vincente as the door closed with a clatter. 'Hardcastle's glorious future is imperilled,' he said, 'and mine doomed to boredom.' He looked at Sir Hilary, an expression of pleading on his freckled face. 'Perhaps you might give us young guns a break, Sir Hilary?'

'And declare the drawings authentic when I believe them false? I'm sorry, young man. One cannot bear false witness about the past in order to satisfy the interests of the future.'

'I guess you're right, sir,' said Browning deferentially. 'I guess you're just goddamned right.'

Dr Vincente, sitting close to the window, had not heard the last exchange of words. He was gazing thoughtfully at Hardcastle who had joined his wife, Maria, outside and was leaning over her shoulder talking to her. Quite suddenly Maria stood up and the two made their way slowly towards the shade of a small tor. They disappeared from sight behind it.

10

Oliver Hardcastle settled himself comfortably on his bed and took out his small personal diary, in which he had listed the names of all the women at the refuge. He had listed them in the order in which he was going to seduce them.

1. Maria
2. Michou
3. Ninette (or is it Nanette?)
4. Nanette (or is it Ninette?)
5. Laura Hutchinson
6. Meryss Jones
7. Lady Compton

8. Dr Blanche
9. Bridget Kilkenny

He had obtained the names from Michou's register and had listed them in order of attractiveness but putting Bridget (whom he considered out of the others' league) at the end as the crowning achievement of his challenge. He would keep her, the best, for last – in the way, as a child, he had kept the best morsel on his plate for last.

He placed a large tick beside the first name, Maria, followed by the words: 'Successful – excellent.'

A knock came at the door. He quickly closed the book and placed it in his jacket pocket.

'Come in,' he called and Michou entered bearing a tray.

'Your mineral water, Mr Hardcastle,' she said deferentially. 'Where shall I put it?'

'Here beside the bed,' he instructed her.

She placed the tray on the bedside table and turned to leave. He reached out and took hold of her hand.

'Don't rush off, Michou,' he said softly. 'Dinner isn't for another hour. Stay and keep me company. I need to practise my French.'

Michou looked down at him hesitantly but her hand remained resting in his.

'I'll have to lock the door,' she said. She giggled. 'In case Mario comes in looking for me.'

Mario, emerging from the lodge common room where he had just changed a spent light bulb, spotted Michou going into the English archaeologist's room with a tray. He waited for her to come out. Then he heard the lock of the door click. He waited several minutes more, then, his face purple with fury, returned to the kitchen to prepare dinner.

After Michou had left his room Hardcastle took his diary from his jacket and marked a tick beside her name. Alongside he wrote the words: 'Successful – mediocre.'

*

A grim-faced Mario served the evening meal in silence. Michou, ignoring her husband's bad temper, was her usual cheerful self. She served the archaeologists at their corner table, mocking them cheerfully for the sober silence that reigned at the table.

'I've never seen such glum faces,' she said. 'You'd think you'd just come back from a funeral instead of the site of a new discovery.'

Hardcastle, Sir Hilary and Lady Compton, Dr Vincente and his wife looked back at her sombrely.

Browning, who had been of the same opinion as Michou, had abandoned the archaeologists and gone to join Bridget and her companions at the tourists' table. Dinner was served inside the dining-room as the temperature in the mountains dropped considerably after sundown.

'Mind if I join you?' he had asked. 'It's as grim as Kafka's castle over there.'

'Of course not, Herman,' Bridget had said, making room for him on the bench next to her. She had then presented him to the table.

'The clouds of war are mustering among the academics,' he whispered. 'I'm keeping out of it.'

'They don't agree about the engravings then, I take it?' said Donaghue.

'Opinions have been expressed – let's put it like that – ' said Browning, 'which are, to put it politely, widely divergent.'

'Dr Vincente looks particularly fraught,' Donaghue commented.

'Dr Vincente?' queried Browning, turning his head to look at the Italian. 'He's the least bothered, as a matter of fact.' He leaned forward conspiratorially. 'It's Hardcastle and Compton who are at loggerheads.'

'Sir Hilary is not sure of the authenticity of the drawings, is that it?' Donaghue asked.

'I can't say too much at the moment,' Browning whispered, 'with the press here.' He indicated Jim Baxter, who was sitting two seats away from Donaghue.

'Don't let me stop you expressing yourself,' said Baxter sardonically. 'I'm here to report facts and Sir Hilary Compton's statement. I'm not interested in hearsay.'

'A good honest reporter, I see,' said Browning in amusement. 'One of the old school – admirable in one so young.'

Baxter glared darkly at Browning then abruptly returned his attention to Meryss Jones, who was sitting next to him.

'As I was saying,' said Browning, 'Sir Hilary has doubts and Hardcastle is hopping around impatiently waiting for him to declare the drawings authentic and thereby render his find the discovery of the decade.'

'And you?' Clothilde asked. 'What do you think?'

'I think they're genuine, but then I do have a vested interest in their being so – like Hardcastle, I guess. But I'm not gonna be as put out as he is by the possibility that they might be fakes. I can't imagine why he's so furious.'

'He's a man of great intensity,' said Donaghue, glancing over at Hardcastle who, every now and again, turned his head in the direction of their table. 'He's the kind, I imagine, who likes to see things through to the end. He's not the type who likes to find obstacles in his path.'

'An obstacle like Sir Hilary Compton is not easily knocked out of the way,' said Browning. 'He is the expert. His word is law. If he says they're fakes then they're fakes, no matter what I, Vincente or Hardcastle think.'

'Is it possible that he could be mistaken?' Clothilde asked.

'No, I don't think so,' said Browning. 'He's spent too many years studying these particular kinds of drawings.'

'If they're fakes, then who did them?' Bridget asked.

'Now there's the sixty-four thousand dollar question,' said Browning. He looked over at Donaghue. 'Perhaps Mr Donaghue here might be interested in finding out? How about it, Mr Donaghue?'

'It would be an interesting investigation,' said Donaghue.

Bridget's eyes lit up. 'I could help you in the field,' she said.

Donaghue patted her arm in a paternal manner. 'If the need arises, certainly, Bridget, my dear.'

'Hey, Bridget,' said Browning, turning to the Irish girl, 'I gotta great idea. You're interested in hieroglyphics, right?'

'Yes, yes I am,' said Bridget, nodding her head of auburn curls.

'Well, waddaya say to working with me on deciphering those symbols? Even if they prove to be fake it could still be fun.'

'A wonderful idea,' said Bridget enthusiastically. 'We could start after dinner.'

'Sure thing,' said Browning. He leaned back contentedly against the bench, his arm stretching out behind Bridget's back.

Oliver Hardcastle, sitting behind them, turned his head sharply in Browning's direction, the expression on his face a curious combination of disquietude and determination.

At the archaeologists' table Dr Vincente sat in reflective silence next to his wife. He was aware that there was something between her and Hardcastle but that knowledge was not the reason for his negative feeling towards the Englishman. He and his wife had entered a marriage contract that allowed mutual liberty. No, it was something else – there was something calculating and uncompromising in Hardcastle that went against Vincente's liberal grain. Hardcastle, he felt, was a *dangerous* man, highly intelligent and cunning – and one had to admire the man's coolness. There was nothing now, for instance, in his behaviour that would make anyone suspect that a few hours earlier he had seduced the wife of the man sitting next to him. A cool customer, Vincente decided; a cool and dangerous customer.

Sir Hilary, sitting with Maria Vincente on one side of him and his wife on the other, was thoroughly enjoying his simple meal of polenta and pork cutlets. He finished eating and sipped his glass of wine while glancing admiringly at Maria Vincente's brightly coloured jumpsuit.

'I don't understand, Beatrice,' he said, turning suddenly to his wife, 'why you don't wear more up-to-date clothes – brighter colours, more modern styles. Why do you always want to look so *insignificant*?'

Beatrice, who was wearing a grey shirtwaist dress of classical design, did indeed look colourless and drab next to Maria Vincente, who resembled a bird of paradise in her yellow and green flowered jumpsuit. Sir Hilary himself was equally bright in another extraordinary T-shirt, this one with rolled-up sleeves and a rainbow of colours in concentric circles painted on it. With it he was wearing jeans cut off at the knee – a totally unsuitable outfit, Lady Compton had felt, for a man of his age.

Beatrice gazed at her husband stricken, her face reddening in embarrassment.

61

Dr Vincente engaged his wife quickly in conversation and Hardcastle regarded Lady Compton curiously. Her discomfiture at being humiliated like this before other people had rendered her speechless.

'I don't know why you don't try it, Bea,' said Sir Hilary, apparently oblivious to his wife's distress. 'Wear something other than dreary creams and greys for a change. It would brighten you up, make you look more alive, more gay.'

The last syllable rang out and the parrot, Petrocelli, sitting on the counter behind Sir Hilary, picked it up. 'Gay,' he called out in perfect imitation of Sir Hilary's resonant voice. 'Gay, gay, gay!'

Beatrice, her face a bright scarlet, stood up, cast a terrible look at her husband and fled from the room.

Sir Hilary gazed after her in puzzlement.

'What on earth did I say?' he asked.

'Say,' repeated the parrot. 'Say, say, say!'

Oliver Hardcastle rose from the table and followed Lady Compton out on to the terrace. Sir Hilary, tutting at the incomprehensibility of female behaviour, turned to the Vincentes with an expression of resigned suffering.

'It's the age,' he said, apologetically. 'Like a second adolescence – ultra-sensitive, like a teenage girl. I was only trying to be helpful. Bloody good job that we men don't have to go through it too, eh?'

'Eh,' repeated Petrocelli, the parrot. 'Eh, eh, eh!'

Oliver Hardcastle caught up with Lady Compton as she reached the archaeologists' lodge. He took her by the arm and steered her to the common room where he insisted that she join him for a drink.

He sat her on one of the room's comfortable armchairs and, pouring two glasses of whisky from the well-stocked bar, placed one in her hand.

Beatrice, unaccustomed to such solicitous attention, put the glass distractedly to her lips and sipped the warming liquid tentatively. Her face was still pink and her hand trembled from her anger and embarrassment.

'You really mustn't feel bad about what your husband said just now,' Hardcastle murmured softly. 'He's as thick-skinned as a rhinoceros. Men like that have no idea that other people can be sensitive or fragile.'

Beatrice gulped her whisky and gazed at Hardcastle in bewilderment. He leaned forward and refilled her glass.

'He's not a man that could ever understand women,' he went on. 'He's too caught up in his own male world of power and achievement.'

Beatrice nodded in agreement, sipping the whisky which by now was leaving a warm glow in the area of her chest.

'He can't help it,' said Hardcastle. 'It's his nature, he has no control over it. He's a man governed by reason – emotion plays no part in his dealings with others.'

Beatrice nodded again and gulped the whisky, emptying the glass.

'He's a brute,' she said through clenched teeth then burst into tears.

Hardcastle moved to her side, placed a comforting arm around her shoulders and wiped her tears with his handkerchief. 'Let me help you,' he said. 'I'll take you to your room.'

He helped her to her feet, then, taking her arm in his, led her to her room. Lady Compton staggered as she walked, half crying and half giggling.

Hardcastle entered the room with her and closed the door after them.

When the meal in the dining-room was over and the tables cleared, Donaghue rose from his seat with the intention of inviting Sir Hilary for an after-dinner drink as he had planned. To his surprise the archaeologist approached him instead.

'Mr Donaghue, Ulysses Donaghue, I believe,' said Sir Hilary, holding out a large thick hand. 'Sir Hilary Compton. I have of course heard of you.'

Donaghue inclined his untidy head modestly and shook the proffered hand. He then presented Clothilde and Bridget and Sir Hilary bowed graciously at the two women.

'I had it in mind to enjoy a cognac with a coffee out on the terrace. Would you care to join me?' Donaghue asked.

'My idea exactly,' boomed Sir Hilary. 'Great minds think alike, eh!'

'Eh,' repeated Petrocelli happily. 'Eh, eh, eh!'

Bridget disappeared with Browning to the archaeologists' lodge to study the inscriptions and Clothilde, having changed her mind about drinking on the terrace, informed the company that she was going to have an early night before the guided visits of the following day. 'One doesn't sleep well in a communal dormitory,' she said, 'so what one lacks in quality one has to make up for in quantity.'

'A character, that one, I'll bet,' said Sir Hilary as the two men took their seats on the terrace. 'I sometimes wish my wife, Beatrice, was a little more *assertive*.' As he spoke he gazed out at the black vista of valley and mountains, the peaks and tors lit palely in the moonlight. Sir Hilary coughed. 'Ahem . . . am I right in assuming that the lady is your wife?'

'Good lord no,' said Donaghue in astonishment. 'A very old and dear friend though. Neither Clothilde nor myself are the marrying kind. In that respect, and probably that respect only, we are very much alike – unmarriageable.'

'I sometimes think that I'm not the marrying kind either,' said Sir Hilary glumly. 'I've been married for thirty years and even now after all this time, my wife sometimes appears to me as a complete stranger.' He paused reflectively, then, shaking his bushy head, said, 'Still, I didn't invite you here to talk about my marriage. You're a detective, I believe, Mr Donaghue.'

'I am that,' Donaghue agreed.

'Will you consider doing a small service for me?' Sir Hilary asked. 'For a fee, of course.'

'I would consider it, yes,' said Donaghue hesitantly. 'But it would depend on the nature of the service.'

'I'd like you to keep an eye on Hardcastle.'

'On Hardcastle?'

'Yes, Oliver Hardcastle – the young chap who discovered the drawings. He was sitting at our table.'

'I know who you mean,' said Donaghue. 'But what exactly do you mean by keeping an eye on him? Do you suspect him of something . . . of being interested in your . . .?'

Sir Hilary looked blankly at Donaghue, then he laughed uproariously. 'My wife, you mean? Good lord, no! Hardcastle and my wife! That'd be the day. No, it's something completely different, a professional problem. I am almost certain that the engravings

64

he found are fakes. I haven't yet come to a firm decision but as I say I am almost sure. Hardcastle places great store by these drawings – too great store, if you want my opinion. I think he sees his future depending on them. I suspect that he might even have faked them himself, although I must hasten to add that I have no concrete foundation for that belief. As a result of my feelings I have a suspicion that he might attempt to tamper with the drawings in order to make them appear more authentic. I'd be most grateful if you could just keep an eye on him during the next two or three days until I make my final statement to the press. I can't remain permanently beside the rock and the guide is occupied with her visits. I can reward you well for your services.'

'I see no reason why I shouldn't be able to keep an eye on him,' concurred Donaghue.

'A discreet eye, of course,' said Sir Hilary.

'The eye of a good detective is always discreet,' said Donaghue. 'As the Bard so wisely instructs us, "Let discretion be your tutor."'

Sir Hilary filled Donaghue's glass with the excellent cognac.

'A well-read detective, eh?' he said admiringly.

'Eh,' echoed Petrocelli from the bar. 'Eh, eh, eh!'

Hardcastle could do nothing to stop Lady Compton's sobbing. She lay with her head buried into her pillow, her body racked by her weeping. He had no choice but to leave her and return to his room where he updated his diary by placing a cross next to Lady Compton's name and alongside the words: 'Unsuccessful – lady willing but flesh not weak enough.'

Then he drew a line through Bridget's name and rewrote it below that of Michou. He would have to seduce the Irish girl next before that damned Browning asked her to marry him!

Lady Compton finally stopped sobbing. In the fuzz of her inebriation it occured to her that her husband might return at any moment. She lifted herself to her feet, pulled off her clothes and dragged her nightie over her head. As her head swam anew she recalled her humiliating experience with Oliver Hardcastle and tears dribbled from her eyes. She could not face seeing the man again. And Hilary – Hilary had gone too far humiliating her in front of everybody in the refuge. She had had enough – things had gone beyond the limits of acceptability. She climbed into bed and lay still, waiting for her head to stop swimming, and drifted into sleep.

11

The long communal dormitory was simply furnished. A wooden structure running the length of one wall provided forty beds – twenty upper bunks and twenty lower. Bridget Kilkenny, Clothilde Blanche, Meryss Jones and the French twins chose bunks at one end of the room, Donaghue and Jim Baxter at the other.

In the dim grey light of pre-dawn the shallow breathing of the seven sleepers was the only sound to break the silence of the early morning. One of the French twins, the one nearest the window, stirred and turned on to her side, the movement waking Donaghue from a rather disturbing dream in which he had found himself hanging over the precipitous edge of the dangerous Lake of Shadows, Sir Hilary Compton grasping his wrists and instructing him to breathe correctly and spit his cigar from his mouth if he expected his life to be saved.

He woke from his dream with great relief and watched with curiosity as a figure rose from the end bunk and moved over towards the window. The female figure stood for a few seconds, then turned, lifted something from the bunk and tiptoed stealthily along the aisle that ran the length of the room.

As she passed his bunk Donaghue was able to make out in the dim morning light the long blonde hair of one of the French twins.

As soon as the girl had left the dormitory, Donaghue rose and made his way silently along the aisle to the spot at the window where she had stood a few seconds earlier. He found himself looking out on to the courtyard that separated the main refuge building from the archaeologists' lodge.

In the half-light Donaghue could discern a tall figure leaning against the gable end of the lodge building and gazing out in apparently deep reflection at the valley beyond, which was bathed now in the crepuscular light of dawn. Donaghue recognised the solitary figure as Oliver Hardcastle. He was dressed in walking boots and a thick anorak. The dormitory was heated and warm but Donaghue knew that the early morning temperature outside was very low. He wondered what Hardcastle was doing out at such an early hour. Could it possibly be, he asked himself, that the archaeologist had gone, as Sir Hilary had suggested he might, to tamper with the drawings? Would the Englishman risk taking uncharted paths in the dark to satisfy his ambitions?

Donaghue's thoughts were interrupted as the blonde twin emerged from the refuge building into the courtyard and made her way uncertainly towards Hardcastle, who turned his head in surprise at her approach.

The girl stopped beside him and the two stood in conversation for a few minutes before moving away and disappearing through the entrance door to the lodge.

Donaghue turned reflectively from the window. His insatiable curiosity forced him to glance at the table beside the last bunk where the girls had placed their belongings. Ninette's metal-framed glasses stood propped against a paperback thriller. So, it was the non-spectacled Nanette who had joined Hardcastle outside. He smiled. There were some things then that the twins didn't do together!

'Well, well!' Hardcastle smiled at the young French girl as she cautiously approached him. 'And what are you doing out at this hour of the morning?'

'I couldn't sleep,' she said shyly. 'I was looking out at the valley when I saw you standing there. I thought . . .'

'You thought I might like some company.' Hardcastle finished her sentence for her with a flashing smile.

'Yes . . . and there's something I wanted to ask you . . . *we* wanted to ask you, my sister and I.'

'Your sister?' Hardcastle peered closely at the girl. 'Let me see,' he said seriously. 'Don't tell me – let me see if I can remember which one is which . . . you're Nanette, is that right?'

The girl smiled coyly up at him. A sudden gust of cold wind blew her hair over her face. She shivered involuntarily.

'It's cold,' said Hardcastle. 'Perhaps we should go inside. You can tell me there what it is you want to ask me.'

The girl nodded and, drawing her anorak over her ears, accompanied Hardcastle into the warmth of the lodge.

Sir Hilary Compton woke, as was his habit, at seven and leapt promptly out of bed. He was doing his regular morning squats when his wife, waking from a fitful sleep, sat up, rubbed her swollen eyes and burst into tears.

'Good lord, Beatrice, what on earth's the matter?' exclaimed Sir Hilary, pausing in mid-squat.

'The most dreadful thing has happened,' said his wife. 'I . . . I . . .' Tears rolled down her cheeks. She placed the bed cover over her face and sobbed into it.

'What dreadful thing has happened?' demanded Sir Hilary, who had abandoned his exercise and placed himself, panting heavily, on the side of the bed. He pulled the bed cover from his wife's face and frowned at her. 'Spit it out, Bea. You're not pregnant?' He guffawed. 'Is that it?'

Beatrice gazed miserably at her husband.

'No, no. It's . . . it's that Hardcastle. I can't face him again.'

'Hardcastle?' queried Sir Hilary. 'Hardcastle? What can Hardcastle have done that is so dreadful?'

Beatrice covered her face with her hands. 'He tried to seduce me last night,' she mumbled. 'It was dreadful. I can't bear to see his face ever again.'

Sir Hilary looked at his wife in incredulity.

'Beatrice,' he said, 'are you mad? Are you telling me that *Hardcastle* tried to seduce *you*?'

'Yes,' Beatrice blurted, averting her eyes from her husband's penetrating gaze.

'Look at me, Bea,' Sir Hilary commanded her.

Beatrice lifted her eyes tentatively to those of her husband. Sir Hilary placed a large hand over her shoulder.

'Listen, Beatrice,' he said gently. 'You've been dreaming – a little too vividly, it would seem to me.'

'I wasn't dreaming,' said Beatrice through clenched teeth. 'I'm telling you the truth. He tried to seduce me last night after I left the table. He gave me some whisky – '

'You drank whisky?'

'Yes, a glass or two. Then he – '

Sir Hilary interrupted his wife, placing a hand on her head and smoothing her ruffled hair. 'What you need, Bea,' he said, 'is a nice hot cup of coffee. In all the years we've been together I've never known you to drink one glass of whisky, let alone two! Alcohol addles the brain. Coffee – it's the only effective antidote. I'll go and order some now.'

He rose from the bed.

'I'm not addled,' protested Beatrice. But her words fell on deaf ears as Sir Hilary had already gone – wearing bright turquoise jogging pants and a fluorescent windcheater – to ask Michou to bring a pot of strong black coffee for his wife.

As he closed the door behind him, Sir Hilary shook his leonine head and tutted to himself. He'd have to keep an eye on Beatrice. Her behaviour was getting a little out of hand. Women, he thought, you can live with them all your life and be not one jot nearer to understanding how they function.

Donaghue, who, after his pre-dawn excursion, had drifted back into a pleasantly dreamless sleep, was woken at seven by the general clamour of the others waking and climbing out of their bunks. The French twins were dressed and ready to leave the dormitory, as were Bridget and Clothilde. Meryss Jones was clambering down from her bunk and Jim Baxter stretched and yawned, making the wooden slats above Donaghue's head creak.

'Come along now, Ulysses,' Clothilde called out to him cheerfully. 'It looks to be a sunny morning. Let's make the most of the little time we have. There are some interesting things to be seen in this valley.'

'To be exact,' said Donaghue as Clothilde approached his bunk, '724 drawings from the Bronze Age, twenty-two Roman inscriptions, fifteen Christ figures and three pieces of graffiti by Napoleon's soldiers.'

'Are you making all this up?' demanded Clothilde suspiciously.

'Not at all,' said Donaghue as he pulled his thick walking socks up over his short calves.

'But how do you know? You haven't even looked at the book I gave you.'

'The information I have is from the horse's mouth. Sir Hilary confided it to me himself last night.'

'You have a brain like a sponge, Ulysses,' said Clothilde, smiling. 'It soaks up seemingly trivial information the way a sponge soaks up water. I can't imagine where you store all your facts and figures.'

'In my IDR – my Irrelevant Data Reserve. It's like an information back-up service. You'd be amazed how useful it can be in the most unlikely circumstances.'

'You know, Ulysses,' said Clothilde humorously as she accompanied her friend downstairs to the dining-room, 'I sometimes think that you weren't made quite like the rest of us.'

Donaghue nodded his unruly head and smiled in reply. It would not occur to him that his friend's words constituted anything other than a compliment.

The dining-room, as they entered it, was warm and sunny, the early morning sun streaming in through the window that gave out on to the courtyard. The nostrils of Donaghue and Clothilde were pleasantly assailed with the odour of percolating coffee.

The Vincentes were sitting in their usual corner in the company of Oliver Hardcastle. Herman Browning sat with Bridget at the same table and, at the table by the door, the guide, Laura Hutchinson, sat with the shepherd, Antonio, sipping a bowl of coffee which she held between long, slender fingers. The French twins sat in their favourite corner by the window.

Donaghue and Clothilde joined Meryss Jones and Jim Baxter at the centre table.

Voices buzzed and a general air of cheerful gaiety prevailed as the diners waited for Michou to serve them their breakfast of hot coffee and crusty rolls. Petrocelli, the parrot, on his perch in the corner, whistled cheerfully between renderings of his repertoire of favourite sounds.

Laura Hutchinson, having finished eating, stood up and addressed the gathering. Her straight brown hair had been brushed back from her face and tied at the nape of the neck, making her angular face appear almost gaunt. There was something intense and determined in the young woman's features that kept the eyes of the men present riveted to her as she spoke.

Hungry, thought Vincente.

Too thin, thought Hardcastle.

Not my type, thought Browning.

A secretive woman, thought Donaghue.

Jim Baxter was the only man in the room who wasn't making a judgement on the guide. He was thinking about Meryss Jones and what a pleasant girl she was, intelligent and passionate, an extrordinary combination of qualities – rarely found together in a woman. It had occurred to him the night before that he might have fallen in love with Meryss. The very idea was novel. He had never felt such a sentiment before. He would have to think carefully about this very unexpected situation.

The guide's voice interrupted his reverie.

'At eight o'clock,' she said, 'there will be a guided visit to the western site, where you will have a chance of seeing the fascinating square and rectangular shapes that have puzzled experts for so long. On this site there are also inscriptions believed to have been made by the soldiers of Hannibal's armies.

'Weather permitting, you can visit the north-east site this afternoon. There you will see the classical horned head symbols, Roman inscriptions and some early Christian engravings.

'Those wishing to visit the western site this morning will meet me at the map board on the terrace at eight. We will be back at the refuge by lunchtime. You will have no need to carry water gourds as we will pass several streams and springs. The water in this valley is particularly pure and free of pollutants.'

'I shall do both visits,' declared Clothilde. 'What about you, Ulysses?'

'I shall give the morning visit a miss,' said Donaghue. 'I have a little job to do for Sir Hilary.'

Clothilde raised a sceptical eyebrow. 'And you, Bridget?' she enquired, turning to Donaghue's tall secretary.

'I'm going to carry on studying the inscription with Herman,' said Bridget brightly. 'It's absolutely fascinating. I'll join you and Mr Donaghue this afternoon.'

Clothilde looked with equal suspicion at Bridget, casting a dour glance at the American who was munching on his third croissant of the morning.

'I don't know,' she grumbled. 'We came to the mountains to walk and all you want to do is sit around. All I can say is you'll regret it later when you're old and arthritic and want to get about but aren't able to!'

Herman Browning grinned, picked up a fourth croissant and led Bridget off towards the lodge. Donaghue remained at his table and Clothilde departed to prepare herself for the morning's walk. Hardcastle, Donaghue noticed, was sitting alone in the corner of the room. Now and again the young archaeologist lifted his head and glanced over at the French twins, who were speaking rapidly and heatedly in French at their table by the window.

'You can go on your own,' Ninette said petulantly. 'Why do you want me with you?' She removed her glasses and polished them, glancing as she did so at Hardcastle in the opposite corner.

'I know what you want,' said Nanette slyly. 'You want to be alone with him.'

'It's nothing to do with that,' said Ninette. 'I just don't feel like walking, that's all. Anyway, for all I know he might be going for the walk himself.'

'That's true,' said Nanette, her face brightening. 'I hadn't thought of that.' She stood up. 'Well,' she said, 'I'm going anyway. You can make your own choice.'

'I have,' said Ninette.

Hardcastle, in his corner, took his diary from his jacket pocket and glanced at what he had written earlier: 'Nanette (no glasses): successful – infantile. Perhaps the one with glasses will be more interesting!'

He closed the book and placed it back in his pocket, then, seeing Ninette rise to leave, he followed her out of the room and up the stairs to the dormitory. A few minutes later the two descended and Donaghue, at a discreet distance, watched them make their way towards the archaeologists' lodge. A movement at one of the lodge windows caught the detective's eye. Maria Vincente was watching the approach of Hardcastle and Ninette. The expression on her face was extraordinary. It was, Donaghue could clearly see, one of intense pain and fury.

12

Maria Vincente, at the window of her room in the lodge, watched Oliver Hardcastle approach the building in the company of the young French student.

Her face took on an expression of pain, derived not only from her anger at Hardcastle's obvious interest in the silly young art student, but from the continued pain in her raw heels. The chafed skin was now so sensitive that she was unable to wear even her lightest shoes and, as a result, was unable to accompany Emilio on the morning visit to the site of the engravings. She had decided instead to visit Oliver Hardcastle in his room and perhaps spend the morning with him. He could try putting some more of the 'second skin' on her blisters.

She had known that he would be in the valley and she had planned to make the most of any opportunity that came her way of being alone with him. But now, to her fury, there he was, responding to the adolescent adulation of a teenager! The girl had obviously coerced him into taking her to his room. And he was falling into her trap like a fly into a spider's web. She would have to stop him doing anything foolish.

She slipped her feet into her mule slippers which looked, she knew, utterly ridiculous with the track suit she was wearing, but her painful heels refused all contact with shoe leather. Wincing with the pain that any movement now caused her, she left the room and approached Hardcastle's door.

In his room Sir Hilary removed his wife's empty coffee cup, placed an aspirin and a glass of water on her bedside table and instructed her to stay in bed until her headache had disappeared. Then he donned his anorak and walking boots and, telling her that he was going to spend the morning studying the new engravings, bade her a cheerful goodbye.

As he left the lodge the door to the bathroom at the end of the corridor opened and Bridget, having brushed her teeth in the icy water provided by the valley's springs, made her way back to Herman Browning's room and the inscription whose curious symbols she found utterly fascinating. As she closed the door behind her she caught a glimpse of Oliver Hardcastle as he entered the lodge followed by the French girl, Ninette Fèvre. Bridget watched curiously as the two entered Hardcastle's room. Then the door opposite Hardcastle's opened and Maria Vincente stepped out into the corridor. The Italian woman smiled half-heartedly at Bridget, who bade her a bright good morning then retreated into Browning's room. As soon as Bridget's door had closed Maria Vincente, her face resuming its expression of tight-lipped anger, approached Hardcastle's door.

'One of those young French girls has just gone into Oliver Hardcastle's room,' Bridget informed Herman Browning as she resumed her seat next to his at the work-table. 'I can understand a girl of nineteen being infatuated with a man like Oliver Hardcastle but what I can't understand is a man of his age being interested in a girl as young as that. You don't suppose he's taking advantage of her, do you?' She looked worriedly at her companion.

Browning smiled at Bridget's rather old-fashioned terminology.

'It takes two to tango,' he said. 'And she's old enough to vote.'

'But they're so childish, those twins,' said Bridget. 'Terribly immature, even for nineteen. It's not the girl's behaviour I find odd – it's his interest in her. He's obviously the indiscriminate type.' She lifted her pretty head in a gesture of spirited resolution. 'I'd have nothing to do with a man like that.'

'Maybe he's just putting the record straight,' suggested Browning. 'I saw him early this morning with the other one. They were taking an early morning stroll together outside.'

'As I thought,' said Bridget, 'utterly indiscriminate – a Casanova. Not the type of man I like at all.'

Browning looked sidelong at Bridget then shifted his gaze rapidly to the work-table on which his copy of the rock's inscription was laid out in enlarged characters.

'Anyone seeing you come into my room might think I was taking advantage of you,' he said humorously.

'But I'm much closer to your age,' Bridget retorted indignantly. 'And in any case we come here to work together.'

'Hardcastle might be working with the French girl.'

Bridget smiled in a maternal manner at Browning. 'You must be terribly naïve if you think that, Herman,' she said. 'Of course they're not working together. She's in love with him and he's taking advantage of her. That's the top and bottom of it, believe me.'

Herman coughed and shifted in his seat. 'May I ask you a . . . personal question, Bridget?' he said. He appeared very slightly embarrassed.

'Of course you may,' said Bridget, smiling at him.

'Are you . . . do you have . . . a boyfriend, a fiancé . . .?' He hesitated. 'A husband maybe?'

'A husband?' Bridget laughed. 'No, I haven't got one of those, not yet anyway. But I will have, no doubt, in the not too distant future – if he doesn't get lost on one of his desert rallies, that is. I'm engaged. He's somewhere in the Sahara at the moment.'

'Ah,' said Herman. 'The Sahara.'

'And you?' asked Bridget.

'I am carefree and unattached,' said Herman a little dejectedly. 'I suppose you could say I'm married to my work.'

'Don't worry, Herman,' said Bridget, patting him comfortingly on the arm. 'You'll meet the woman of your dreams one of these days. Just think – she's out there . . .' Bridget waved a long slender arm at the world beyond the lodge. '. . . waiting for you right now. It's only a question of being in the right place at the right time.'

Herman, who thought that this place at this moment was just about the most perfect he had ever been in, glanced dismally at Bridget, then, smiling with mock cheerfulness, turned his attention to the inscription.

Maria Vincente hesitated before knocking on Hardcastle's door. She could hear voices from within. She glanced over her shoulder to make sure that nobody was watching, then pressed her ear to the door. The conversation in the room was muffled but just audible.

'Which of us do you prefer?' she heard the girl saying coyly.

'You, definitely,' Hardcastle replied.

'How can you tell us apart?' the girl asked. 'If I take my glasses off people say we are exactly alike.'

'Every woman is unique,' said Hardcastle, 'even identical twins. Your features may be the same but you are more intelligent. It shows in your face. In your expressions you are far from identical.'

The girl laughed, a trill of pleasure. Then there was silence.

Maria knocked on the door and opened it brusquely. She stood angrily in the doorway.

The two, who had obviously been in an embrace, leapt apart. Hardcastle gaped at Maria and the girl let out a shriek of laughter as her eyes took in the apple-green jogging pants and purple-bobbled mules.

Maria's face turned slowly red with fury and embarrassment.

'I came to see if you could do something with my feet, Oliver,' she said, 'but you obviously have more important matters to deal with.' With that she turned on her stinging heels and ran, limping, back to her room.

'I'd better go,' said Ninette. 'She looked at me as though she wanted to murder me.' The girl giggled. 'I thought she was going to take off one of those purple mules and hurl it at me. If I were you . . .' She paused and pecked a surprised Hardcastle on the cheek. '. . . I'd stick to one woman at a time. You'll find that life will be a lot simpler.' Then she popped her glasses on to her small nose and left the room.

Hardcastle sat confusedly on his bed. Was it possible, he thought with incredulity, that he had overstepped the mark with this challenge he had set himself? It was obviously going to be difficult to keep his activities hidden. It hadn't occurred to him to lock his door. But what was Maria so furious about? She wasn't his wife, after all. As far as he was concerned she constituted an occasional dalliance, nothing more. Who the hell did she think she was? His features set into an expression of angry determination. If she thought that she could dictate to him she could think again! He shook his head as if engaged in a private debate. No, he was not going to let a bit of stupid female jealousy stop him from doing as he pleased. A married woman could hardly demand fidelity from her lover!

He smiled at the irony of his observation then he took his diary from his pocket. Alongside the name Ninette he wrote: 'Didn't work out – but would have been marginally better. They're clones. If it wasn't for the glasses I couldn't tell them apart. Perhaps I'll try again another time.'

He rose to close the door which Ninette had left open and spotted Herman Browning emerging from the bathroom at the end of the corridor. Browning had been washing his hands. He held them up for Hardcastle to inspect. Dark blue stains dotted the palm of the left hand.

'My damned pen leaked,' said Browning. 'You can't get ink-stains out no matter how much you scrub them.'

Hardcastle pulled Browning to one side. 'Can you spare a moment?' he asked. 'I wanted to have a word with you.'

'Go ahead,' said Browning pleasantly.

'I believe you're working on the inscription?'

Browning nodded. 'Sure am,' he said.

'Have you come to any conclusions about its authenticity?'

'Until it's deciphered it'll be difficult to say with any degree of certainty whether it's authentic or not. But I have to admit that the damned inscription is fascinating me. I've never seen anything like it. Some of the symbols are decipherable but some are completely new to me. I'll have to do a fair bit of research before I can suggest any kind of coherent significance.'

'Sir Hilary seems to have made up his mind that the engravings are fakes,' said Hardcastle.

'He's erring on the side of caution,' said Browning. 'It's only natural. He hasn't studied them enough yet to be sure. He's up there now, as far as I know, giving them a thorough going-over. He is the acknowledged expert. He'll know whether they're fakes or not.'

'I know they're not,' said Hardcastle fervently. 'I discovered the blasted things!'

'I understand how you feel,' said Browning. 'But why should Sir Hilary make a deliberately false statement? He has no vested interest in pronouncing them fakes if he knows them to be real. On the contrary – look at the publicity it will bring him.'

Hardcastle looked gravely at Browning. 'It's not that I think that he'd deliberately make a false statement . . .' He paused and leaned conspiratorially towards the American. 'What I fear is that he might make a false statement *unwittingly*.'

'I'm not sure that I follow you,' said Browning.

'What I'm trying to say,' said Hardcastle, 'is that I'm not sure that Sir Hilary is altogether sane.'

Browning's sandy eyebrows rose in surprise.

'He seems perfectly sane to me,' he said. 'Eccentric, perhaps, but then the British tend to become eccentric with age. It's a national characteristic, I believe.'

'Look at the way he dresses,' said Hardcastle disdainfully. 'Like a college student! He puts gel on his hair, for God's sake!'

'Not a mark of insanity, as far as I know,' said Browning with a grin. 'Sorry, Hardcastle, I can't say I agree with you on that one.'

'Haven't you seen the way he hangs around Vincente's wife? It's not exactly discreet behaviour for a man in his position.'

Browning looked humorously at Hardcastle. 'Interest in younger women can only be considered insanity if the girl is under age. Signora Vincente is hardly that!'

Hardcastle frowned in irritation. 'Well, I consider it close to insanity when a respected sexagenarian dresses and behaves like a sixteen-year-old. I would hesitate to trust his judgement.'

'Maybe so,' mused Browning. 'Maybe you're right.'

At that moment the door to the American's room opened and Bridget's head popped out.

'Herman,' she called excitedly. 'Come here quickly.' She nodded at Hardcastle in acknowledgement of his presence. 'I've had an idea . . .'

'I'll be with you in a second,' Browning called and Bridget disappeared from the doorway, evidently in haste to return to her discovery.

'Maybe this is the breakthrough we've been waiting for,' said Browning in amusement. He grinned at Hardcastle. 'She's an amazing girl, Bridget. You wouldn't think a girl as beautiful as that could have brains but she has. Maybe she'll decipher the inscription and prove one way or another whether the drawings are authentic or not.'

A curious expression crossed Hardcastle's face. 'Wait one moment, Browning, will you . . .?' he said. 'I have something to show you.' He disappeared into his room, leaving Browning standing patiently in the corridor.

While waiting for Browning, Bridget peered excitedly at the sheet of paper on which she had been listing possible meanings of the engraved symbols. The inscription lay before her, set out in large characters, copied to scale from the original:

The symbols had then been listed vertically with any possible meanings alongside:

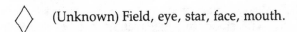 (Unknown) Field, eye, star, face, mouth.

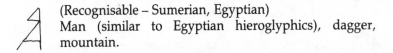 (Recognisable – Sumerian, Egyptian)
Man (similar to Egyptian hieroglyphics), dagger, mountain.

(Unknown) Field, face, star, eye, grain.

(Recognisable – common to Bronze Age cultures) Star, god.

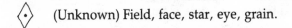 (Similar to Egyptian symbol meaning big)
Fork, tool, lightning, plough, crown.

(Common in inversed form) Meaning uncertain, possibly abstraction – arm, leg, tool, plough.

(Unknown) Field, sun/moon in heavens, habitation.

The inscription was divided into three distinct groups of four symbols. She noted down the first four and beneath each marked one possible significance:

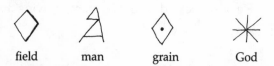

| field | man | grain | God |

Beneath this she wrote the sentence: 'From the field of man comes the grain of God.'

She gazed at what she had written and her face lit up into a bright smile. Was it possible . . .? Was it conceivably possible . . .?

The door opened behind her.

'Herman . . .' she said excitedly, turning her head. She was surprised to see, not Herman, but Oliver Hardcastle, standing in the doorway. He was frowning, his eyebrows knitted in agitation.

'Miss Kilkenny,' he said, 'you'll have to come. Browning seems to have passed out.'

'Herman . . . passed out?' exclaimed Bridget. She jumped up and followed Hardcastle quickly along the corridor to the spot where Browning had stood in conversation a few moments before. The American was no longer standing but lying slumped inelegantly on the tiled floor of the corridor.

'I was talking to him – you saw me,' Hardcastle explained. 'Then I went into my room to get a book I wanted to show him and when I came out he was like this. One minute he was standing up and the next he was in a heap on the floor.'

Bridget had bent to look at Browning. She patted his face brusquely with her hands. 'Wake up, Herman,' she said anxiously. But the American remained immobile.

'He seems to be in a sort of coma,' she said. 'It's more than just a faint.'

'Help me lift him,' said Hardcastle. 'We'll take him into my room.'

With Bridget's help the archaeologist hoisted Browning and then lifted him through the open doorway of his room and on to the bed. Browning's face was pale. It bore an expression that amounted almost to surprise.

'There's no doctor at the refuge,' said Bridget. 'Only Dr Blanche, and she's gone on the walk. What could possibly have happened to him?'

'He'd been washing ink from his hands,' said Hardcastle. 'Perhaps the ink has poisoned him. Maybe he's allergic to it. You don't suppose he's had a heart attack, do you? He's a bit overweight.'

Bridget looked worriedly at Browning. 'What can we do?' she said. 'There must be a way of waking him up.'

'There's nothing we can do until the doctor comes back,' said Hardcastle, shaking his head.

'We ought to tell the refuge keeper,' said Bridget. 'He could call a doctor from the village.'

'I'll do that, then,' said Hardcastle. 'You stay here with Browning in case he wakes up.'

Hardcastle left and Bridget sat tentatively on the bed beside Browning, watching his face avidly for any sign of reanimation. After a few minutes Hardcastle returned.

'There's no one in the refuge,' he said. 'They must have gone down in the jeep for supplies. But I phoned the village doctor. He's out on a call but his secretary said she'd give him the message as soon as he returns.' He took Bridget by the arm and lifted her to her feet. Her face was pale with anxiety.

'There's no point in fretting here,' he said. 'He's breathing regularly.' Hardcastle smiled reassuringly. 'Maybe he was up all night worrying about the inscription and he's having forty winks.'

Bridget smiled half-heartedly as she allowed Hardcastle to lead her back to Browning's room. He sat her at the table where she had been working and placed a comforting arm around her shoulder.

'You mustn't worry, Bridget . . . do you mind if I call you Bridget?'

Bridget distractedly shook her head.

His hand squeezed her shoulder. 'He'll be all right.'

'But he was all right ten minutes ago,' Bridget said. 'I just don't understand it.' She looked up imploringly at Hardcastle. She appeared to be on the verge of tears. Her lips trembled prettily and Hardcastle found himself unable to resist the temptation of leaning forward and kissing her on the mouth.

Bridget's reaction was instantaneous. She fell backwards from her chair. Hardcastle fell with her. He had no other option as his nose was gripped painfully between Bridget's teeth. As he had leaned towards her Bridget, who attended weekly classes in self-defence in London, had done exactly as her instructor had suggested for such circumstances and bitten her aggressor's nose.

The two landed in an untidy heap on the floor, Hardcastle yelping in pain.

This was the spectacle that met Donaghue's eyes as he opened the door to Browning's room.

Donaghue coughed to attract their attention to his presence and Bridget released Hardcastle's nose. The archaeologist scrambled hurriedly to his feet and gazed, horrified, from the detective back to Bridget then back again to Donaghue.

'I . . . I . . .' he stammered. He held a hand over the tip of his nose, which bore the marks of Bridget's teeth and was beginning to redden and swell. 'She . . . she bit me . . . it was an accident.'

Bridget, who by now had lifted herself to her feet, adjusted her sweater, which had become crumpled in the débâcle, and stood up to her full height of five feet nine inches, regarding Hardcastle with an expression of grim resolution. She threw back the mass of red curls which had fallen over her face. 'If it was an accident,' she said primly, 'I apologise for biting you. I reacted instinctively. I thought you were going to attack me.'

Hardcastle gazed at Bridget with a mortified circumspection. There was no admiration in his regard, only extreme wariness. He backed away from her towards Donaghue at the door.

'Perhaps you wouldn't mind telling me what's going on?' Donaghue enquired.

'It's a little complicated,' said Hardcastle hesitantly. 'There was an accident. Browning passed out. He's in my room. Bridget . . . Miss Kilkenny here was, naturally, distressed. I was attempting to reassure her when . . .' He touched his swollen nose gingerly and glanced uneasily at Donaghue. '. . . she bit me.'

Donaghue looked quizzically at his secretary, who stared defiantly back at him.

'As I said, I thought he was going to attack me. If I was mistaken in that respect I apologise.'

Her tone of voice, although polite, implied strongly that she did not consider that her judgement had been wrong. At the same time her Irish intonation became noticeably marked.

'You say that Browning passed out. Is anyone attending him?' Donaghue asked Hardcastle.

'I called the village surgery but they have no idea when the doctor might turn up.'

'Hadn't we better go and look at him then?' said Donaghue, turning to leave.

Hardcastle, in apparently great relief, left the room and led

Donaghue, followed by a stern-faced Bridget, to his room. They found Browning sitting up on Hardcastle's bed, his crew-cropped head in his hands.

He gazed in puzzlement from one to the other.

'One minute I was standing up wide awake in the corridor and the next I'm flat on my back in here. What the hell's going on?'

'You seem to have fainted, Herman,' said Bridget.

'Fainted?' The American scratched his head. 'I've never fainted in my life. Why in God's name would I faint?'

'Lack of oxygen to the brain,' suggested Donaghue.

'But why would my brain lack oxygen all of a sudden?' asked Browning in mystification.

'There are various reasons,' said Donaghue. 'Sudden shock, vertigo, low blood pressure, low blood sugar level. Do you suffer from low blood pressure by any chance?'

'Not as far as I know,' said Browning. 'As I told you, I've never fainted before in my life.'

'Did anything occur that could have caused you a shock?' Donaghue asked. 'Did you see or hear anything unusual?'

'Absolutely nothing at all. I was standing in the corridor waiting for Hardcastle here to come back with whatever it was he wanted to show me and that's it – I don't remember anything else after that.'

'And up to that point you can't remember anything, even some small thing, that might, unconsciously, have caused you a shock?'

'I told you,' said Browning. 'Nothing. There was nothing in the corridor, no sound coming from anywhere. Bridget closed my door behind her – she was looking out to see where I'd gone – and I turned my head at the sound. That's the last thing I remember.'

'Nothing hit you – touched you?'

'Nothing bigger than a mosquito.'

'A mosquito?'

'A mosquito buzzed by my ear. I've no doubt it had a good meal while I was down.'

'I suppose it's still warm enough for mosquitoes,' Donaghue mused. 'But one wouldn't expect them at this altitude.'

'Could have been a fly, I suppose,' said Browning. 'But there was nothing bigger than that in the corridor, I can assure you of that.' He shook his head in puzzlement. 'I just can't understand it. It was like a bolt out of the blue – like some invisible force that wiped me out.'

'There'll be a reason,' said Donaghue reassuringly. 'You'll have to get a doctor to examine you. There's bound to be a very simple physical cause.'

'Well, I'm darned if I know what it is,' said Browning, shaking his head. He lifted himself unsteadily from the bed. Bridget placed her arm on his and led him towards the door. Passing Hardcastle, Browning held out an inkstained hand.

'Thanks for the use of your bed, Hardcastle,' he said. He peered closely at the Englishman's face. 'What on earth have you done to your nose? Looks like someone's tried taking a bite out of it!' He laughed aloud at his joke, then, realising with embarrassment that nobody else had found his comment amusing, allowed Bridget to lead him from the room.

'I don't know what's going on,' he said to her as they passed along the corridor, 'but it's darned weird, whatever it is.'

'Did you see Mr Browning fall?' Donaghue asked Hardcastle as they left the archaeologist's room.

'No, I told you, I'd gone into my room to get a book to show him. He was lying on the floor when I came out.'

'It's very curious,' said Donaghue.

The little Irishman bent and picked something invisible from the floor just inside the open doorway. He held out an apparently empty palm to Hardcastle.

'A contact lens,' he said. 'Is it yours?'

'No,' said Hardcastle, shaking his head as he peered at the tiny transparent lens in Donaghue's hand.

'It must be Browning's,' said Donaghue. He took a paper handkerchief from his pocket and carefully wrapped it around the fragile object.

'This business with Browning is the strangest thing I've ever seen,' said Hardcastle. 'I'd advise him to have a check-up. He's carrying a bit too much weight for his own good. The Americans eat badly – all those hamburgers. Bad for the heart. Dangerous, one could say without exaggeration.'

Hardcastle's words made Donaghue painfully aware of the burgeoning rotundity of his own midriff. Hardcastle was lean and muscular, a picture of health and physical perfection. Donaghue smiled a little wistfully. 'The pleasure of the flesh can be life-curtailing, that is true,' he said. 'But they can also bring in their wake problems other than those of health.'

Hardcastle looked sharply at Donaghue. Involuntarily he touched his smarting nose. The detective turned to leave.

'One must take one's pleasures where one can,' Hardcastle said. 'Don't you agree, Mr Donaghue? Life is short.'

'I most certainly do agree,' said Donaghue. 'Life sometimes can be pitifully short.'

13

By 11 a.m. the temperature had risen to a comfortable twenty-four degrees Centigrade. Donaghue, wearing his favourite Fair Isle sweater and a pair of colonial-style shorts to the knee, settled himself at the wooden table on the terrace and took his long-range binoculars from their case. He had promised himself a pleasant scan of the valley from the relative safety and comfort of the refuge terrace.

The parrot, Petrocelli, was sitting on his perch at the end of the table, having been placed there in the sunshine by Mario before he and Michou had set off down to the village for extra candles and oil. It was not inconceivable that a storm might come up and very often the valley's storms cut off the refuge's supply of electricity. The ancient emergency generator in the shed beside the kitchen had refused to show any sign of life when Mario tested it, and their stock of candles and oil would not be adequate for the unexpected number of visitors.

Donaghue looked over at the parrot. An African Grey – dull-coloured, not brilliant like the macaw but, as Donaghue knew, this drab, unremarkable-looking bird was the best speaker of all in the parrot world, making up in verbosity and perfect mimicry what it lacked in colour.

Petrocelli looked back at Donaghue. Then it spoke: one word in Italian, *puttana*, which it spat at the detective, making him start. Donaghue's reaction was involuntary; he knew that Petrocelli was only an animal of limited intelligence, yet he could not help but wince at hearing the bird's accusation in vulgar Italian that he was a woman of loose morals.

The parrot was, of course, imitating its master who had, no doubt, addressed his wife earlier in the day with the same term. Was it possible, Donaghue mused, that Michou Santinelli had been another one flirting with the handsome Oliver Hardcastle? A jealous tension underlay the otherwise convivial atmosphere at the refuge. Donaghue had felt it from the first meal on the day they arrived. The thought had crossed his mind as he had come on to the terrace this morning that he would like to sit and read *Othello*. Of course it would have to be *Othello* – a drama of jealousy and the paranoia that jealousy brings in its wake.

Was Clothilde right, perhaps? Was he himself feeling jealous and therefore seeing jealousy all around him? Mentally he shook his head. No, his celibate state had left him free of sentimental problems. One did not suffer jealousy if one was without a partner.

Donaghue's celibate state was not a matter of choice. He had never married quite simply because he had never met the right woman for him. Donaghue, a lapsed Catholic since the age of twenty, had had one or two love affairs as a young man but the shackles of his Jesuit education, which had taught him that marriage was a sacred institution, made him seek that state as the natural framework for a sexual relationship. He sometimes thought that he should have become a priest like his college friend, O'Malley. O'Malley was now the priest of a quiet parish in East Anglia and was a happy, satisfied man. Donaghue was, on the whole, a cheerful individual, a man never happier than in the process of discovery – but he had never been, and knew he never would be, satisfied. Somewhere hidden deep in his psyche lurked a longing for romantic love but the idea of a relationship outside marriage left him with a foreboding sense of guilt.

This did not, however, prevent him from nursing a secret admiration for his secretary, Bridget, although he would never dream of pursuing his desire as long as Bridget was engaged to another man. And, knowing Bridget as he knew her, she, in turn, would never consider infidelity. Bridget, unlike her employer, was a practising Catholic.

Donaghue, if asked, would have to admit that he cherished also a secret desire that Bridget's fiancé might find another woman or quite simply fail to return from one of his frequent rallies abroad. Such thoughts, Donaghue knew, were dangerous. He knew only too well from his professional experience that such unspoken desires could lead to acts such as murder.

Donaghue smiled to himself. He, of course, would not be tempted to murder Bridget's fiancé, Tim, but not everyone had his control or his morality. There were people who saw no reason why their desires should not be satisfied and who would allow nothing to stand in the way of that satisfaction. Several of the people at the refuge he had recognised as of that type – people without a strict code of morality, people with a single-minded determination to achieve their own ends. Oliver Hardcastle was one, Jim Baxter another, Sir Hilary Compton a third; among the women, Maria Vincente and possibly the guide, Laura Hutchinson, although it was difficult to judge her (she was a very secretive woman), also one of the French twins – the one called Ninette – and the refuge keeper's wife, Michou.

And yet, Donaghue reflected, he had discovered during his career that murder was committed by every type of person, moral as well as amoral, religious as well as atheist. It seemed that the human animal possessed an infinite capacity to rationalise his acts. Donaghue had dealt with murderers who believed that their crimes were religious acts. Such a murderer was designated insane, the cold-blooded killer evil, but Donaghue was not sure that the epithets were satisfactory. He sometimes felt that every human being was capable of killing his fellow. The mechanism that prevented one and permitted another was inadequately explained by the terms 'sane' and 'insane'.

Donaghue brought his rather morbid train of thought to an end and picked up his binoculars. He stretched out his short legs with satisfaction, sighing as he did so. The parrot sighed with him. He put the powerful binoculars to his eyes and scanned the valley before him. The tor with the newly discovered inscription was, he knew, to the right of his centre of vision. He caught it suddenly, recognising the bent figure of Sir Hilary. He focused on the archaeologist's thick head of hair and hawk-like profile. He was poring over the left-hand side of the rose-coloured rock studying the drawings. He appeared to be inserting an implement of some kind into the indentations, measuring the depth of the incisions, Donaghue deduced. It was obvious to

Donaghue, as an unseen observer, that Sir Hilary was immersed totally in what he was doing, displaying that single-minded determination that he had thought of earlier. Right now, at this moment, there might well have been nobody else alive in the whole world as far as this elderly man intent on his research was concerned.

He moved the binoculars further to the right to the spot where the Lake of Shadows lay hidden from sight. The water could not been seen from this level – only from above, on the top – but he knew it was there to the north-east of the peak, its treacherous banks concealed behind outcrops of rocks and clumps of bushes. He caught a movement, something darting. Could it possibly be a marmot? He knew there were a number of the shy creatures in the valley and that they rarely showed themselves to people. He trained the binoculars carefully around the vicinity of the pool. One of the bushes moved. There was certainly something behind or in it. He waited several seconds in excited anticipation but there was no further movement. The animal must have burrowed or scuttled away behind the adjacent rocks. He spent fifteen minutes happily scanning the valley for marmots but without success.

Then his pleasurable pastime was interrupted as the refuge jeep appeared, filling his field of vision with its large green and black fenders. The vehicle pulled up in front of the refuge door and Michou and Mario descended to offload their supplies. Having deposited the boxes in the kitchen, Mario appeared on the terrace with a tray bearing a bottle and two glasses. He settled himself at the table and offered Donaghue an aperitif of mulled wine.

Donaghue happily accepted and sipped the aromatic wine with pleasure. Mario gulped his glass and poured another. He looked a little dejected.

'You're not a married man,' he said to Donaghue. This was a statement rather than a question.

'No,' said Donaghue. 'I never have been.'

'And right you are too,' said Mario. 'Marriage only ever brings problems. Look at me.' He tapped his balding forehead where faint furrows indented the olive-complexioned skin. 'It's worry that makes you get old – and what do you worry about most when you're married?'

Donaghue shook his wiry head.

'What your wife's up to – that's what you worry about,' said Mario dismally. 'What she's up to and who with.' He shook his head sorrowfully. 'Women are faithless creatures.'

Donaghue shook his head again in commiseration. He declined to make a comment. There would have been no point in trying to convince Mario that not all women were faithless: such an observation would not have made the man feel better. Instead he told Mario about Herman Browning's fainting fit of an hour earlier.

Mario dismissed the incident as unworthy of investigation. Walkers, he said, were forever fainting at this altitude. They forgot that the air is rarer at 2500 metres. The serious walkers trained for such an altitude, learned to breathe correctly, but people like this Browning, who were obviously not sportsmen, were at risk at these heights – not only from lack of oxygen, but from vertigo and general lack of experience.

'Mr Hardcastle called in a doctor from the village,' said Donaghue. 'Perhaps he should be told not to come.'

'Mr Hardcastle will be needing a doctor himself soon,' grumbled Mario menacingly, 'if he messes about with my wife again.'

'Mario!' Michou's voice called shrilly from the kitchen. 'Come and put the boxes away. I can't lift them – you're the man around here.'

'Here,' repeated Petrocelli in the same shrill tone.

Mario rose reluctantly. Donaghue could see that Michou had gained the upper hand in their dispute. Mario could hardly deny that he was the man around the place!

Donaghue picked up his binoculars once again, pleased that the refuge keeper had obeyed his wife's summons and returned to work. He had no inclination to get involved in a conversation about the couple's marriage problems.

He found himself focused once again on the rose-coloured rock at the top of the tor. Sir Hilary was no longer there – probably on his way back down to the refuge for lunch, Donaghue deduced. He panned on to the rock which gleamed a pale pearly-pink in the midday sun, wondering whether the glasses were powerful enough to afford him a clear image of the rock drawings. Happily they were. Slowly he panned across the surface of the rock from right to left, marvelling at the clarity and brightness of the drawings and accompanying inscription.

He focused on a tiny horned-head figure standing with arms raised next to a smaller, circular shape. Donaghue smiled to himself. The figure's stance could almost have been that of a contemporary goalkeeper, arms stretched to catch a ball. It was not inconceivable of course that Bronze Age man had devised ball games similar to those played by contemporary man. Perhaps their drawings represented nothing more than a rugby or football league final!

It was astonishing, Donaghue thought, that such simple drawings etched into a rock could cause the furore and sensation that they would undoubtedly cause if and when authenticated.

Donaghue moved his binoculars from the rock, then stopped suddenly, hesitating. He moved them back on to the tiny figure. Something, some little thing, irked him.

In that part of his memory bank that he called his IDR – his Irrelevant Data Reserve – something stirred. He sat reflectively, allowing his brain to sift the data.

Donaghue had been endowed from a very early age with a capacity to store seemingly trivial data that he accumulated on the whole unconsciously. Some such trivial observation was making its way now to his conscious brain. Quite suddenly he knew what it was. A frown crossed his leathery features.

He brought the binoculars down the side of the tor and caught Sir Hilary in his sights as he stepped nimbly down the makeshift track to the bottom. A movement to Sir Hilary's right sent Donaghue's head swivelling and he caught sight of Laura Hutchinson, leading a straggling group of walkers back from their morning visit.

Sir Hilary joined the returning group at the intersection of the paths. Donaghue was about to put his binoculars away when the movement of a figure hurrying from the refuge caught his attention. He recognised Oliver Hardcastle as he picked up the Englishman's handsome features in his sights.

Hardcastle approached the guide and, taking her arm, drew her to one side. When the others had disappeared from sight the archaeologist said something to the girl, smiling charmingly as he did so. Quite suddenly, to Donaghue's surprise, Laura Hutchinson lifted her arm and slapped Hardcastle resoundingly across the cheek. Hardcastle recoiled, an expression of fury on his face, then reached forward and grasped the guide's arm. Whatever he intended, his action went no further as, at that instant, the shepherd, Antonio, appeared, as if from nowhere, and pulled Laura Hutchinson from Hardcastle's grasp. Antonio stood menacingly between the guide and the archaeologist, his face, close up in the binoculars, a mask of determination. Hardcastle put his hand to his reddening cheek, while Laura Hutchinson turned on her heel and walked angrily back towards the refuge.

The shepherd, Antonio, keeping his eyes on Hardcastle's face, stepped backwards off the path into the shadows of the rocks from which he had come.

Donaghue could not prevent himself from smiling as he regarded Hardcastle's face in close-up. The Englishman's nose still bore the marks of Bridget's teeth from the débâcle of the morning and now one cheek had turned a livid red from the violent impact of Laura Hutchinson's hand. Donaghue wondered what on earth Hardcastle could have said to her to provoke such a reaction. He had said very little, had scarcely opened his mouth, when the woman had hit him.

Hardcastle, an expression of bewilderment on his face, and his hand nursing his smarting cheek, made his way hesitantly back to the safety of the archaeologists' lodge.

Donaghue finally packed his binoculars away and vacated the terrace, leaving the table free for Mario and Michou to prepare lunch. He ambled down along the track to welcome Clothilde back from her outing.

'A splendid walk,' Clothilde enthused. 'Marvellous weather and the guide is excellent. It's so nice to meet a young person who takes her work seriously – a rare thing nowadays, I'm sad to say.'

'She does appear a very serious young woman,' Donaghue concurred. 'And before you say anything, Clothilde, I will be benefiting from her experience this afternoon. I shall accompany you on the visit to the north-east site.'

'Excellent,' said Clothilde as she took Donaghue's arm so that he would be obliged to keep up with her more rapid pace. 'We shall be setting out at two, immediately after lunch. Miss Hutchinson advised an earlier rather than later start as there are clouds on the distant horizon which could herald a late afternoon storm.'

Donaghue looked up at the clear blue cloudless sky.

'There appears to be no storm in the offing,' he said. 'But one has to bow to the superior wisdom of experience. At two o'clock it will be, then.'

'Which means a light lunch and no wine,' said Clothilde authoritatively. 'One cannot attempt a walk in the valley in an inebriated state. There are too many slippery rocks and areas of marsh. One could easily slip, crack one's head on a boulder and, if one didn't kill oneself, end up in a nasty coma.'

'Which reminds me, Clothilde,' said Donaghue. 'Could you spare a few minutes before lunch to give Herman Browning a quick look-over? He passed out this morning for no apparent reason and was a little concerned about it.'

'The sedentary type,' said Clothilde. 'Malnourished and over-weight. He's bound to have health problems.'

They had reached the terrace of the refuge where Mario was setting out plates and glasses on the long wooden tables.

'I shall avail myself of the primitive washing and toilet facilities,' said Clothilde to Donaghue as she headed for the wash-room. 'Then I'll meet you at Browning's room.'

Hardcastle went straight to his room in the lodge, anxious to inspect his smarting face before joining the others for lunch. He was feeling intensely embarrassed and bewildered by the guide's behaviour of a few minutes earlier. He had done nothing more than ask her to remind him of her name, with the intention of inviting her to sit with him at lunch, when she had lashed out and slapped him across the face. An utterly unwarranted and unprovoked attack. The woman was obviously not in her right mind – a definite no-go area as far as seduction was concerned! He would cross her immediately off his list. There was no doubt about it, he reflected – women, all of them, were incomprehensible and irrational creatures, ruled, it would seem, by a matrix of emotions over which their brains had no control whatsoever!

As he passed Browning's door he stopped and, after a few moments' reflection, tapped lightly on it.

Browning opened the door and looked enquiringly out. Bridget, sitting inside at the desk, turned her handsome head and looked suspiciously at Hardcastle.

'Do you think I could have a word with you – privately?' Hardcastle said, his voice low.

'Sure,' grinned Browning. 'Will the corridor be private enough?' He turned his head. 'Back in a sec, Bridget,' he called to the girl as he closed the door behind him and stepped out into the corridor.

'Listen, Browning, I've been thinking,' said Hardcastle urgently. 'I think it's fairly sure that Sir Hilary is going to pronounce the drawings fakes. Perhaps you could have a word with him. If you could convince him that the inscription is genuine he'll have to agree that the drawings are as well.'

'But I'm not sure myself of the inscription's authenticity,' said Browning. 'I'd have to decode it first.'

'But you must have an idea one way or another.'

'It's difficult,' said Browning. 'Especially an inscription such as this, the like of which has never been seen in Europe before.'

'Look,' said Hardcastle, 'all I'm saying is that if you tell him that you're convinced it's genuine he'll have to reconsider his decision.'

Browning looked at Hardcastle quizzically. 'Are you asking me to lie, Hardcastle?' he said.

'Not lie exactly – just express an opinion. You must want them to be genuine as much as I do.'

'What one wishes and what one gets, sadly, do not always coincide,' said Browning somewhat glumly.

'There's no reason why one shouldn't, in the end, get what one wishes,' said Hardcastle, his tone terse.

'Milton's "unconquerable will", eh?' said Browning.

'I prefer Swift,' retorted Hardcastle. '"Take the will for the deed."'

'I'm a Wendell Holmes man myself,' said Browning, grinning. '"Man has his will but woman has her way" – I'm afraid that Bridget, Mr Donaghue's admirable secretary and an extremely moral young woman, would never allow me to lie about the inscription. She knows I'm not sure about it, though she is as keen as I am to see it authenticated – and when it's a case of a woman having her way . . . well, who knows?'

'So, you're not prepared to talk to Sir Hilary?' said Hardcastle.

'Not at this stage, no,' said Browning. 'But the way Bridget is going it looks like she might come up with an answer to the riddle of the inscription, and if she does then I'll be a lot surer of my ground.'

He turned and grasped the handle of his door. 'Back to the grindstone, then – though one can't really call it a grind working with a girl as beautiful and intelligent as Bridget. By the way, Hardcastle,' he added as he opened the door, 'you've got a red mark on your cheek – looks like someone's taken a poke at you.' With that Browning grinned amiably and turned to enter his room.

At that moment Donaghue, who had been making his way along the corridor, approached the American and, nodding politely at Hardcastle, accompanied Browning into his room.

'Hardcastle seems to be in the wars,' Browning commented. 'He's got marks all over his face – must be accident prone.'

'With regard to your accident of this morning,' said Donaghue, 'my friend Clothilde Blanche is a doctor. She is willing to give you a brief check-over. She's on her way now if that's convenient with you.'

'Fine by me,' said Browning.

'By the way, Mr Browning,' said Donaghue as he unfolded a paper handkerchief and held out the contact lens he had found. 'I found this in Hardcastle's room. I take it it's yours?'

'A contact lens?' said Browning. 'Nope, not mine. I've never needed the things. My vision's perfect. Twenny-twenny.' He leaned forward and whispered conspiratorially. 'Probably belongs to one of his lady friends. There's been a stream of them knocking on his door this morning.'

Donaghue decided that Browning's conjecture was probably correct. He would have to seek out the owner very discreetly.

A knock came on the door and Clothilde entered. She shook Browning's hand with a firm grip.

He briefly recounted the events of the morning. Clothilde then sat him on the bed and proceeded to inspect his eyes, tongue, throat, pulse and the rhythm of his breathing.

'There appears nothing major untoward,' she said finally. 'A few kilos to lose but you appear to be in good general health. You say that before you fainted nothing hit you, as far as you can remember?'

'I'd remember if something had hit me,' said Browning. 'If it was a blow strong enough to knock me out I'd have felt it.'

'There is a slight discoloration at the back of your neck.' Clothilde indicated a small circle of reddened skin behind Browning's ear. 'Have you always had it?'

'Not that I know of – but it's there that the darned mosquito or fly or whatever it was must have nipped me. I told you, Donaghue, something buzzed by my ear.'

Clothilde bent to inspect the mark. 'I suppose it could be an insect bite, although I see no head. Some people react violently to insect bites – anaphylactic shock. They usually experience skin prickles, increased body temperature, breathing difficulties and violent nausea. Did you have any of these symptoms?'

'None,' said Browning, shaking his head. 'As I said to Mr Donaghue here, one minute I was wide awake and the next I was out.'

'In any case,' said Clothilde, 'if you had had an anaphylactic reaction you'd be dead now unless someone had rapidly administered adrenalin.' She shook her head. 'I can see no obvious reason why you should have passed out. I can only suggest that you have a full medical examination when you return home to the States.'

'Sure will,' agreed Browning cheerfully.

He resumed his seat next to Bridget at the table and Clothilde and Donaghue took their leave of the industrious couple.

As they opened the door and stepped out into the corridor the sound of raised voices assailed their ears.

Maria Vincente was standing at Oliver Hardcastle's door. The archaeologist in the open doorway was frowning at her, his voice raised in anger.

'. . . no right to interfere in my affairs,' he shouted. 'Don't think you can impose your will on mine!'

Spotting Donaghue and Clothilde, Hardcastle closed his door quickly with a clatter and Maria Vincente turned and marched furiously along the corridor, brushing past Clothilde and Donaghue, tears welling uncontrollably from her large dark-lashed eyes.

'Mr Hardcastle seems to be raising an emotional furore among the women here at the refuge,' Donaghue commented as the refuge door closed behind her. 'One can only deduce that their heightened feelings stem from unrequited passion. I wonder who'll be the next to attack him?' He gave a brief description of

Bridget's and Laura Hutchinson's encounters with Hardcastle that morning.

'Well, I won't be the next, that's for sure,' said Clothilde grimly. 'I have never, even when young, been attracted to good-looking men.' She linked her arm affectionately in Donaghue's, propelling him rapidly along the corridor. 'You know as well as I do, Ulysses, that the benefits of ugliness far outweigh those of beauty. Ugliness can be fascinating and its fascination only increases with the passage of time, while that of beauty rapidly fades.'

'But', said Donaghue, who was never quite sure whether his friend's comments constituted insult or compliment, 'it seems that young women are inexorably attracted to men like Hardcastle.'

'Not all women,' retorted Clothilde. 'Not the intelligent ones. Bridget, your secretary, for instance, is not attracted to him in the least. Nor am I for that matter – and I doubt whether that young Welsh girl, Meryss Whatever-she's-called, is either. Imagine, Ulysses, that you are a young girl – a great leap of the imagination, I know, but try nevertheless. Who would attract you, Oliver Hardcastle with his good looks or a man like yourself with a fine mind and a scrupulous morality?'

Donaghue tried to do as Clothilde had asked but failed. She had been right. To imagine himself as a young girl was a leap far too great for even his fertile imagination.

'I can only guess', he said, 'that if I were a young woman I would think as my secretary Bridget does.'

'And of the two you know who she would choose?'

'You think she would choose me?'

'Of course,' said Clothilde. 'She would never choose a man like Hardcastle.'

Donaghue's monkey face deepened very slightly in colour. He smiled embarrassedly.

'Now don't go entering into futile fantasies, Ulysses,' said Clothilde reprimandingly. 'Don't imagine that that's the only choice she'd have!'

She squeezed his arm playfully. 'Shall we go to lunch? I'm ravenous!'

14

Mario and Michou served a lunch of cold meats, salad niçoise and wholewheat bread. Donaghue, at Sir Hilary's invitation, joined the archaeologists at their table. He found himself sitting opposite his secretary, who was seated next to Browning. Oliver Hardcastle sat somewhat morosely next to Maria Vincente. Lady Compton was noticeable by her absence.

Browning, between mouthfuls, beamed around at his fellow experts and addressed them enthusiastically. 'You might be interested to hear that Bridget here . . .' He stopped to smile admiringly at the beautiful Irish girl. '. . . has come up with a possible significance of the inscription. Of course the idea cannot as yet be verified but it is plausible in terms of our existing knowledge. We are, of course, guessing the significance of the unknown symbols. Show them, Bridget.'

Bridget held up an enlarged version of the inscription, a definition of each group of symbols written beneath:

From the field of man comes the grain of God.

From the tool of man comes the fruit of God.

From the mind of man comes the knowledge of God.

'Is it not a little far-fetched to think that primitive man thought in such abstract terms as mind and knowledge?' said Dr Vincente. 'All the Bronze Age art that we have seen up to now depicts the concrete artefacts of everyday life: the plough, tools, above all the ox.'

Browning spoke eagerly. 'Why should that mean that they lacked the capacity to think as we do? All they lacked were the means of expressing such thoughts. They lacked an alphabet. Who's to say that some bright Bronze Age spark living in this valley didn't come up with the idea of an abstract symbol? I've no doubt that primitive man produced the odd genius every now and again as we do.'

Sir Hilary Compton coughed politely and interjected, 'I'm sorry to have to put a damper on your enthusiasm, Browning, but I discovered something this morning that has almost certainly confirmed my opinion that the drawings are fakes.'

'Really?' said Browning, unable to conceal his disappointment. 'Can you tell me what it was?'

'Certainly,' said Sir Hilary. 'It's no secret. It's there at the top of the tor for all to see. This morning I discovered an additional engraving that was not there yesterday. There is a joker in our pack – a cat among us pigeons.'

Everybody at the table stared at Sir Hilary in shocked silence. Donaghue was the first to speak.

'Would the new engraving be that of a small circle positioned next to a human figure to the left of centre of the rock?'

Sir Hilary turned to look at the little Irishman in surprise.

'As a matter of fact it is. How on earth did you know?'

'I spotted it myself this morning. I was looking at the rock through my binoculars. You must have just left for lunch, Sir Hilary. I noticed the additional symbol.'

'How extraordinarily observant of you,' said Sir Hilary in admiration. He turned to his fellow experts. 'The quality of the new engraving is such that I can only say that it was done by an expert. As it was not there yesterday and I discovered it early this morning I do not have to be a great detective – like Mr Donaghue here – to deduce that it must have been done during the night.'

'Am I right in thinking, Sir Hilary,' said Browning quietly, 'that you are implying that either Vincente, myself or Hardcastle did it?'

'I am implying nothing,' said Sir Hilary. 'I am simply stating an observation. If the new drawing corresponds in style and execution to the others then I will have no choice but to pronounce them all fakes.'

'Does it appear to resemble them?' Vincente asked.

'That I cannot say. I'm still comparing measurements. I shall continue working this afternoon.'

Hardcastle spoke quietly. 'What I don't understand, Sir Hilary, is why, if someone among us faked the original drawings, he or she would add another, thereby exposing the forgery.'

'I cannot say anything about the forger's motive,' replied Sir Hilary. 'I can only talk about the engravings themselves.'

'But it's crazy,' said Hardcastle heatedly. 'What possible motive could there be? I can see no rhyme or reason in it. To go up there in the middle of the night and carve out another drawing in the rock – what purpose could that possibly serve?'

'You were out last night, Hardcastle,' said Browning softly. 'I saw you. What were you doing?'

Hardcastle looked darkly at Browning.

'I was out before dawn and what I was doing is no concern of yours.'

He rose from the table, his face flushed. 'Well, it looks like Sir Hilary has made up his mind,' he said curtly. 'I see no reason to stay in this godforsaken valley a day longer.'

'Do calm down, Hardcastle,' said Sir Hilary, 'and stop jumping to conclusions. My mind is not yet made up. As I said, I haven't yet completed my analysis.'

Hardcastle sat down hesitantly, evidently reassured by Sir Hilary's words. Coffee was served and drunk in a reflective silence. At the end of the meal Laura Hutchinson announced that the afternoon visit would start at two and that the prospective walkers were to bring capes and sweaters in case of storms. She advised the women not to wear any metal jewellery or hairclips.

Browning, who had intended accompanying Bridget on the outing, expressed his wish to look instead at the new faked engraving. Dr Vincente said that he too would accompany Sir Hilary back up to the tor.

At two o'clock a small group gathered at the map board for the afternoon walk: Donaghue, Clothilde, Bridget and Ninette Fèvre. They waited for Meryss Jones and Jim Baxter whose names were also down for the trip.

Meryss arrived at five past two, alone, her face animated and flushed. 'I'm sorry I'm late.' She giggled embarrassedly. 'But I've just found myself at the centre of male rivalry. Mr Hardcastle invited me to go and look at the fake drawing with him and Jim punched him.' She giggled again, her small intelligent eyes bright with amusement. 'I've never been fought over before,' she said.

'And Mr Baxter, is he coming?' asked the guide.

'No,' said Meryss. 'He felt obliged to go and photograph the new engraving – and I think he wants to keep an eye on Mr Hardcastle in case he follows me up here.' She giggled again. Laura Hutchinson regarded her grimly before calling the group together and setting off at a leisurely pace in a north-easterly direction.

After ten minutes of walking the guide suddenly stopped. She looked distractedly at the group. 'I am really most terribly sorry,' she said, 'but I've forgotten my walkie-talkie. It's absolutely essential if there is any risk of storms. I'll have to go back and get it.' She glanced at her watch. 'It's two twenty. I can get there and back running in fifteen minutes. There are no drawings to be seen in the immediate vicinity but there are marmots. If you are quiet and discreet in your movements you might be lucky enough to spot one while you're waiting. Don't wander too far from the path and avoid the marshy area to the west. The Lake of Shadows lies thirty metres or so west of this spot and is practically invisible until you are on top of it.'

She set off running on her slim well-muscled legs. Meryss, Ninette and Bridget wandered off to the shade of a nearby rock and settled themselves on the grass. Meryss extracted from her rucksack a bar of chocolate which she offered around, and the girls, nibbling happily, entered into an animated discussion of the desirability or otherwise of Oliver Hardcastle.

Donaghue and Clothilde wandered back along the path to the place where, Donaghue calculated, he had spotted the marmot that morning through his binoculars. 'There,' he said excitedly, pointing to an invisible spot some ten metres from the path. 'A marmot hole!'

Clothilde squinted. 'I can't see anything,' she said.

'It's barely discernible,' said Donaghue. 'Marmots are very discreet creatures. If we sit here quietly we might see one come out.'

They positioned themselves comfortably against a rock and, setting sun-hats on their heads against the midday sun, watched and waited in silence. The valley was extraordinarily still, the sky blue and cloudless, the only sounds to break the silence the buzz of an insect by Donaghue's ear and the bleating of sheep from a nearby hillside, accompanied by the tinkling of their bells.

After ten minutes Donaghue whispered disappointedly to Clothilde, 'They probably know we're here – they're not coming out to play. The guide will be back any minute. We'll have to start back. You go on ahead. I have to . . . ahem . . .' Donaghue coughed embarrassedly, '. . . answer the call of nature.'

Clothilde set off and Donaghue walked a few metres off the path and behind an outcrop of rock.

To his surprise he heard the murmur of voices coming from behind a further, much larger boulder. Beyond the boulder, he knew, lay the treacherous Lake of Shadows. Curious, he moved forward. A man's voice came, distant but audible. He recognised it as that of Oliver Hardcastle.

'. . . interfere,' Hardcastle was saying angrily. 'You're trying to impose your will on mine. It won't work. You don't know who you're dealing with.'

It struck Donaghue that what Hardcastle was saying was curiously similar to what he had said to Maria Vincente earlier in the day. Had Signora Vincente climbed all the way up here with blistered feet?

The answering voice was so quiet as to be inaudible.

Hardcastle's voice rose in pitch and anger.

'I'm warning you – you'd better change your tactic. You're treading on dangerous ground.'

Again an indiscernible answer, then silence followed by a prolonged rustling sound. Donaghue heard a voice calling his name. He turned his head. It was Laura Hutchinson, standing on the path. He turned and followed her back to join the others. As he hurried along, trying to keep up with the athletic young woman's stride, he shivered involuntarily. He had not noticed the sun go in. Laura, he noted, had put on a sweater, a rather

101

bright, violet-coloured hand-knit in wool. He looked up and was astonished to see half of the sky laden with clouds, a dark billowing mass of cumulo-nimbus that scudded swiftly from the east.

'Don't worry,' Laura Hutchinson said, looking up at the darkening sky. 'The site isn't far. We have time to get there and back before the storm sets in.'

The small group returned from their walk early in the evening cold and wet. The rain had set in on the return journey but they had managed to get back to the refuge before the imminent storm broke. While visiting the site they had seen lightning flash over the distant hills to the east. By the time walkers and experts sat down to dinner at seven an electric storm was lighting up the vista beyond the refuge terrace.

The temperature outside had dropped to a chilly two degrees but inside, the dining-room was cheerful and warm, heated by the cooker in the kitchen and an old-fashioned wood-burning stove. Oil lamps and candles were out ready in case the electricity supply was cut by the storm.

A lively discussion animated the archaeologists' table. Hardcastle was absent, presumed by Browning and Vincente to be peeved by Sir Hilary's implication at lunchtime that an archaeologist had faked the additional engraving.

Sir Hilary, accompanied finally by his wife, took his seat next to Donaghue whom he had invited to join him. He had spent the whole afternoon at the tor, carefully comparing the new engraved circle with the other drawings. He looked over at Browning and Vincente, an amused glitter in his eye.

'You know,' he said, 'this new, obviously fake little drawing has forced me to rethink my opinion that the other drawings are false.'

Browning's face broke into a happy smile. Bridget, sitting next to him, beamed. An expression of relief crossed Emilio Vincente's dark, handsome features.

'The forged circle is very different in execution and style from the others. If my hypothesis that they are all forged is correct then I have to conclude that there are two forgers. That, I feel, is highly unlikely. If the drawings are genuine then they were probably executed one or two centuries later than the other drawings in the valley – hence their slight difference in style. Perhaps, for some reason unknown to us, they were deliberately hidden – possibly, as Browning suggested, because of the inscription. As to who added the fake circle and why, I am not qualified to offer an opinion.'

Sir Hilary lowered his voice and nodded his large head in the direction of the French twins, who were gazing avidly out of the refuge window at the growing storm. 'Perhaps one of those girls did it. You know what students are for pranks.' Then he turned and clapped Donaghue on the back, making the little detective almost choke on the olive that he was munching. 'Perhaps our detective here will conduct an investigation into the identity of the mystery forger.'

'I'm inclined to agree with you, Sir Hilary,' said Donaghue, 'that it's nothing more than a prank.'

The meal continued in an atmosphere of heightened conviviality. The storm raged outside. Great forks of lightning lit up the valley's distant hills. Booms of thunder crashed above the refuge making the thin walls tremble and the lights flicker. As a precaution Mario lit one oil lamp on the counter so that they would have light if the electricity failed.

'Someone should go and warn Mr Hardcastle that the electricity could go at any moment,' said Donaghue. 'He should at least have a torch ready if it does.'

'I'll go,' said Mario hurriedly before his wife had time to volunteer. He donned his waterproof cape and departed for the lodge, returning a few minutes later, a surprised expression on his face.

'He's not there,' he said, perplexed. 'I tried all the rooms in the lodge and in the rest of the refuge. He's in neither building. Where on earth can he be? Has anyone seen him recently?'

'He didn't come up to the tor with us,' said Browning. 'I expected to see him. For some reason he got waylaid at the bottom. I heard him speaking to someone on the way down. That was about two fifteen.'

'I heard him but didn't see him shortly after that,' said Donaghue.

'Did anyone see him here this afternoon?' Mario asked.

The diners, looking round at one another, shook their heads.

'Well, I didn't see him at the refuge this afternoon,' said Mario. 'Where exactly did you hear his voice, Mr Donaghue?'

'At the bottom of the tor, to the north-east side. From where I was standing I guess he was not far from the pool – the Lake of Shadows.'

'That's right,' said Laura Hutchinson. 'The spot where you were standing is fifteen metres or so from the edge of the pool.'

A hushed silence fell over the room at the guide's words. Each head turned towards her. Then Meryss Jones spoke matter-of-factly, addressing the room: 'If Mr Donaghue heard Mr Hardcastle speak, then there must have been someone with him. Perhaps that person knows where he went?' She looked enquiringly round at her fellow diners. There was no response. Nobody moved and nobody spoke. Donaghue, who had supposed that Hardcastle's interlocutor had been Maria Vincente, chose the side of discretion and said nothing.

A sudden booming crash of thunder broke the silence, making one of the French twins squeal. At the same time the refuge walls trembled and the lights flickered on and off.

Nanette Fèvre giggled nervously, then spoke. 'What on earth can he be doing out there in this storm?'

'No one in their right mind would stay out in a storm like this,' said Meryss. 'He must have come back.'

'If he came back, then where is he?' asked Mario. 'He's not here in the refuge nor in the lodge – there's no other shelter.'

'He could have sheltered from the storm in Antonio's hut,' said Laura Hutchinson. 'But I can't understand why he didn't return when the storm started brewing. He knows the valley well enough. He's an experienced walker. Perhaps we should go out and look for him.'

'In this?' said Michou. 'Won't it be dangerous?'

'If he's fallen and is trapped somewhere he'll never survive the night out in the open,' said Mario. 'I agree that we should go and look.'

A search party was quickly organised. All the men present agreed to go out as well as Laura Hutchinson, Clothilde and Meryss Jones, the experienced walkers among the women.

It was agreed that they would spread out in pairs, concentrating on the tor and the area around the Lake of Shadows where Hardcastle had been last seen and heard.

Mario and Dr Vincente headed for the shepherd's hut while the rest of the group, led by Laura Hutchinson, made their way towards the base of the tor where they split off in different directions. Laura Hutchinson, holding a powerful flashlight, went with Sir Hilary Compton in the direction of the lakeside. Donaghue, Clothilde and Browning took the area around the base of the tor and Jim Baxter and Meryss Jones made their way up the side of the tor itself.

Each searcher carried a torch and was protected from the driving rain by a calf-length rubberised cape. The torches were lit but their light was scarcely necessary as searing zigzags of lightning lit up the landscape every few seconds.

Hardcastle's name rang out as each searcher called him, their cries drowned out much of the time by the great crashing boom of thunder that accompanied each flash of lightning as it zig-zagged from the heavens to the valley below.

As Browning, Clothilde and Donaghue searched diligently behind each rock and boulder at the base of the tor they suddenly heard Laura Hutchinson's voice clear above the others, her tone strident and urgent.

'He's here!' she called. 'I've found him – in the lake.'

The message was transmitted from searcher to searcher and within a few minutes they were all gathered around the guide at the edge of the deep-sided pool.

Laura Hutchinson, standing next to Sir Hilary, directed the powerful beam of the flashlight on to the dark water below.

Hardcastle lay floating on his back, his face gleaming a ghostly white in the light of the beam playing on it. The expression visible to all above was one of great fury and determination as if his struggle against death had been ferocious in the extreme.

The searchers watched the floating body in shocked silence, then Mario said, his voice trembling, 'We'll have to get him out. I'll go back for ropes and harnesses.'

Antonio, who had accompanied Mario and Dr Vincente back from his hut, returned to the refuge with Mario. Laura Hutchinson suggested that the less experienced walkers, namely Browning, Donaghue and Jim Baxter, accompany the women back to the refuge. Dr Vincente, Sir Hilary, Mario, Antonio and herself would be able to hoist the body out and carry it back.

Sir Hilary turned, shaking his leonine head.

'A dreadful accident,' he said. 'A sorry and dreadful accident.'

As he spoke a great flash of lightning lit up the grisly spectacle in the pool. The grey angry face of Hardcastle, the eyes opened and furious, glared up at the small group looking down at him. It was almost as if he were still alive. They stared back at him transfixed. Then the body bobbed unnaturally as the lashing wind and rain drove the icy waters of the pool into surging eddies.

15

Using rock-climbing equipment of harness, ropes and pitons, Mario descended the steep-sided banks of the pool. An eddy of water, driven by the howling wind, pushed the bobbing body close to the bank so that Mario was able to secure a rope around Hardcastle's neck without immersing himself in the icy water. Pulling the body towards him, he looped the rope under the oustretched arms and called for Sir Hilary at the top to haul it up.

Antonio and Sir Hilary hoisted Hardcastle up and Mario climbed nimbly back up to the top. They wrapped the body in a tarpaulin sheet that Mario had brought for the purpose and, with Laura Hutchinson leading the way, the four men, Vincente, Sir Hilary, Mario and Antonio, carried the body on their shoulders like pall bearers back to the refuge.

On Mario's instruction the corpse was placed in the generator shed and Laura Hutchinson suggested that Dr Blanche be called to examine it.

Clothilde came immediately, accompanied by Donaghue, Browning and Baxter. As she bent to inspect the body the light suddenly went out. Clothilde tutted in annoyance and Browning swore. Mario, a stream of verbose Italian issuing from his lips, disappeared and returned within a few seconds with an oil lamp which he placed next to Hardcastle's body.

Clothilde began her examination. She closed the staring eyes but not before everyone present had noted once again the expression of fury that seemed to glare from them even in death.

Hardcastle was dressed simply in a T-shirt, knee-length shorts and open leather sandals. His lean body was so tanned that the pallor of death was scarcely noticeable. With the eyes closed he could have been sleeping, caught up in a dream of great intensity.

After her examination Clothilde stood up.

'Well,' said Jim Baxter. 'Death by drowning, I suppose.'

Clothilde frowned. 'Curiously, no,' she said.

Baxter's face took on an unaccustomed expression of animation.

'What on earth do you mean? He's found dead in a pool and he didn't drown?'

'He didn't drown,' said Clothilde. 'There's no water in his lungs. He would have been face down in the pool if he'd drowned. He was dead when he hit the water.'

'Dead when he hit the water?' repeated Baxter excitedly. 'What did he die of, then?'

'I don't know,' said Clothilde, the furrows of her brow deepened by a frown. 'It's very curious. There is some swelling around the nose and cheek but that could not have caused his demise. There appears no apparent reason for his death.'

'Struck down by God, perhaps,' said Baxter grimly. 'Divine retribution. His type never fall foul of human justice.'

Clothilde looked deprecatingly at Baxter. 'If he was struck by anything,' she said, 'it would have been lightning. It's the only thing that could possibly explain his death. He's wearing nothing metallic but if he'd been standing close to a rock with pockets of iron ore he could have received a shock strong enough to send him reeling backwards over the edge.'

'What time would you estimate his death?' Donaghue asked.

'I'd say between two thirty and three thirty, not much later. He's been dead about six hours.'

'And you can give no definite clinical reason for his death?'

'There is no sign of an accident – a fall or a blow. There is, as I said, bruising to the face but nothing that could explain his expiring, then falling into the lake.'

'Perhaps he passed out like I did,' suggested Browning.

'If he had fainted he would have woken on impact with the water,' said Clothilde. 'He would have surely called for help.'

'Antonio would have heard him,' said Laura Hutchinson.

107

Antonio, in the corner, nodded gravely, the bell around his neck tinkling as he did so.

'His death will have to be reported,' said Clothilde. 'I would be interested to hear another doctor's opinion.'

Mario's voice came from the dark recesses of the small room: 'With the electricity cut the telephone line will be dead. During a storm like this no one will be able to go down to the village. Even by foot the track will be treacherous. We won't be able to get a doctor up here until the storm passes. We'll have to leave the body in here. In any case,' he added, shivering as he spoke, 'he's not going to deteriorate rapidly in these temperatures.'

Clothilde covered the body with the tarpaulin and the small group left the shed to return to the warmth of the oil-lit dining-room. Before closing the shed door Donaghue pulled Clothilde to one side.

'Have you really no idea as to the cause of death?' he asked.

'Absolutely none,' replied Clothilde. 'The only possible explanation is that he was struck by lightning!'

Donaghue reflected. 'The storm came up at about four. Could there have been any lightning over the lake at three thirty? We would have seen it, surely? We weren't that far away.'

'There wasn't any as far as I remember,' said Clothilde. 'But then we might not have noticed. We were intent on looking at the rock drawings.'

'Did you see anything on his body that might indicate foul play – apart from the bruises on his face? I know how he got those.'

'The thought had crossed my mind,' said Clothilde. 'A young man in the prime of life found dead in a pool. But there is absolutely no sign of a struggle of any kind – no bruising or lesions. The man died of no apparent cause!'

'Could he have committed suicide?'

'You mean by taking a lethal dose of barbiturates, passing out and falling into the lake? A rather theatrical and precarious method of killing oneself. But only an autopsy would reveal that.'

'There's something odd about Hardcastle dying,' said Donaghue. 'Something aberrant.'

'It's always aberrant when the young and healthy die,' Clothilde agreed.

'The young and fit die only through accident or design,' said Donaghue.

'Either way the cause of his death is not obvious,' said Clothilde. 'But one thing is certain – something killed him. One does not die from no cause at all!'

She closed the door of the generator shed and stepped out into the icy wind-driven rain. The storm had travelled westward but, as Mario had pointed out earlier, another would follow quickly in its wake.

Mario, as soon as he entered the refuge, made for the bar and opened a bottle of cognac. He poured a small tumbler for each person in the room.

In the corner by the window Michou was comforting a tearful Nanette.

'He can't be dead,' the girl sobbed. 'He's too young.'

'There there, my dear,' said Michou, whose own eyes were moist with tears. 'It's not as if he was a close friend.'

'No, but I was going to get to know him,' wailed Nanette. 'I didn't even get a chance to talk to him.'

She put her head in her hands and sobbed anew.

Ninette, dry-eyed, sat to one side of her sister in the company of Bridget and Meryss.

Mario served the small tumblers of cognac and urged them all to drink.

'It'll warm you up,' he said in his singsong Italian accent, 'and take the edge off this nasty business.'

Nanette wiped the tears from her eyes and sipped the warming liquid.

Jim Baxter and Browning joined the girls at their table while Donaghue and Clothilde joined Sir Hilary and Lady Compton, who were already in the company of Laura Hutchinson and Antonio, the shepherd.

Dr Vincente left the dining-room to find his wife, who had preferred to remain alone in the archaeologists' lodge.

'A nasty and tragic business,' said Sir Hilary as Donaghue and Clothilde took their seats at his table. 'You'd think someone as young and fit as Hardcastle could have climbed out of that pool instead of drowning in it the way he did.'

'He didn't drown,' said Clothilde. 'He was dead when he fell in.'

Lady Compton gasped, her face paling.

'Good God!' exclaimed Sir Hilary. 'Heart attack? One would hardly expect cardiac problems in a man like Hardcastle. Lean and fit, not the type, I'd say – but then I'm not a doctor.'

'I suppose cardiac arrest is possible,' said Clothilde. 'But, as you say, he hardly appears the type. As a matter of fact I have no idea how he died, but he certainly didn't drown.'

'It doesn't make sense,' said Laura Hutchinson. 'A young man in perfect health just dropping dead. He looked perfectly all right at lunchtime. There's something awfully tragic about it.'

'He was a bad lot,' said Sir Hilary. 'Is it so tragic when a bad lot comes to an end?'

Lady Compton looked, horrified, at her husband.

'That's a terrible thing to say, Hilary,' she said almost inaudibly.

'A terrible thing to say, I agree,' said Sir Hilary, 'but the truth nevertheless. The truth, sadly, is sometimes terrible to hear.' He looked at his wife pointedly. 'As far as I am concerned he was a bad lot and bad lots generally come to a bad end.'

'What makes you say he was a bad lot, Sir Hilary?' Donaghue asked.

'He was . . . how can I put it . . . frantic. Yes, that's the word – frantic – in his ambition. A bad sign. Didn't want to take the time it took to get where he wanted to go. Would stick at nothing to achieve his ends. My feelings are based more on intuition than fact, that I have to admit. For instance, I felt strongly when I first met him that he had faked the engravings.'

'You no longer feel that way then, Sir Hilary?' said Laura Hutchinson.

'As I said at lunchtime, I'm more of the opinion now that they are genuine. The newly added one is obviously fake. Perhaps he did that one.'

'But why?' asked the guide. 'For what possible reason?'

'To spite me perhaps. Who knows?' said Sir Hilary. 'A gesture of frustration because I had suggested that the engravings might be fake. Vandalism, I'd say, pure and simple. I told you he was a bad lot. An educated hooligan.' Sir Hilary smiled grimly. 'Hardcastle was not a young man who loved life – he was a young man who *took* life and gave nothing back in return. As far as I am concerned, and I've lived a long time, life is not to be simply taken, it is to be enjoyed, played with – above all, it is to be laughed at.'

His voice gained in volume, became booming so that those at the other table turned their heads to look at him.

'Life is absurd,' he said 'a practical joke on a cosmic scale. Hardcastle was too serious, far too serious. He had no sense of humour – no sense of *fun.*'

The last word rang out and the parrot picked it up. 'Fun, fun,' it repeated. 'Fun, fun.'

The parrot's repetition sent Sir Hilary into great booms of laughter with the effect of instantly dissipating the tension that had pervaded the refuge since Oliver Hardcastle's body had been brought back.

Mario poured a second round of cognacs and a babble of animated conversation started up.

'Fun,' called Petrocelli from his perch. 'Fun, fun, fun.' Then he added as if in rhyme: 'The gun, hide the gun. The gun, hide the gun.'

'There's no gun, Petrocilli,' Mario called out humorously. 'This isn't a case of murder.'

At the word 'murder', inexplicably, a hush fell over the room.

'What's the matter?' asked Mario as he looked around at the silent faces in puzzlement. 'I didn't say it *was* a murder, I said it *wasn't*. Nobody killed Hardcastle as far as I know, did they? He died of natural causes – isn't that right, Dr Blanche?'

'As far as I could tell, yes,' said Clothilde. 'There was no sign of foul play.' She smiled. 'He certainly wasn't shot by a gun.'

'Hide the gun,' called Petrocelli. 'Hide the gun.'

'What are you talking about a gun for, Petrocelli, you dumb parrot?' said Mario as he placed the bird's large cage over its perch and threw a towel over it. He smiled around at the assembly. 'I got him from a Sicilian,' he explained. 'He thinks he's back with the Mafia.' He burst into a loud guffaw of laughter and Sir Hilary joined him, chuckling in amusement.

'A gangster parrot,' he chortled. 'That reminds me of a story. There was a Mafia gunman who went to see the Pope . . .'

He proceeded to tell his story to the table and the atmosphere of merriment was quickly restored.

A clap of distant thunder heralded a new storm and Mario proposed a hot punch before the gathering retired.

The parrot beneath its towel said no more, a large boom of thunder overhead shook the refuge walls and Sir Hilary finished his story, leaving his listeners laughing uproariously. Even the usually dour Laura Hutchinson managed a smile. The only person at the table who hadn't laughed was Lady Compton. She had heard her husband tell humorous stories before – it was an old habit of his – but she had never heard him tell one like this. Not only had this one been irreverent, it had been *indecent*. She looked, stricken, at her husband.

In their room at the lodge Dr Vincente found his wife sitting beside the window gazing out at the now ferocious storm. Her face was pale, her lips set into a firm angry line.

Dr Vincente squatted at her side and took her hand in his. At his gesture she burst into tears.

'Were you in love with him?' he asked quietly.

Maria turned and gazed tearfully at her husband. Then she laughed. 'In love?' she said, her voice quivering slightly. 'Do you seriously think I was in love with him?'

'I wasn't sure.'

'You've lived with me all these years and you hardly know me,' she said, smiling. She reached out and gently stroked her husband's hair. 'You intellectuals are all the same,' she said. 'You live in a world of ideas. You see nothing of what is going on around you. How could any woman love a man like that? I was infatuated with him, that's all. He cast a spell on me.'

'And you had no control over it?'

She spoke softly again. 'No, I had no control over it. You must know what I mean, Emilio.' She took his hand and caressed it gently. 'You must meet women sometimes who captivate you.' She looked at him slyly. 'The guide, perhaps. I know she interests you.'

'Of course,' said Emilio. 'Of course I meet women who fascinate me.' He smiled. 'You were the most fascinating of all. But no other interests me enough to . . . get involved.'

'You mean', said Maria smiling, 'that no one interests you enough to tear you away from your books.'

'No one interests me enough to allow them to control me.'

'You're scolding me,' she said. She turned her head and gazed out at the black valley which was lit up every few seconds by the zigzag lightning of the storm. 'He couldn't bear to be controlled. In that you were alike.'

She spoke as if addressing the valley and not her husband, and so quietly that her words were barely audible.

'I could never have loved a man like that,' she said. 'I hated him.'

16

Storms came one upon the other throughout the night. In the communal dormitory the walkers slept fitfully, disturbed by the regular crashes of thunder that shook the building and by the knowledge that Oliver Hardcastle's inert body lay cold and rigid a few metres away in the generator shed.

Only Donaghue slept soundly, the rumble of his snoring adding to the general cacophony of coughs, creaking bed slats and bodies turning fretfully in their sleep.

Donaghue, having had a good night's sleep, was the first to wake in the morning, which dawned grey and overcast. He could hear the rain hammering relentlessly on the roof of the refuge and, looking out of the dormitory window, he saw that the sky was still laden with black storm clouds. There was not going to be an immediate improvement in the weather, that was obvious.

Flicking the light switch by the door, he noted that the electricity was still off. A cable must have been brought down. The cognac and punch of the night before had left his head a little fuzzy. A cup of hot milky coffee would do the trick.

Anxious not to wake the others he padded silently downstairs in his thick walking socks and was surprised to see the light of an oil lamp in the dining-room. Maria Vincente was sitting alone at the table by the window. She held a bowl of coffee in her hand. The coffee pot stood on the table before her.

'The coffee's hot,' she said. 'I've just made it. Please help yourself.'

Donaghue shivered involuntarily as he took a bowl from the stack behind the counter.

'It's cold down here,' he said conversationally. 'The dormitory's surprisingly warm.'

'The window was wide open just now when I came in,' said Maria. 'That's why it's cold.' She indicated the long window, now closed, at the end of the counter. 'The wind must have blown it open.'

Donaghue looked at the towel-covered parrot's cage which stood on the counter beside the window. A frown creased his leathery brow. 'The parrot is next to the window – did you check it?' he asked.

'No,' said Maria. 'Why on earth should I?'

'Parrots don't take too well to draughts,' said Donaghue. 'Their feathers are meant to be ruffled by warm tropical winds not wet icy ones.'

He lifted the towel from the cage and uttered an exclamation of distress. The parrot lay inert at the bottom of the cage.

Donaghue reached into the cage and touched the frozen plumage. The parrot was dead, icy to the touch and rigid. Donaghue picked up a sprig of something green that lay beside the bird then he replaced the towel and, lifting the cage, carried it through the kitchen and placed it outside the kitchen door. An expression of disquiet crossed his monkey-like face as he returned to the dining-room.

'I had no idea . . . I didn't think to look,' said Maria, her face distraught as Donaghue took a seat beside her at the terrace window.

'I feel quite distressed,' said Donaghue. 'That parrot was an excellent mimic. I'd become quite fond of it. It was as if it had a personality of its own.'

'Mario and Michou will be upset when they hear the news,' said Maria. 'I think they've had it for a long time.'

'It surprises me that Mario hadn't closed the shutters,' Donaghue murmured. 'I suppose Hardcastle's death must have perturbed him.'

'Yes,' said Maria. Her tone was bitter. 'Not only him. It has perturbed me as well.'

She looked fixedly at Donaghue as if weighing him up.

'Mr Donaghue,' she said, 'I came here early for a reason, not just to drink coffee. I was hoping to see you.' She smiled, her teeth shining brilliant white against the even tan of her unmade-up face. When she smiled, Donaghue noted, Maria Vincente was a stunningly beautiful woman.

'I guessed you would be an early riser,' she said. 'You have that kind of enthusiasm – the type who doesn't like to waste the day. Am I right?'

Donaghue inclined his head modestly. He looked at her admiringly. Signora Vincente was as astute, it seemed, as she was beautiful.

'We spend a third of our lives in sleep,' said Donaghue. 'Why? One of those great unanswered questions. I try to keep my sleeping time to a minimum so that I can spend what waking hours I have trying to find some answers to life's mysteries.'

'It's for such an answer that I wanted to speak to you,' said Maria. 'You're a detective, I believe – a private investigator?'

'I am,' Donaghue agreed.

'Would you . . . could you investigate Oliver Hardcastle's death?'

Donaghue looked at her quizzically.

'On whose behalf?' he asked.

'On mine. I will pay you, of course.'

'And what exactly do you want me to investigate? The exact cause of his death?'

'The cause of his death and why he died.' Her eyes suddenly filled with tears. 'He shouldn't have died,' she said, her tone furious. 'He should not have died!'

'Dr Blanche said that the exact cause of death could only be ascertained by an autopsy. There would not normally be an autopsy unless there was suspicion of foul play.'

'There is such a suspicion. I suspect foul play.' She paused. 'I think Oliver Hardcastle was murdered.'

Donaghue's untidy eyebrows rose. 'Can you tell me why you suspect such a thing?'

'Because there is no other possible explanation for his death.' She repeated what she had said before. *'He should not have died.'* Her voice quavered as she spoke. 'He was in the prime of life, full of vigour, fit and healthy. Men like that do not just drop dead.'

'That is generally true,' Donaghue agreed. 'But, as I said, only an autopsy can reveal the true cause of death.'

Maria turned her head and looked out at the deepening gloom of the valley beyond. 'Look at the weather,' she said. 'It's not going to clear. We could be stuck here for days. By the time we get a doctor up here it might be too late to ascertain the true cause of his death. The doctor might say that there are insufficient grounds to suspect foul play and the death will be registered as heart failure or natural causes. It won't be the truth. *He could not have died of natural causes.*'

'Do you have any concrete reason to suspect someone of killing him?'

Maria Vincente hesitated. 'I have no concrete evidence, if that's what you mean. I've heard no one threaten him or anything like that, but I have a powerful feeling, an intuition I suppose one must call it, that he was killed.' She hesitated again. 'I knew him well – intimately. He was a man easy to dislike. He made enemies more easily than friends. He was a man who unwittingly caused strife among those around him.'

'Enough, you think, for someone to kill him?'

'It seems so.'

'Do you know anybody here who might have hated him enough to kill him?'

'Just about everybody,' she said grimly. 'In the short time he was here he made an enemy of practically everybody – excluding yourself perhaps.'

'Do you include yourself in the number?'

'I include myself,' she retorted sharply.

'And you think that somebody here at the refuge killed him?'

'Yes, I do. It's highly unlikely that somebody came up to the valley, killed him and then disappeared without being seen. It was one of the people here now.' She lowered her voice. 'There is a murderer among us, Mr Donaghue. I am sure of it. I am worried that whoever it is might kill again. You know what they say about murderers, that they usually strike twice. Please find out who it is – or at least try and find something that will provide the police with the grounds for an autopsy. Whoever killed him thinks they have got away with it. They must not know that murder is suspected or that an enquiry is being made. Can you work as discreetly as that?'

Donaghue smiled. 'I can perhaps make a supreme effort.'

He looked at Maria Vincente reflectively. 'A death without apparent cause is always suspicious, particularly, as you said, when it is that of a healthy young man. Before I make my decision, would you be prepared to answer one or two pertinent questions?'

'Certainly,' said Maria. 'Ask whatever you like.'

'You said you knew Oliver Hardcastle well. Tell me what you knew of him.'

'I've known him for ten years. We met at university. I had a scholarship to Cambridge. He was two years younger than me, a gifted student.'

'You were an archaeology student too?'

'Yes, but I didn't complete my degree. I dropped out.'

'Might I ask for what reason?'

Maria Vincente averted her eyes. 'The reason was personal,' she said. 'I'd rather not divulge it.'

'Hardcastle as a student – what was he like?'

'Much as you saw him now, handsome, intelligent, an incorrigible flirt, utterly unscrupulous in his dealings with women. He had a private harem of lovers – students, lecturers, even one or two of the cleaning ladies! He believed that he was such a master of discretion that not one of his lovers knew about the others. He was wrong, of course. They all knew. Everyone in the department knew of his exploits. The only person unaware of his reputation was Oliver! But he was too arrogant to see himself as anything other than utterly accomplished in everything he did.'

'You are not painting a very pretty picture,' said Donaghue.

'He was not a very pretty character.' Maria's tone was acerbic. 'He had a handsome face but a despicable arrogance.'

'Did you number among his lovers at university?'

'Yes.'

'And on and off for the next ten years?'

She looked at Donaghue in surprise. 'Yes,' she said.

'Might I ask an indiscreet question?' Donaghue ventured.

'I know what you are going to ask,' Maria interjected quickly. 'Was my husband aware of my infidelity? Yes, he was. Our marriage is based on truth not dissimulation. He accepted my relationship with Oliver because he knew it posed no threat to him. He knows I would never love a man like Oliver Hardcastle.'

117

'Are you sure, Signora Vincente, that you did not love him?'

She looked sharply at Donaghue.

'I could never have loved him,' she said curtly.

'Were you jealous of his interest in other women?'

Her sensual blood-coloured lips quivered very slightly before she spoke.

'Naturally I felt jealous sometimes – it's only human. He was such a terrible *user* of women – saw them only in terms of their physical attractiveness. One sometimes felt one was compared. That made me terribly angry.'

'Jealousy is seen by some as a manifestation of love,' said Donaghue.

'Not by me,' retorted Maria. 'I love my husband, Emilio, but I am never jealous of other women who catch his eye. I think the opposite. I think jealousy is only ever a manifestation of hate.'

'Your concern about his death – might that not be construed as a token of love?'

'You're trying to trap me into professing love for him. You won't succeed. I never loved him and I never would have. I didn't even like him. But that doesn't stop me from feeling outraged that he should be killed.'

'Naturally,' said Donaghue. 'Any intelligent and compassionate person is outraged by the taking of a young and vital life. Tell me, Signora Vincente, do you know if Oliver Hardcastle had an intimate relationship with any of the women present at the refuge?'

Maria smiled grimly again. 'He had planned to have such a relationship with just about every woman here.' She picked up her bag and withdrew a chunky book bound in black leather. It was Oliver Hardcastle's personal diary. She opened it and handed it to Donaghue.

'He had planned, it seems, to establish a harem of all the women at the refuge, including Lady Compton and Dr Blanche!'

Donaghue scrutinised the list of women's names and the comments that Hardcastle had made alongside them.

'Unscrupulous, as you said,' he commented.

'He was never as discreet as he believed himself to be,' said Maria. 'So any of the husbands or boyfriends could have found out and felt animosity towards him.'

'You think then that if he was killed it was from a motive of jealousy?'

'Absolutely. He created an atmosphere of jealous tension from the moment he arrived. Didn't you feel it, Mr Donaghue?'

'I must admit that I did sense both jealousy and tension,' Donaghue concurred. He leaned back in his chair, sipping his bowl of coffee. 'To find out exactly what happened to Hardcastle I will have to discover the identity of the person who spoke to him last. I will have to know the movements of each person during the time leading up to his death. Dr Blanche puts his death between two thirty and three thirty. Can you tell me when you saw him last?'

'I can't say exactly what time it was but it must have been two or a little after. I spent about half an hour at the tor with Emilio from one thirty to two. I spotted Oliver at the bottom of the tor. He was on the path that leads to the lake. He was upturning rocks. I asked him what he was doing and he said he was looking for more hidden drawings. He wanted to prove to Sir Hilary that the drawings he had found were genuine. He said that there were bound to be more of the same type in the vicinity of the tor. He sounded rather desperate. It seems that Sir Hilary had, at that point, more or less made up his mind that the drawings on the tor were fake. Oliver couldn't see himself being the laughing stock of the archaeological world. That idea didn't please him at all!'

'Did you argue with him?'

'Argue? No, we didn't argue. I tried to reassure him that Sir Hilary's decision would be based on an objective analysis, nothing else, and that he would have to accept it.' She paused. 'Oliver and I only ever argued over personal matters. In that particular instance we didn't discuss our relationship.'

'How long did you stay with him?'

'About five minutes, I'd say. My feet were killing me. I have blisters on my heels – new boots that I hadn't broken in properly. I went back to the lodge to bathe my feet.'

'Can you say what time you arrived?'

'As I said, I can only guess the time. Perhaps two fifteen. I was back at the lodge before two thirty, that I know. I picked up my watch and put it on not long after I arrived in my room. It said

119

two twenty-five. Hobbling as I was, it must have taken me fifteen minutes to get back.'

'Did you see anybody on your way?'

'Not on the way, but I saw the guide leaving the lodge as I arrived. She was running, carrying something in her hand.'

'Did you see anyone in or around the refuge?'

'Curiously enough, apart from the guide, no. There seemed to be nobody about, no sign of life at all. I had the impression that I was alone at the refuge. Of course I didn't check it – it was only an impression.'

'And so, between two thirty and three thirty where were you exactly?'

'I was in my room, nursing my feet, until Emilio came back from the tor.'

'What time was that?'

'Not long after me – five minutes or so. He couldn't have been far behind me.'

'I have to ask you another indiscreet question, Signora Vincente,' said Donaghue. He held up Hardcastle's leather-bound diary. 'How did you come by this?'

'I went to his room to look for a tube of ointment that treats blisters. He put some on my feet yesterday. The diary was lying open on the bedside table.'

'His bedroom door was unlocked then?'

'Yes. We leave the doors open for Michou to clean the rooms although I noticed that Oliver had left a note on the bed asking her not to move any of his things. He is always very concerned about his privacy.'

Donaghue's eyebrows arched imperceptibly but he said nothing. Maria Vincente was obviously no great respecter of other people's wishes.

'If you don't mind, I shall keep hold of the diary,' he said. 'There might be something in it that will give me a clue to a possible assassin.'

'I'm sure that every woman he ever had dealings with would have wanted to kill him at some time or another. Only the fact that I was happily married stopped me from feeling murderous towards him.'

She leaned towards Donaghue, her eyes dark with intensity. 'I was privileged,' she said. 'I was able to desire him without loving or hating him. In that, I was like him. Oliver Hardcastle was incapable of feeling passionately about anyone other than himself. He loved and hated no one. The emotional reactions of the women he got involved with confused him. I was the only woman who matched him in his dispassion. I am the only woman who really understood him. It's for that reason that I want to find his killer. I feel I owe him at least that.'

Donaghue eyed Maria Vincente speculatively. Much of what she had said mirrored his own thoughts and conclusions about Oliver Hardcastle, who, it seemed, was as disturbing a character in death as he had been in life.

'I'll take on the enquiry,' he said.

Maria Vincente smiled and sat back with a sigh in her chair. She sipped her coffee with satisfaction.

17

Signora Vincente, her mission accomplished, left the dining-room to return to her husband in the lodge. As the door closed behind her Michou descended the wooden ladder from the mezzanine above the kitchen where she and her husband slept.

Donaghue, lost in thought as he gazed out at the gloom of the rain-lashed valley, was unaware of her presence until she uttered a loud exclamation.

'Petrocelli!' she called loudly. '*Où est* Petrocelli?'

Donaghue quickly rose from his seat. His monkey face bore an expression of great sorrow. 'I'm sorry to have to tell you, Madame Santinelli,' he said, 'but the parrot is dead.'

Michou's plump, beringed fingers flew to her mouth.

'Dead?' she gasped. 'Petrocelli dead?'

'It seems that the window blew open during the night. An African Grey could not survive such a cold draught. I put the cage outside the kitchen door.'

Tears welling from her eyes, Michou fled to the kitchen and thence to the small terrace beyond. She returned distraught. Donaghue suggested that she drink a hot coffee and she sat tearfully at his table. She spoke in heavily accented English:

'Mario will be much, much upset. He has that parrot since he was a child. It was as old as he is. They live as long as human beings, did you know that?' She sobbed. 'I don't understand how it happened. Mario knows that a parrot cannot support the cold. That's why he always closed that window and the shutters.'

'He must have forgotten last night, perhaps because of Oliver Hardcastle's death.' Donaghue spoke gently.

'But I don't think it was open. In cold weather we keep the shutters closed during the day.'

'Somebody opened it perhaps and forgot to shut it again.'

'Perhaps,' said Michou distractedly. Then she burst into tears, sobbing uncontrollably, her large bosom beneath her heavy velour dressing-gown rising and falling ponderously. 'It's so dreadful,' she wailed. 'Mr Hardcastle dead and now Petrocelli. It is as if the refuge is – how you say? – cursed. I had a feeling this weekend would turn out bad – too many people for so late in the season, and the weather unpredictable. There has been an atmosphere here I have never felt before.'

She shivered. 'I don't like it. I had nightmares last night. It's unusual for me. I usually sleep like a marmot but last night I was disturbed. I dreamt that something – an invisible presence – came into the refuge during the night and pulled me from my bed and dragged me to the Lake of Shadows. It pushed me in and pressed my head beneath the water. When I tried to scream my voice came out as the voice of the parrot.'

She looked at Donaghue, her eyes wide with fear. 'It's as if my dream was a premonition.'

'I don't think that is the case,' said Donaghue reassuringly. 'What I imagine is that you heard the window blowing open and the parrot squawking. You incorporated the sounds into your dream. We all do that.'

'Do you think so?' asked Michou with a degree of relief. 'But why would I imagine that someone was trying to kill me?'

'A man has died in unusual circumstances. It's perfectly normal to be perturbed by death.'

Michou leaned forward across the table. 'You know, Mr Donaghue, there's something not right about Mr Hardcastle dying like that. It gives me the *frissons* to think of a handsome young man like that lying dead in icy cold water. There's

something not natural about it. It makes you think he might . . .
he might . . .'

'Have been murdered?' suggested Donaghue. 'Is that the word
you wanted to say?'

Michou's puffy face paled. She nodded. 'It's been on my mind
since it happened,' she said. 'I imagine someone pushing him
over the edge, watching him struggle to keep his head above the
water . . .' She shivered again and pulled her thick dressing-
gown tightly over her chest.

'He wasn't drowned,' said Donaghue. 'He died before he fell
into the lake.'

Michou's sleep-puffed eyes opened wide. 'What could he have
died of – at his age?' she said. 'I've never seen a fitter man. Not
even my Mario. He looks after himself but he smokes. I've never
seen Mr Hardcastle smoke. There's something not right about it.
Don't you think there's something strange about it, Mr Donaghue
– as a detective, I mean?'

Donaghue's shaggy head nodded in agreement. 'I do indeed,'
he said.

'Do you think', Michou asked, her voice lowered to a whisper,
'that he was killed?'

'There's nothing to suggest such a thing,' said Donaghue.
'There's no sign on the body of a struggle of any kind. In fact it's
impossible without an autopsy to say how he died.'

'It gives me the *frissons*,' repeated Michou. She sipped the hot
coffee, holding the bowl cupped in both hands. 'A dead body in
the generator shed and us stuck here at the refuge without
electricity. I don't like it. I will not sleep soundly until the storm
is over and we can call the police up.'

'Don't worry, Madame Santinelli,' said Donaghue comfortingly. 'I'm sure you are in no danger. As soon as the storm lifts
and the sun shines again you'll feel completely different. I have
no doubt that there is a perfectly satisfactory explanation for Mr
Hardcastle's death. Naturally, as a detective, I am intrigued by
anything curious or unexplained. Mr Hardcastle must have had
some health problem that was perhaps unknown to himself. I
would be interested to know who was the last person to see him
alive. They might have noticed something amiss.'

'Well, it wasn't me,' said Michou firmly. 'The last time I saw

123

him was at lunchtime before he went up to the tor with Sir Hilary and the others. He didn't come back with Sir Hilary – that I know for sure. I was polishing the corridor in the lodge when Sir Hilary came in.'

'What time would that have been?'

'Oh, I don't know. Between two thirty and three. Nearer quarter to, I'd say. I usually finish at three. It was a waste of my time – polishing the floor, I mean.' Michou's tone was complaining. 'He left wet footprints all over the clean polish – *en plus*, he didn't even notice or apologise. I suppose the English aristocrats have the habit of servants to clean up after them. They probably never even consider saying thank you! I didn't clean up the mess he'd made. The weather had changed and soon everybody would be coming in with wet muddy feet.'

'You must know Sir Hilary well,' said Donaghue conversationally. He smiled. 'Elderly academics are not known for their practical sense.'

'Mario and I started work at the refuge in the year Sir Hilary discovered the drawings – that is, twenty years ago. We have cooked and cleaned for him each time he came to the valley. But do you know, Mr Donaghue, if you asked him, I'm sure he wouldn't know our surname. During all these years he has never invited us to sit at his table and converse as we are now. In his eyes we are just servants . . .' She spoke with a note of deprecation. 'Not the kind of people to socialise with. I think his wife would be more sociable but she is weak – she lives under his wing.'

'He is an extraordinary man,' said Donaghue. 'Would you say that he has changed since you saw him last?'

'Not since I saw him last – that was only last year – but I suppose he has changed since he retired. He certainly dresses differently but I suppose he feels he can dress as he pleases now. But he is as loud as ever. Petrocelli loves imitating him.' She stopped, tears welling in her eyes as she remembered that the parrot was no longer alive. 'For some reason Petrocelli always liked his voice. Petrocelli was always choosy about who he imitated.' She burst into uncontrollable sobs, burying her head in her hands.

'Please don't distress yourself, Madame Santinelli,' Donaghue implored her. He rose and placed a stubby arm comfortingly

124

around her hunched shoulder. 'I'll make some more coffee,' he said and hurried over to the kitchen.

Having put water on to boil he threw the old grounds into the dustbin. As he did so something caught his eye. He inserted a hand gingerly into the rather insalubrious plastic bin liner, rummaged around and withdrew what appeared to be a television remote control device. He held the black plastic rectangle in the palm of his hand. He uttered two exclamations incomprehensible to Michou who, having watched him rummage in the bin, had come over to see what he had found.

'Bedad!' and 'The divil take it!' he said aloud.

Michou peered at the simple, rather elegantly designed article in Donaghue's hand. 'I've seen that before,' she said.

'Didn't you put it in the bin?' he asked.

'No,' said Michou. 'Mr Hardcastle must have put it there. It's his. I saw it in his room yesterday when I was tidying up. A funny-looking thing. You'd think it was a remote control but it hasn't any buttons. I suppose it must be broken if he threw it away. They have some strange instruments, these archaeologists.'

'It's probably used for dating rocks or minerals,' said Donaghue. 'I shall keep it and take it apart. I am a great one for mending things.'

'It's all the same to me,' said Michou. She looked up as Mario descended the ladder from the mezzanine, tiredly rubbing his eyes.

He bade Donaghue good morning and looked quizzically at his wife's puffy red-rimmed eyes.

'Is anything the matter?' he asked, glancing suspiciously at Donaghue.

Michou tearfully told him of the parrot's demise and led him through the kitchen to view the bird's carcass.

Donaghue returned to the table by the window and proceeded to examine the rectangular object that he had found in the dustbin. Then he delved into his pocket and extracted the dried sprig of parsley that he had found at the bottom of the parrot's cage. He looked from one to the other. 'The divil take it!' he said to himself under his breath.

*

Clothilde, an inveterate early riser, was the next to wake. She made her way down the dark stairway to the shower room and washed her face and hands in the icy spring water. Refreshed and lured by the aroma of freshly made coffee, she entered the dining-room and spotted Donaghue at the table by the window.

'The Santinellis?' she asked. 'Are they not up yet?'

'They're outside burying their parrot which, very unfortunately, died during the night.' Donaghue explained that the window had blown open and Petrocelli had frozen to death. Then, having offered Clothilde a bowl of coffee and a croissant, he gazed thoughtfully out at the gloomy valley. Clothilde regarded him speculatively.

'You're up to something, Ulysses,' she said. 'I can see it. Don't tell me, I know – you think that Hardcastle was murdered and the parrot too!'

'I'm not so sure about Hardcastle,' said Donaghue, 'but I am sure the parrot was.'

Clothilde looked dubiously at her friend.

'Ulysses,' she said, 'one cannot *murder* a parrot. One can kill it intentionally or otherwise but one cannot murder it.'

'If murder can be defined as unlawful killing with malice aforethought, then the parrot was murdered.'

Donaghue retrieved from his pocket the sprig of parsley. 'Someone gave the parrot parsley. They did so knowing that the bird would surely die if he ate it. Then they opened the window in case the parrot failed to eat the herb. Parsley is deadly poisonous to a parrot. So are icy draughts. Petrocelli was killed by somebody here at the refuge last night. I would very much like to know who that person was.'

'Do you think it has anything to do with Hardcastle's death?'

'I think it might have.'

'But you said you weren't sure that Hardcastle was murdered.'

'There's nothing to suggest that he was.' Donaghue paused. He looked reflectively out at the valley again. 'I would like to go up and look at the spot where Hardcastle fell into the lake.'

'That would be terribly dangerous, Ulysses,' said Clothilde. 'You're not the most sure-footed person I know.'

'But you are,' said Donaghue. 'Would you consider coming with me? Look.' He pointed up at the sky. 'There's a lull in the

126

storm. We could go now – as soon as you have finished breakfast, of course.'

Clothilde smiled, her face creasing into myriad folds. 'I can see how much the idea of snooping around a dangerous spot in a thunderstorm excites you,' she said. 'You are still a small boy at heart, Ulysses, always seeking adventure. Well, at least your adventures are not the romantic kind which, it would seem, can be life-imperilling!'

'Do I assume from what you say that you think Hardcastle was murdered by a jealous lover or lover's mate?'

'The thought has crossed my mind, I must admit – as, I imagine, it has crossed the minds of everybody at the refuge. In the few days he was here that extraordinarily good-looking young man had gained himself a large number of enemies. Perhaps even you, Ulysses. I bet you were just a teeny weeny bit put out by his obvious interest in your secretary.'

Donaghue bristled. 'You've known me for a long time, Clothilde,' he said. 'You should know me well by now. I am ruled first by my heart, then by my head and lastly by the intuition of others, particularly that of women. I would never allow base self-interest to upset that equilibrium. It has stood me in good stead over the years and I'm not going to change it now.'

Clothilde nodded approvingly and patted her friend on the arm. 'As always, my dear Ulysses,' she said, 'you are implacably correct. I cannot argue with you.'

'So, will you come with me up to the lake?'

'Now?' asked Clothilde.

'I think now would be the best time, before the others wake and before another storm sets in. Ah,' he said as the door to the hallway opened to admit a dishevelled Antonio. 'Perhaps I should ask the shepherd first if another storm is imminent.'

He beckoned to Antonio who came hesitantly over to the table.

'Tell me, Antonio,' he said, 'would you say there'll be another storm within the hour?'

Antonio pressed his face against the window pane and peered out.

He shook his matted head then held up two fingers of his left hand. The index finger was bent at the knuckle.

127

'I think he means in an hour and a half,' said Clothilde.

'Thank you, Antonio,' said Donaghue as the shepherd, wearing the same shapeless pants and sweater that he had worn since they had arrived, weaved his way through the tables to the counter where he helped himself to a croissant from the pile on the plate.

'We'll go now,' Donaghue whispered and Clothilde nodded.

Within ten minutes they were ready, dressed in warm sweaters, walking boots and full-length rubberised capes. They carried rucksacks which contained torches, water, chocolate and flare rockets in case of emergency.

They left the refuge building quietly and set off to the north-east along the track that led to the lake. They walked slowly. The rain was still driven by a violent wind. The ground, even on the track, was treacherous, muddy and slippery.

At the window of the refuge dining-room a face was pressed against the pane, its weather-beaten features impassive. Antonio watched them until they turned the first bend, then returned to the plate of croissants on the counter.

And, at a window of the lodge, another face watched too, its expression as impassive as that of Antonio. It remained gazing out at the grey valley long after the two walkers had disappeared from sight.

Herman Browning, anxious not to wake the Comptons or the Vincentes, crept along the lodge corridor dressed in his protective cape. Once outside in the courtyard he lowered his head against the driving wind and rain and hurried over to the refuge buidling. He went directly up to the dormitory and found Bridget's bunk, which was the last on the lower row. He gazed wistfully at the beautiful sleeping face before shaking her gently by her shoulders and whispering, 'Bridget, wake up. I've had an idea?'

Bridget's green, slanted eyes opened sleepily.

'Herman,' she said. 'Is it morning?'

'It sure don't look like it,' said Herman smiling. 'But it is.'

She sat up on the bunk wearing green flannel pyjamas. Her mass of auburn curls spread out from her head in a halo of tousled disorder.

Herman blinked. 'You look . . . you look wonderful,' he blurted.

'Really?' yawned Bridget, rubbing her eyes. 'I usually look terrible in the morning.'

'Listen,' said Herman urgently. 'Get dressed quickly and come down to the dining-room. I'll fix breakfast for you. I've got something to show you. An idea about the inscription. It's incredibly exciting. I had a brainwave during the night.'

'OK,' said Bridget as she clambered out of bed. She stood and stretched at the foot of the bunk then crossed her arms and waited.

'Well?' she said.

'Well?' repeated Herman.

'You don't think I'm going to take off my pyjamas in front of you, do you?' she said indignantly.

'N-no,' stammered Herman, who had hoped she would do exactly that. He turned clumsily, bumped into the wooden bunkpost and stumbled out of the dormitory.

'I'll be down in two minutes,' Bridget called.

Clothilde kept hold of Donaghue's arm as they followed the path to the lake, the two treading with great care. Large pebbles and rocks had been driven by the rain down on to the path and were slippery underfoot.

The light was crepuscular, the sky laden with banks of grey, almost black clouds. When they finally reached the small clearing around the lake Donaghue sat on a boulder with great relief. The grassy area that surrounded the border of the pool was wet and spongy. Donaghue's sturdy walking boots sank into the water-logged turf.

'What exactly do you expect to see here?' Clothilde asked. 'Apart from rocks, marshy ground and a rather uninviting-looking lake?' She was gazing down on to the grey troubled surface of the water below.

Donaghue had risen and was now pacing around the small marshy area at the lake's edge. He stood still and pointed in an easterly direction. 'I'd say it was about fifteen metres due east from this spot that we were sitting watching for marmots, wouldn't you, Clothilde?'

Donaghue seemed to be pointing at a large outcrop of boulders.

'I've absolutely no idea,' said Clothilde. 'It's difficult in these conditions to say where east is.' She stopped and looked at her friend in astonishment. He appeared to be doing a rain dance – standing on one spot and treading the sodden ground with his two short stubby legs.

'Ulysses,' she said, 'are you feeling all right?'

'I've never felt better in my life,' said Donaghue in a lyrical Dublin brogue. He beamed at her from beneath the hood of his rubber cape.

She looked at him suspiciously. For a moment she had the impression that she was looking at one of those dwarf-like creatures from a children's fairy tale. A leprechaun, she thought, that's what he's like – an overgrown leprechaun. She smiled. 'Ulysses,' she said, 'is dancing on turf in the rain some ancient Irish custom or do you have a rational reason for doing so?'

Donaghue finished his jig with a flourish. 'Would you say, Clothilde, that this particular spot would still be wet when it's dry?'

Clothilde cocked one eyebrow. 'Is this an Irish riddle?' she asked.

'I think this spot would remain permanently wet even when the rest of the valley is dry, don't you agree?'

'Yes, it's marsh,' said Clothilde. 'Fed by underground springs.'

She shivered. Black clouds loomed ominously over the crests of the distant peaks. 'Shall we be long?' she asked.

'I shall just have a quick scout around the site,' he said. 'Perhaps you can help – keep an eye out for anything that appears out of place.'

After a few minutes' search Clothilde called Donaghue. 'Ulysses, come and look at this.'

Clothilde was kneeling, inspecting the smooth surface of a boulder. In the left-hand corner, etched into the oxidised surface was a tiny star:

'One of the symbols of the hieroglyphic,' said Donaghue as he peered closely at the engraving. 'And unaccompanied.'

The boulder was situated close to the entrance of the clearing. He moved to the next rock. In the same left-hand corner was a second, barely discernible engraving:

'Bedad!' exclaimed Donaghue aloud. Then he hurried back along the path, bending to inspect each flat-surfaced rock. On the two adjacent boulders he discovered, again in the left corner, two further symbols: a fork and a humanoid figure:

'Remember the sequence, Clothilde,' he said. 'A fork, a humanoid, an open rectangle and a star.'

'Is it the same as the hieroglyphic on the tor?'

'Similar but not the same,' said Donaghue.

He reached forward suddenly and plucked something from a twig of gorse behind the boulder. Clothilde peered at the tiny scrap of violet-coloured material that he held in his hand.

'Tie-dyed silk,' she said authoritatively. 'Very fine and fragile, the kind that would catch easily on a twig.'

Donaghue didn't answer. He appeared to be deep in thought. Quite suddenly he spoke in lyrical verse, his voice low and soft:

> 'Sweet are the uses of adversity,
> Which like the toad, ugly and venomous,
> Wears yet a precious jewel in his head;
> And this our life, exempt from public haunt,
> Finds tongues in trees, books in the running brooks,
> Sermons in stones and good in everything.'

He turned to Clothilde, his piercing blue eyes bright, 'There are not sermons but secrets in these stones,' he said. 'I've found enough. We can be getting back now.'

18

By the time Bridget and Herman Browning had finished their breakfast of warmed croissants and hot coffee, the dining-room had begun to fill. Jim Baxter sat with Meryss Jones and the French twins in the corner by the window. Laura Hutchinson and Antonio, at the long central table, were joined by the Vincentes and Sir Hilary and Lady Compton.

Browning, having finished his third croissant, took Bridget by the arm and lifted her to her feet.

'Come over to the lodge,' he said, 'and I'll show you my idea.'

The two donned anoraks and capes and left the refuge building for the lodge.

Browning's room was warm. He had left the oil heater burning. He lit the oil lamp on the table so that Bridget could see what he had written. On the table lay two copies of the inscription. The one on the left bore Bridget's suggested interpretation:

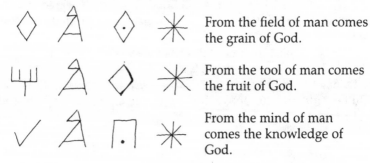

From the field of man comes the grain of God.

From the tool of man comes the fruit of God.

From the mind of man comes the knowledge of God.

'You suggest that only the last four symbols are an expression of an abstract concept but *what if all of them represent abstract concepts?*' He grinned excitedly at Bridget, his eyes gleaming with fervour. 'I woke up last night with the idea. I sat bolt upright in bed, the way they do in Marx Brothers movies. Suppose, Bridget, just supposin' that the whole goddamn inscription expresses an abstract thought. Some neolithic Einstein who'd worked out that we are more than bipedal carnivores. Look – this is my idea, though I have to admit it was your idea that inspired it. Look, Bridget, what do you think?' He lifted his interpretation for Bridget to inspect:

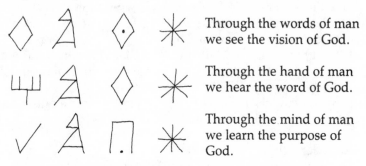

Through the words of man
we see the vision of God.

Through the hand of man
we hear the word of God.

Through the mind of man
we learn the purpose of
God.

Bridget's eyes glittered like those of a cat in the dark.

'It's a marvellous idea, Herman,' she said. 'But do you really think it's possible? I was only letting my imagination run wild.'

'Of course it's unlikely – only speculation,' said Browning. 'But as you say, isn't it a marvellous idea? That early man could have seen himself in relation to the eternal. How do we know that he didn't have the language to express it? We assume that he communicated through grunts. All our assumptions about early man are only that – assumptions. Boy!' he said as he sat at the table and gazed reverently at the drawings. 'Boy! Am I going to enjoy the next five years researching these!'

'So, Sir Hilary has definitely pronounced them authentic?' queried Bridget.

'He said as much to me. I don't know whether he's made another statement to that journalist Baxter but he said that he's more or less sure. I'll have my work cut out with this one.' He hesitated. 'Perhaps, Bridget, you might be interested in coming over to the States from time to time and helping me out – when that fiancé of yours is away on a rally, maybe?'

Bridget's eyes widened with delight.

'What a marvellous idea, Herman,' she exclaimed.

Then to Browning's great delight she flung her arms around his neck and kissed him gratefully on each cheek.

'Clothilde,' said Donaghue as he trudged behind her along the path, his eyes glued to his feet. He had been silent since they had left the clearing at the edge of the lake where he had uttered the few lines from *As You Like It*. 'I know that the clinical cause of Hardcastle's death is not sure but I have a strong suspicion that his death was not a natural one.'

'I won't bother asking you why,' said Clothilde dourly, 'as you won't reveal anything to me until you are sure. But you can tell me what you suspect.'

'I suspect that his death was induced not by natural causes but by some agent outside himself.'

'Do you think he committed suicide?'

'No, I don't think that's the case.'

'Struck by lightning?' suggested Clothilde hopefully.

'Unless he died considerably later than you calculated, that is impossible.'

'You think he was killed by someone, then?'

'I think he was probably killed by someone, yes.'

'Someone here at the refuge?'

'I would imagine so.'

'Do you have any idea who that person might be?'

'As to that, there are many possibilities. Perhaps you could help me there, Clothilde. During your long years as a doctor you have acquired an invaluable insight into human behaviour. Among the people at the refuge, for instance, do you think there are any who felt hateful enough towards Hardcastle to kill him?'

'Who didn't is the question,' said Clothilde dourly. 'But let's look at it systematically. Think back to the first day we arrived. You yourself said that you felt animosity at the archaeologists' table.'

'I felt animosity directed towards Sir Hilary Compton – from Hardcastle and Browning and Lady Compton.'

'I noticed that Mario was very cool towards Hardcastle after the first morning. Perhaps he caught his wife *in flagrante delicto* with the Englishman.'

134

'The idea of infidelity would certainly upset a man like Mario,' Donaghue concurred.

'And Michou, having been seduced by Hardcastle, might have been venomously jealous of his flirtation with the other women. It was obvious to anyone that he was involved in some way with Signora Vincente – although her husband didn't seem to mind at all!'

'She believes he was murdered,' said Donaghue. 'As a matter of fact she has asked me to investigate his death.'

'That could be a bluff, of course,' said Clothilde. 'She could have murdered him herself.'

'Quite possibly,' agreed Donaghue. 'In fact I had reason to believe that she was the last person to see him alive. When we were waiting for the guide yesterday afternoon, just after you left, I heard Hardcastle talking to someone. I didn't hear the other voice but the conversation was remarkably similar to the one we overheard between Maria Vincente and Hardcastle in the lodge that morning. I assumed she had followed him up to the tor and was still telling him off. That conversation occurred just before his death – if your calculation was correct.'

'It couldn't have been far wrong. Rigor mortis had set in.'

'She says she was back in the refuge at two twenty-five, before Hardcastle died.'

'If it wasn't her, perhaps it was her husband,' ventured Clothilde. 'He could have suppressed his jealousy over the years. Or it could have been Jim Baxter. Hardcastle had attempted to seduce the plain and spotty Meryss Jones and, as everyone must have noticed, Mr Baxter is madly in love with her. There again, I suppose one of the French twins could have done it because he showed more interest in one than the other.'

'You're being facetious, Clothilde,' said Donaghue. 'But what you have said is perfectly true – he did show more interest in one than the other.'

'In the one without glasses, I suppose?'

'No, the other one – the one with glasses. The one called Ninette. I don't think her sister, Nanette, even got to speak to him.'

'So she could have killed him from jealousy?'

'I'm not sure about that. She seemed genuinely distraught by his death.'

'The guide,' said Clothilde. 'She seemed cool towards him.'

'Yes, her attitude is curious. I'd be interested to speak to her.'

'Then there's Browning. I think you'll agree that he's fallen head over heels for Bridget, although he appears to be discreet in his relationship with her.'

'Which cannot be said for his relationship with his colleagues,' said Donaghue. 'In the domains of men and work Browning is blunt and sometimes downright rude. I could see that there was no love lost between him and Hardcastle.'

'His motive could be either jealousy of Hardcastle's interest in Bridget or professional jealousy. And if it wasn't him, that leaves the Comptons. Perhaps Sir Hilary worried that Hardcastle was going to topple him from his pinnacle. It's hardly likely that Hardcastle was interested in his wife!'

'In my opinion the latter is more likely. Hardcastle had attempted to seduce Lady Compton.'

'Good lord!' exclaimed Clothilde. 'Did the man have no scruples at all? Was he going to seduce every woman at the refuge, for God's sake?'

'As a matter of fact he was,' said Donaghue. 'Even you, Clothilde.'

Clothilde stopped in her tracks. 'Me? He was going to seduce me!' Her face deepened in colour, whether from embarrassment or fury Donaghue was not sure. 'What on earth makes you say that?'

'Maria Vincente showed me his diary. He had planned to seduce every woman at the refuge. A kind of frivolous pastime while waiting for Sir Hilary to pronounce on the drawings. He didn't get round to all of them and he didn't succeed with all those he tried. Bridget gave him a swollen nose and Laura Hutchinson a smarting cheek – the reason for the bruising you saw on his face.'

'Well!' spluttered Clothilde. 'It's fortunate he never got round to me. He would have got more than he bargained for!'

'He did get more than he bargained for – in the end,' Donaghue added gravely.

'So Lady Compton could have killed him from fury. If he had attempted to seduce her she would have known it was only for a game. She would have felt horribly insulted.'

'I've no doubt she did,' Donaghue agreed. 'So, you can see

how difficult it is. He could have been killed by almost anybody at the refuge. And I am sure that if I were to question each person separately I would find that almost all of them could have been the last to speak to him up at the lakeside. I have a feeling that nobody will have a sure alibi for the time Hardcastle died.'

'Do you intend to question everybody?'

'Discreetly,' said Donaghue. 'I wouldn't want them to think he'd been murdered.'

'I'm sure the thought has crossed a lot of minds,' said Clothilde. 'Few people slept soundly last night. There was a lot of to-ing and fro-ing and walking about.'

'Yes. Somebody walked about the dining-room and opened the window. They then fed the parrot parsley. I was the only one to have slept soundly – which is a great pity.' He looked sadly at Clothilde. 'A very great pity indeed.'

19

In the crowded dining-room Mario announced the news of the parrot's death. His voice quivered as he spoke. He advised the inhabitants of the lodge to make sure their shutters were securely locked at night.

'I'm not saying that a cold draught is as dangerous to a human being as it is to a bird, but it can bring on a nasty cold.'

'Or let in a murderer,' said Nanette quietly from her corner.

There was a ponderous silence for a few moments before Laura Hutchinson spoke.

'There is absolutely nothing to indicate that Mr Hardcastle died other than by natural causes.' She looked grimly over at the pink-eyed French girl. 'Talking about murder is not going to make our enforced stay at the refuge any easier. You are letting your imagination run away with you.'

Antonio's bell tinkled as he nodded in agreement. Laura went on: 'We may be obliged to stay confined to the refuge buildings for two or more days. We shall have to try to make the time pass as pleasantly as possible in the circumstances. Perhaps Mr Santinelli will tell you what recreational facilities are available.'

Mario stood up.

'There's not much in the way of indoor activities, I'm afraid. Visitors to the valley do not usually spend much time inside the refuge. There are cards, chess and backgammon. The lodge has a small supply of books and magazines in the common room which I'm sure the archaeologists will be willing to share with the walkers. We have enough supplies of food for a week but I don't think the storm will last more than three days so we won't starve to death. All I can say is to make the most of your stay in the refuge to get to know each other.'

'Bloody great,' grumbled Jim Baxter in the corner. 'Three days in close confinement with a bunch of eggheads. I'd rather do a week in Wormwood Scrubs!'

'Do you play cards?' Meryss asked.

'Can't stand gambling.'

'What about backgammon?'

'Stupid game.'

'I'll bet you play chess, though.'

Baxter hesitated. 'As a matter of fact I've never learned.'

Meryss smiled brightly. 'Well, now's your chance. I'll teach you. I'll bet you're a fast learner.'

Bridget and Herman Browning were poring over a book on Egyptian hieroglyphics when a knock came on the door.

'Come in,' called Browning and Donaghue's tousled head appeared around the doorjamb.

'Can I have a word with you, Browning?' he asked.

'Sure,' said Browning cheerfully. 'Come on in and take a seat.'

Donaghue sat on an uncomfortable swivel chair at the table. His eye was caught by the two sets of drawings with their respective interpretations. He studied them briefly before looking enquiringly at Browning.

'Great idea, isn't it?' said the American. 'Perhaps hardly credible but a nice thought, dontcha think?'

Donaghue was looking intently at the drawings again.

'Yes,' he said almost absently. 'A nice thought.' He turned to the archaeologist. 'I am curious to discover who was the last person to see Hardcastle alive. Can you tell me when you saw him last?'

138

Browning's eyes narrowed. He looked inquisitively at Donaghue. 'Are you investigating his death or something? Has that old buzzard Sir Hilary commissioned you?'

'Not at all,' said Donaghue. 'I am merely trying to satisfy my own curiosity.'

Bridget smiled. 'Mr Donaghue can't help it. He likes to find things out. He usually does too.'

'OK,' said Browning. 'I'm game to help. Let me see. Last time I saw Hardcastle was at lunch. But I heard him after that. I left the tor sometime before two. We'd all looked at the fake drawing – not much to see as far as I was concerned. Someone had scratched a circle next to a humanoid figure. It looked like a bit of idle graffiti to me, the kind of thing a child would do.'

'Few people idly pass by at the top of the tor,' said Donaghue.

'That's true,' agreed Browning somewhat sheepishly.

'Do you have an idea as to the perpetrator?'

'Haven't a clue. I think we all assumed it was Hardcastle.'

'What would have been his motive?'

'Who knows? To spite Sir Hilary, perhaps? Had Sir Hilary pronounced the drawings fake we would have assumed that Hardcastle had faked them.'

'So, the last time you saw him was in the dining-room?'

'Yes, but as I said I heard him later. I left, as I said, sometime before two with the intention of joining you lot on the afternoon visit – thought I'd catch you up. When I reached the bottom of the tor, at the point where the paths intersect, I heard Hardcastle's voice. He must have been on the path that leads to the lake. He was talking to a woman. Can't say who, though.'

'Were they at the lakeside?'

'No, not as far as that. I wouldn't have heard them from where I was. They were quite close – not far from the intersection.'

'Were they arguing?'

'I didn't actually stop to listen to their conversation, so I've no idea what they were talking about – but I don't think it was an argument. I just recognised Hardcastle's hoity-toity British accent.'

'Did you recognise the woman's voice?'

'No, as I said, I wasn't interested in listening but I assume it was Vincente's wife. It was pretty obvious that something was going on between them. I guessed it was some kind of secret rendezvous – but Hardcastle's private affairs were of no interest to me at all.'

'You didn't join us after all?' said Donaghue.

'No, I saw clouds in the distance so I changed my mind. I'm no great trekker in the best of weather. I came back and carried on working here.'

'What time would you say you heard Hardcastle speak?'

'I'd guess just after two – I was back here at two fifteen.'

'Was anybody else at the lodge when you arrived?'

'I thought there wasn't anybody. It seemed empty. Though, once I was in my room, I heard the lodge door open and close. So someone else came in or went out.'

'You didn't see who it was?'

'No, but . . .' He stopped, looking speculatively at Donaghue. 'Now this is a curious thing, Donaghue, when I look back on it. I went along to Hardcastle's room to borrow his calculator – mine had just conked out – and through his window I caught sight of someone heading for the tor. I thought my mind was playing tricks on me because my first impression was that it was Sir Hilary – but of course it couldn't have been as I'd left him up at the tor.'

'What made you think it was Sir Hilary?'

'I don't know. I just got a fleeting glance but I suppose it was the bright colour of the shirt. Whoever it was, they were wearing a vivid shirt like the ones Sir Hilary is prone to wear – bright colours, flamboyant pattern, the kind of thing that stands out a mile. This one was a mixture of purple, red and yellow! No one else wears that kind of thing as far as I know.'

'Maria Vincente wears brightly coloured clothes,' Bridget ventured.

'But skimpy,' said Browning. 'She doesn't usually wear big baggy T-shirts but this person was definitely not Maria Vincente. She is far too petite. I don't think I would confuse Sir Hilary with a small dark woman half his age! Come to think of it now,' Browning mused, 'I wonder who the hell it was.'

'I wonder too,' said Donaghue. He paused reflectively. 'Yes indeed – I would be most interested in knowing the answer to that question.'

*

After leaving Browning's room, Donaghue slipped across the lodge corridor and into the Comptons' room. In the surreptitious manner of a cat burglar he made for the wardrobe and rapidly scanned the contents, then he opened the drawers of the dressing-table, taking note of what lay within. Then he hurried out, closing the door behind him, and entered the Vincentes' room next door. There he followed the same procedure, noting with admiration the much greater order in Maria Vincente's wardrobe where her numerous outfits were colour co-ordinated and arranged with a perfect symmetric neatness.

This time he was interrupted by Michou who appeared in the doorway in the company of Lady Compton. Both were wearing dripping waterproof capes, having traversed the courtyard that separated the two buildings in the driving rain. Michou, who was carrying a bucket filled with cleaning utensils, looked at Donaghue in surprise. Lady Compton's regard was one of open disbelief.

'Were you looking for something, Mr Donaghue?' Michou asked.

'Yes. I had lent Signora Vincente a pen. I came to retrieve it. As she was not here I thought I might see if it was on her table.'

An expression of puzzled suspicion crossed Michou's face as she glanced at the open wardrobe.

'And did you find your pen?' Lady Compton asked curtly.

'I didn't,' Donaghue replied.

'Perhaps you should go and ask her. She's in the dining-room,' Lady Compton suggested before turning and heading for her room.

Donaghue slipped past Michou and, pulling his cape over his head, prepared himself for the freshly raging storm outside.

With head bent he battled his way across the few metres between lodge and refuge. He was scarcely aware of the ferocity of the storm which sent icy rain in almost horizontal sheets and great streaks of vivid lightning searing from the heavens. His thoughts were concentrated on the puzzle he was trying to resolve.

As he opened the dining-room door a huge crash boomed from somewhere to the west. The sound carried on, boom after boom, increasing in volume.

'*Dio mio!*' he heard Mario exclaim. 'That's not thunder. That'll be a boulder struck by lightning. It sounds like an avalanche.'

The distant booming crashes continued, accompanied by intermittent claps of thunder directly above the refuge roof.

'It sounds like a rockfall,' said Laura Hutchinson, who was standing at the window. 'It's coming from the west. The road could be affected.'

'We'd better go and look,' said Mario worriedly.

'I'll go with you,' said Laura. 'Perhaps Antonio will come too?'

Antonio rose, his bell tinkling as he moved. The three prepared themselves hurriedly for the storm – capes, torches, climbing equipment and flares.

A tense silence reigned for a few moments after they had left.

Maria Vincente's lips set into a tight line.

'I'll go mad, Emilio,' she said quietly to her husband, 'if we have to stay here locked up in this primitive shack for much longer. I shall get an attack of claustrophobia and go crazy.'

'In that case you'll have to brave the storm and go outside,' her husband suggested sensibly.

'What? And get struck by lightning or pushed by some unseen hand into that awful lake?'

Sir Hilary, who was sitting at the end of the same table, chuckling every now and again at the book he was reading, looked up reprimandingly.

'Maria, my dear,' he said, 'you mustn't let the oppressive weather get you down. Take advantage of the time on your hands. Write letters you meant to write a year ago or read a book.' He held up the paperback he was reading. 'The secret diary of a thirteen-year-old boy. Read something amusing like this. It's marvellously entertaining and hysterically funny – certainly takes the mind off death and storms.'

Maria gazed at him miserably.

'We have books in the lodge,' he said. 'I'll accompany you over if you'd like to choose one.'

'Go on,' Emilio urged her. 'Get a book to read. It's a good idea.'

Maria rose hesitantly. She donned her anorak and cape and, holding Sir Hilary's arm, accompanied him out into the storm.

Dr Vincente, now alone at the table, took a notebook from his haversack and began to write.

Donaghue joined Clothilde at the corner table where the French twins sat gazing out at the raging storm. Jim Baxter and Meryss Jones had gone up earlier to the dormitory to play chess.

Ninette's eyes glittered behind her spectacles.

'I love a storm,' she said. 'I love its uncontrollable power.'

Her sister, Nanette, shivered.

'I hate it,' she said.

She looked at Ninette, then at Donaghue. 'They say that identical twins are the same in everything but we're not. I can't stand being cooped up but Ninette doesn't mind.'

'Nanette was in love with Oliver Hardcastle,' said Ninette, 'but I saw right through him. I saw him for what he was. Nanette is a romantic. I am a hardened realist, isn't that so, Nanette?'

Nanette glared at her sister and Donaghue interjected before the discussion developed into a sibling argument. He looked, smiling, from one to the other.

'Would you mind very much if I asked you both a question or two? I am passing my time in a little amateur detection. I am intrigued to find out who was the last person to see Oliver Hardcastle alive. Can you tell me when each of you saw him last?'

Ninette looked sharply at Donaghue, then her eyes turned quickly to her sister.

'We saw him at lunch. Neither of us saw him after that.'

'N-no,' Nanette stammered. 'We didn't see him again after he left for the tor.'

'You didn't see him return to the refuge at any point?'

Nanette shook her head.

'Did you stay at the refuge all afternoon, Nanette?'

The girl looked puzzled. 'I don't remember. Perhaps I did. No . . . I think I went for a walk – just the paths around the refuge. I didn't stray from the paths.' Her eyes misted over and she started to sob.

Ninette moved towards her sister and placed a comforting arm around her shoulder.

Donaghue and Clothilde moved discreetly away to an adjoining table.

'You'll get over it, Nanni,' Ninette said gently. 'It was only a childish crush. He really wasn't worth it.'

'It's curious,' said Clothilde. 'Did you notice, when that girl cried just now, *there were no tears in her eyes*? Does that mean that her sobbing was insincere?'

'Not at all,' said Donaghue. 'She is genuinely distraught. She didn't cry tears because she's wearing contact lenses. You can peel onions wearing contact lenses and you won't cry tears. I noticed it too and it confirms a little question that has been niggling at me. I picked up a contact lens in Hardcastle's room yesterday morning. I guessed it belonged to one of the women who had visited him. As Maria Vincente has no lens-cleaning equipment I guessed it must belong to one of the twins. I just wasn't sure which.'

'So it belongs to Nanette, then?'

'No, to Ninette.'

'But she wears glasses.'

'I'm sure she has a pair of contact lenses for parties or going out with a boyfriend.'

'Why don't you ask her if it's hers?'

'She'll say it isn't.'

'You're being mysterious, Ulysses,' Clothilde chided. 'What are you up to now?'

'I shall announce at lunchtime when everyone is here that I've found a lens. You'll see – nobody will claim it.'

'Why on earth wouldn't she claim it? You don't have to say where you found it.'

'She has a reason.'

'And you know what it is?'

'I can guess.'

'Sometimes your discretion can be exasperating,' said Clothilde crossly. 'I know it's boring being cooped up indoors when we could be out enjoying the flora and fauna of the valley but don't let your fertile imagination run away with you.'

'My brain, much to the great regret of my parents, is not in any way a creative one. It is not, I am sad to say, a great one for the imagination. On the contrary. It refuses obstinately to work with anything other than data directed to it by the senses. I gave up trying to control or change it long ago. It functions of its own accord and according to its own unfathomable logic.'

'What you're trying to say in your very Irish eloquence and circumlocution,' said Clothilde drily, 'is that you notice things

144

and that you cannot prevent yourself from coming to conclusions about what you observe.'

'Exactly that.'

'Some might choose to call it nosiness,' said Clothilde.

'They would be wrong,' Donaghue assured her. 'Inquisitiveness is a conscious activity of which I am never guilty. I would describe myself as incorrigibly curious – a condition, as I said, that I have no control over.'

He stood up.

'I am now going to attempt to satisfy my curiosity by going upstairs to speak to young Meryss Jones and her rather morose companion, Jim Baxter. I wonder if they'll be good enough to tell me when they last saw Oliver Hardcastle alive?'

Meryss Jones was in the process of checkmating Jim Baxter when Donaghue approached her bunk.

'Don't worry, Jim,' she was saying. 'You'll get the hang of it soon. Everybody has to start somewhere. That was remarkably good for a first game.'

Baxter looked glumly up as Donaghue coughed to gain their attention.

'May I interrupt you for a moment?' he asked and Meryss cheerfully invited him to join them on the bunk.

'It's less stuffy up here,' she said. 'The dining-room gets a little crowded when everyone is in it.'

Baxter looked warily at Donaghue. 'I hope you're not going to tell us that that noise we heard was an avalanche and that we're stuck here until someone comes up to dig us out. I saw the guide and the others going off.'

'Mario thinks it might be a rockfall. They've gone to check,' Donaghue explained. 'No, I haven't come about that. I've come about something completely different. I am interested in discovering who was the last person to see Hardcastle alive.'

'Why's that?' Baxter asked suspiciously. 'Do you think someone bumped him off? Tell me if you find out who it was. I can add it as a footnote to my report.'

'I take it from your tone that you were no great admirer of Oliver Hardcastle,' said Donaghue.

'It would be difficult for anyone to admire a man as egotistical and unscrupulous as Hardcastle.'

'Can you tell me when you spoke to him last?'

'I don't think I've spoken to him since I came here,' said Baxter diffidently.

'That's true,' said Meryss. She giggled. 'Jim didn't say a word when he punched him. He just tapped him on the shoulder and when Mr Hardcastle turned his head he punched him square on the nose.'

Baxter glanced disparagingly at Meryss before addressing Donaghue: 'The last time I saw him was when I lost control and punched him. It was after lunch. He was trying to persuade Meryss to go off with him. I saw red.' Baxter's face deepened in colour. 'The bastard knew I was . . . I was interested in Meryss. He just didn't give a damn about anybody or anything that wasn't in his interest. But I don't think I was the last to see him. On my way up to the tor I saw Maria Vincente coming from the path that leads to the lake. In retrospect I assume that she was on her way back from a rendezvous with Hardcastle. They were lovers, I believe.'

'Have you any idea what time that would be?'

'About two fifteen or thereabouts. I was too furious with Hardcastle to go up to the tor with the archaeologists. I waited till I had calmed down a bit, then went up and took a few quick snaps of the sensational faked drawing which turned out to be nothing more exciting than a crudely etched circle. Hardly worth mentioning in my report. One of those art students probably did it for a joke.'

'What time did you leave the tor?'

'I don't know. I stayed there about ten minutes. As I said, there was nothing spectacular to see. Let me see, by the time I got to the top . . . then I took the photos and a few notes . . . I must have left about two forty-five.'

'Was there anyone still up there when you left?'

'No. That I do know. Dr Vincente was leaving as I arrived.'

'On your way down did you see or meet anyone?'

'Not a soul. I went straight up to the dormitory and wrote up my notes.'

'You would have got back at, say, three, is that right?'

'About that, I suppose. I didn't check the time.' He looked

dourly at Donaghue. His tone when he spoke was sardonic. 'As I hadn't chucked Hardcastle into the lake, I didn't have a guilty conscience. As a result of that, I didn't check my watch to make sure my alibi was watertight.'

Donaghue smiled ruefully. 'I am interested in discovery not accusation,' he said.

He turned to the Welsh girl. 'And you, Meryss, when did you see him last?'

'At the same time as Jim.' She smiled. 'I didn't sneak away when we were waiting for the guide and wreak my revenge on him – or worse, accept his invitation and meet him secretly at the lakeside.'

Jim Baxter frowned at her. 'This is not the time to be facetious, Meryss,' he said. 'Mr Donaghue here is probably looking for someone to hang a murder on. Private detectives are forever trying to root out the baddies among us. I can only suppose that they need constant reassurance that they themselves number in the opposite camp.'

Donaghue smiled as he rose from the bunk. '"There is nothing either good or bad but thinking makes it so." I'm inclined to take the Bard's thought a step further: people are neither good nor bad but judgement makes them so.'

With that he moved up the dormitory aisle to his own bunk.

When he had settled himself comfortably Donaghue withdrew a notebook from his pocket and began to write:

Hardcastle last seen:
Maria Vincente: spoke to H at 2.05.
Michou: lunchtime.
Browning: saw H at lunch, heard him shortly after 2. Thinks he was talking to Maria Vincente.
Nanette: lunch (possibly lying).
Ninette: lunch (telling truth).
Jim Baxter: 1.50 punched H for soliciting Meryss.
Meryss Jones: 1.50.

He put his notebook away and closed his eyes. Two questions were niggling at him. Hardcastle had not gone up to the tor with the other experts to look at the faked circle. Why? Had he delayed his visit because Jim Baxter had added an extra bruise to his already battered face? Or had he decided not to go because he had faked the engraving himself – or knew who had faked it?

The second question was related to the tiny symbols that he had found on the rocks close to the lakeside. Maria Vincente had said that Hardcastle had been looking for more drawings of the type he had discovered on the tor. He must have discovered the tiny symbols at the lakeside. Could it possibly be that he had faked them? And if so, why? If he had faked all the drawings as Browning had suggested, why had he not 'discovered' them all at the same time? And why the obviously faked circle?

Donaghue found himself shaking his head. There was something not consistent – something out of place. There was something Donaghue did not quite see. It was related to the tiny circle – and to Hardcastle's character, to the Englishman's intrinsic egoism. Hardcastle had been a man who took himself seriously. He had been burdened with a sense of his own importance that had been so profound and so all-encompassing that it had cost him his life – or so it would seem. But that tiny circle . . . one couldn't really take that circle seriously . . .

In moments of reflection such as this Donaghue liked to indulge in one of his favourite slim Havana cigars. But on this occasion he would have to forgo the pleasure – one couldn't smoke in a communal dormitory and Clothilde would never allow him to smoke in close proximity to her nose in the dining-room. He continued his reflection in smoke-free solitude until a loud exclamation from Meryss Jones roused him from his reverie.

'An excellent move, Jim,' the girl exclaimed happily. 'You've checkmated me. Do you know you've just played the classic Gunsberg Steinitz game of 1890?'

'Really?' said Jim dubiously. 'If I did I wasn't aware of it.'

'You're a natural, Jim,' enthused Meryss. 'You play instinctively. If you put in the practice I'm sure you could reach championship standard in no time.'

Jim Baxter's normally morose features suddenly underwent an extraordinary transformation. They found themselves rearranged into an expression to which they were utterly unaccustomed – Baxter smiled. In his whole life nobody had ever told him he was champion material.

20

Antonio reached the rockfall first. They had followed the sound of crashing rocks and, as Mario had feared, found that the fall had indeed blocked the road at the point where it levelled out to join the valley. A granite slab, pocketed with iron ore, had been struck by lightning and shattered. The force of the strike had triggered a minor avalanche which had resulted in the road being blocked by a substantial mound of boulders and fragments of broken rock.

'There's no point in attempting to move this lot until the storm passes,' said Mario glumly. 'They say lightning never strikes twice in the same place but knowing our luck this year it'll happen for the first time in the whole of the bloody universe if we clear this now.' He cursed volubly in Italian, then turned and headed back along the track.

'It'll take two days to clear,' he grumbled as they made their way back, treading carefully on the slippery pebbles of the track. 'That's two more days with that body in the shed. It'll be a week before the death can be reported. The police are going to think it a bit suspicious. It'll be impossible to tell what he died of. They're bound to think one of us killed him.'

'Or all of us,' said Laura. 'They might think it was some kind of plot. After all, it is unusual to have so many visitors in the valley so late in the season. They might think that's more than a coincidence.'

Mario stopped and looked fearfully at Laura.

'Do you think we should get rid of the body?' he said. 'Weigh it down maybe and throw it back into the lake? We did haul him out of there after all. He would have just disappeared and nobody would be any the wiser until he was reported missing – which could take months. That way there'll be no comeback on us.'

Laura looked rather disdainfully at Mario.

'There'll be a comeback if they find that he'd been deliberately thrown into the lake. A weighted body would be a clear case of murder. As far as I'm concerned it's quite simple. Hardcastle died from natural causes. If it turns out that he died otherwise then I'm sure the police will be capable of finding out how and why. As things stand now no crime has been committed and therefore there's no need for anybody to be anxious about it.'

'I'm not anxious,' retorted Mario. 'I was just looking to what might happen.'

'Who knows what might happen?' said Laura.

She strode along on her muscular legs, keeping up easily with the longer stride of the two men. 'The storm might clear up tonight and we'll be out of the valley in two days after we've cleared the rocks, or sooner if we can get the fire brigade up to help. And we might discover the truth about Oliver Hardcastle's death quicker than we thought. I'm almost certain that that little Irish detective is conducting a private investigation into it. So, if you're innocent, Mario, you'll have nothing to fear.'

Mario glared angrily over at Laura Hutchinson's angular profile. Snooty bitch, he thought, thinks she's talking to a barman. He set his lips and, saying nothing, walked ahead of the guide in a furious silence. There was nothing he could have said that wouldn't have left him feeling ignorant and inferior in the face of the tall, aloof, arrogant Englishwoman.

The three battled their way back to the refuge against the icy driving wind and rain. Not another word was said. Only the tinkle of Antonio's bell could be heard above the continued booms of thunder.

Lady Compton sat alone in her room. The shutters were closed and the room was lit by an oil lamp. She could not bear to see or hear the storm that was keeping her imprisoned in what had become for her a valley of nightmare. Since her arrival in the Vallée des Prêtres she had had to face the terrible fact that her husband, her dear Hilary, was insane. Not only had her worst fears come true when he started criticising her publicly, but on top of that he was now showing himself up too, telling indecent jokes and laughing aloud while reading cheap paperback bestsellers!

But that was not the worst. When Oliver Hardcastle had humiliated her she had wished him dead but she had not wished him to die the way he had. It was all too awful – as if suddenly her world had been turned topsy-turvy. The control she'd always exerted over her life had been taken from her hands. After an uneventful life as a dutiful wife and mother suddenly things were happening to her.

Distractedly she picked up the small pile of magazines that Hilary had left on his bedside table. If only this dreadful storm had not come up. They would have been able to leave today after Hilary had made his statement to the press. She would have to find a way of taking her mind off the awful situation they were in.

She idly flicked through the magazines then started with shock as she realised what she was looking at. They were not the usual archaeological reviews and Sunday supplement magazines that Sir Hilary had always taken with him on journeys. These were journals of a very different nature altogether – magazines one would have expected to find on the bookshelves of an adolescent boy! A football journal, an outrageous fringe satirical magazine, a paperback book of puerile jokes and an adult comic strip that, as she flicked through the pages, Lady Compton realised was indecent to the point of obscenity!

She shook her head in distress. She was right, Hilary was going mad, but he was convinced he was sane. What could anyone do? Hilary had always had a will of iron. Whether mad or sane his will did not change. How on earth was she to save him from himself?

She replaced the magazines. There was only one missing – one containing pin-ups! He had stopped short of that at least! Suddenly she heard the loud boom of her husband's laughter. He was in the corridor. She opened the door to see Sir Hilary, an arm protectively around Maria Vincente's shoulder, accompanying the Italian woman into the lodge common room. Lady Compton hurried along the corridor after them to hear Sir Hilary say to Maria, 'Have a look at the books on the shelf, my dear. If you find them a bit too stuffy I can give you a selection of magazines – light reading, humour, *risqué* stories, that sort of thing. I don't suppose football interests you?'

Maria smiled broadly. 'As a matter of fact it does,' she said. 'I'm hoping Italy will win the World Cup. My home team is Milan.'

'An excellent team,' said Sir Hilary. 'Do you go to see them play?'

'When I'm home, yes,' said Maria. 'I adore the atmosphere, the power of the crowd – that almost religious adoration and chanting. I find it almost pagan. I imagine it can't have been very different among the crowd at the Colosseum for the Roman games. The phenomenon of the crowd fascinates me – how the individual will submit to the uniform mentality of the mass.'

Sir Hilary's eyes lit up. 'It's exactly that that fascinates me – the game as well, of course. I get an extraordinary thrill when my team wins but I suppose that is part of – as you say – the religion of the game. It's a very curious phenomenon, the passion and self-sacrifice that football arouses in a multitude of people all over the globe.' He smiled. 'You are a perfect example of how extraordinary the phenomenon is – a beautiful young woman fascinated by the game.' He paused. 'I have some magazines with me on the World Cup. Perhaps you'd like to look at them?'

'I'd love to,' said Maria enthusiastically.

Sir Hilary turned towards the door and spotted his wife who was standing, pale-faced, in the doorway.

'Beatrice,' he said, 'while you're there, run back to our room and fetch the football magazines I left on the bedside table. I think there are two or three. Could you bring them for Signora Vincente, there's a dear.'

Beatrice, her eyes misting in distress, turned and dutifully went back to her room to fetch the magazines.

Having borne witness to Meryss Jones' second defeat by Jim Baxter – this time he had unwittingly used the Karpov Kortchnoi game of 1978 – Donaghue returned to the dining-room to find it in an unusual silence.

Clothilde, in the corner, had engaged the French twins in a game of pocket Scrabble. Michou was in the kitchen preparing lunch, sobbing every now and again as she remembered that Petrocelli, the parrot, was dead. She missed his raucous imitation of Antonio's bell and the voices of the louder guests. Dr Vincente sat at the central table, his dark head bent over his notebook.

He looked up as Donaghue approached him.

'Can I speak to you, Dr Vincente?' Donaghue enquired.

'Certainly,' said Vincente, smiling. He appraised the stocky little figure before him. There was something *uncoordinated* about the Irishman's appearance. His clothes, khaki-coloured linen trousers and an Aran sweater, were of that excellent British quality but, like all quality clothing, when hung on a Celt or an Anglo-Saxon, they appeared to lose whatever degree of chic they possessed. Were he, an Italian, to wear them they would look entirely different. Vincente, as an anthropologist, was fascinated by racial and cultural peculiarities. And the Irishman's face – a quite ugly, monkey-like face that would have made one laugh were it not for the sharp intelligence of the small vivid blue eyes. There was no co-ordination between the leathery features and the unruly mop of grey-streaked hair and yet one felt one was in the presence of a personality of great mental coherence and order.

Dr Vincente found such contradictions utterly fascinating.

'Shall we talk here?' he said. 'Or in the privacy of my room?'

'I think in private,' said Donaghue.

'I suppose you want to speak to me about my wife's notion that Hardcastle was murdered,' said Dr Vincente as they traversed the rain-lashed courtyard to the lodge.

'It is something to do with that,' Donaghue agreed.

Having ensconced his guest in one of the two straight-backed armchairs that furnished his room, Dr Vincente offered Donaghue a glass of port from a decanter on the bureau. Donaghue gladly accepted. A little warming aperitif before lunch would go down well, he said with a smile.

'So, you're investigating Hardcastle's death?' said Vincente. 'Do you agree with my wife that he might have been murdered?'

'Murdered? That I cannot say. But his death certainly bears investigation.'

'Have you come to any conclusions as yet?'

'I have some ideas but no, I have come to no conclusions.' He sipped the excellent port with pleasure. 'What I am interested in discovering is the identity of the person who last saw or spoke to Hardcastle alive. I'm sure that person will have some idea as to how he died. Can you tell me when you saw him last?'

'I saw him last at lunchtime. I expected him to accompany us up to the tor but he didn't. I must admit his absence surprised me. I would have expected him to be as interested in the faked drawing as we all were.' Vincente hesitated. 'Unless of course he faked it himself.'

'But wouldn't he have given himself away by showing no interest?' Donaghue queried.

'Yes, one would have thought so. As I said, I thought it strange that he hadn't come. But then Hardcastle was never an easy character to fathom.'

'Did you know him well?'

'I can't say he was a close friend – not to me anyway. My wife, Maria, was much closer to him than I was.' Vincente smiled, his dark handsome features creasing into a boyish grin. 'But then she is a woman and I am a man – although I am sure that her feelings towards him were those of a mother to a child rather than of a mature woman to a mature man.' Vincente hesitated. 'I think I should explain something. She met Hardcastle at university. She became pregnant by him, had an illegal abortion at his insistence and since then has been unable to have a child. Hardcastle took on the role of a surrogate son. He fitted the role well. He was emotionally immature, his behaviour towards women was that of an adolescent boy. He and I had little in common. He was an archaeologist and I am an anthropologist. As a character he was secretive and jealous. I am neither. He was very typically English in that he was incapable, I think, of ever expressing his true feelings. I, as a Latin, can do nothing else.'

'Do you think he was professionally honest?'

Vincente looked gravely at Donaghue. 'Do you mean, do I think he faked the drawings as everyone else seems to think he did? I'm not sure. I think I believed him to be honest in his professional dealings if not in his personal ones.'

'Do you think it's possible that somebody hated him enough to kill him?'

Vincente's dark eyes scrutinised Donaghue. 'That's a difficult question to answer,' he said. 'It's possible, although I'm not sure that it's what happened.'

'Did Hardcastle, as far as you know, go up to the tor yesterday afternoon?'

'Not as far as I know. I was the last to leave after Sir Hilary. I'm not counting the journalist, who arrived as I left.'

'What time was that?'

154

'It was at two thirty exactly. I remember looking at my watch.'

'And Sir Hilary, what time did he leave?'

'Not more than five, ten minutes before.'

'Do you know, Dr Vincente, whether your wife went out towards the tor to see Hardcastle yesterday afternoon?'

There was, Donaghue noticed, an almost imperceptible hesitation before Vincente answered. 'My wife? No, as far as I know she didn't go to see him.'

Dr Vincente's head turned suddenly as the sound of raised voices, followed by a loud thud, came from the direction of the Comptons' room.

The sound of Lady Compton's voice, high-pitched in hysteria, came to the ears of the two men.

'I can't stand it any longer. This place is driving me mad. I think I'm going crazy.'

She began to laugh hysterically then screamed, a long piercing cry. There followed a sharp slap and the cry stopped abruptly.

Dr Vincente and Donaghue, who had jumped up and run out into the corridor, saw the Comptons' door open and a pale, tearful Lady Compton rush out and along the corridor to the lodge entrance. Her cape covered her head but it was evident from her red-rimmed eyes that she had been sobbing.

Sir Hilary stood somewhat sheepishly in the doorway.

'Have to apologise for all that,' he said. 'But this confounded storm is cracking her up. She suffers from claustrophobia and being cooped up like this is doing her no good at all.'

Vincente nodded in sympathy and, taking leave of Donaghue, returned to his room. Sir Hilary invited Donaghue to join him for an aperitif.

'My apologies for the dreadful noise,' he said as he closed the door. He picked up a heavy onyx ashtray. 'She threw this at me. Fortunately it hit the wall and not my head or there would have been another, not so mysterious, death in the valley!'

He replaced the ashtray and sighed. 'Women are difficult at the best of times but at the worst . . . Let's hope that this damned storm clears up and we can get out of here without delay.'

'Have you come to a decision, then, about the drawings?' Donaghue asked.

'Yes, finally. I shall make a public announcement at lunch.

That glum-faced Barker or Baxter or whatever he's called will have plenty to report when he gets back to London. Bourbon?' he enquired, holding out a bottle.

'A tot,' Donaghue agreed. A nip of bourbon to follow the port would warm his appetite nicely for lunch.

'A lot of people, particularly the women, have been profoundly disturbed by Hardcastle's death,' said Donaghue. 'One hardly expected a death to occur during a week such as this.'

'It was certainly the last thing I expected,' said Sir Hilary. 'But several unexpected things happened: the storm, that wasn't predicted, the appearance of an obviously forged drawing, so many visitors so late in the season and then Hardcastle dying.' Sir Hilary chuckled. 'It's amazing, the older one gets the more one should be used to the unexpected. After more than three score years on this planet one should have learnt that life is anything but predictable. In fact one should *expect* the unexpected – but one is always surprised by it.' He smiled grimly. 'I'm sure Hardcastle didn't expect to die, for instance. I'll bet when he came here that was the last thing he expected to happen. He was an arrogant, foolish young man. I can imagine that he thought he would live for ever.'

'The young do.'

'Hardcastle was more arrogant than most. He took himself for a demigod.'

'Do you think, then, that he was destined to die young, Sir Hilary?'

'I am no great believer in destiny,' the archaeologist replied. 'I don't believe we are puppets manipulated by some unseen deific hand.'

'Are you an atheist?' Donaghue asked.

'I wouldn't go so far as to say that.' Sir Hilary smiled. 'It would take as much arrogance to deny a God as to be sure there is one. In the perilous territory of the unknown one can only believe or not believe. I tend to the belief that there is a creator and that we humble mortal beings have been invested with the creative spirit. We are limited, however, by our physical weakness and the roles we are obliged to play.'

'Do you perhaps think, as the Bard did, that we are mere players on a stage?'

'No, I think rather that life is a game and that we are its toys –

highly sophisticated, computerised toys, perhaps, with a degree of freedom. Wind us up and off we go in our own anarchic way! I can imagine that God, if such a God exists, must have a whale of a time watching us in action!'

Sir Hilary's tone was unexpectedly sober. He looked sombrely at Donaghue. 'And you, Mr Donaghue?' he asked. 'Which camp do you fall in or do you stand in the no man's land of ignorance like me?'

'Fortunately or unfortunately as the case may be,' said Donaghue, 'I am shackled with the unbreakable bonds of a Jesuit education. I am bound to a belief in a benign creator and the sorry lot of his free-thinking but muddled creation. I am, as a consequence, burdened also with a profound belief in the power of good.'

'It's curious,' said Sir Hilary, 'but during my whole life the concepts of good and evil have meant very little to me. The objectivity of the scientist perhaps. What is good for one man is evil for another and vice versa. As far as I'm concerned morality is that which is in the self-interest of the moraliser.'

'You are perhaps a little cynical, Sir Hilary,' said Donaghue. 'Am I right in that?'

'No, not cynical,' Sir Hilary replied. 'I am a realist. I have learnt with advanced age to see life through the realistic eyes of the child. Watch the child at play. He's without morality, without any notion of good and bad. He's guided only by the principles of pleasure and justice. It is our natural state, one that gives way to the conscience of the adult. Now that I am retiring from the adult world of responsibility I am happy to regain that pleasurable childish state. My wife thinks I am mad, returning to a state of infancy. In a way she's right, although of course I'm not mad as I am perfectly conscious of what I am doing.'

He laughed, a hearty, booming laugh. 'It's a curious world we live in. My wife thinks that I am mad. If you ask her, she will say that a man like Oliver Hardcastle was sane – a perfectly normal intelligent, successful young man – *but she will be wrong*. I am sane, Oliver Hardcastle was mad.'

'When you saw him last, was he behaving strangely then?'

'I have always seen his behaviour as strange – too determined, too *serious*. He was a young man without humour – that is what I call strange.'

'As a character he fascinates me,' said Donaghue. 'I am intrigued to know why he didn't go up to the tor after lunch to look at the faked engraving. Did he perhaps go up later?'

'Not while I was up there,' said Sir Hilary.

'Perhaps he went up after you left. Can you say what time that was?'

'Haven't a clue – didn't have my watch with me. You'll have to ask Vincente – he left after me.'

Sir Hilary looked humorously at Donaghue. 'What's all this, Mr Donaghue? A private investigation?'

'You might call it that,' said Donaghue. 'I can't help myself. Hardcastle was a mysterious character. He died in a curious way. I am irresistibly drawn to the unravelling of mysteries.'

'It's the child in you struggling to get out,' said Sir Hilary with a chuckle. 'Fire away, ask any questions you like.'

'When did you see Hardcastle last?'

'At lunch – like everyone else, I suppose,' said Sir Hilary. 'He looked a bit distracted but then he'd been put out because I was taking my time in coming to a decision about the drawings, and if you want my opinion I think he'd had a bit of a to-do with a lady friend.'

'Do you think, Sir Hilary, that he could have been murdered?'

'Murdered? Sir Hilary let out a bellow. 'Who would be bothered to murder a man like Hardcastle? What utter nonsense. Is that what you're investigating? You're wasting your time, Donaghue. You're on the wrong tack. You'll get more fun playing Cluedo!'

'You're probably right, Sir Hilary,' said Donaghue as he finished his glass and rose to leave. 'Oh, there's something else. Just by chance, on the path that leads to the lakeside I discovered four tiny replicas of the symbols of the inscription. Did you know they were there?'

'Yes, of course,' said Sir Hilary. 'Hardcastle discovered them shortly after he discovered the drawings on the tor but due to their rather dangerous position we did not encourage anyone to advertise their presence.'

'And the faked circle? Do you have an idea who did it?'

'Not a clue, but it's unimportant. There's graffiti all over the valley – one piece more won't make any difference.'

Sir Hilary lifted his heavy bulk, impressing Donaghue with his agility and strength. He glanced at his watch. 'It's almost twelve – lunchtime. I'm starving, aren't you, Donaghue?'

21

Maria Vincente emerged from the lodge bathroom just as the door closed behind Donaghue and Sir Hilary. Having changed into a brightly coloured winter track suit she entered her room and suggested to her husband that they go across to the dining-room for lunch.

They were joined by Herman Browning and Bridget. As they crossed the courtyard Browning looked up at the sky and exclaimed, 'There's a break in the cloud – look!'

The others looked up and to their great delight saw that the black cover of cloud was considerably thinner to the east and that there was indeed a tiny patch of blue over the furthest peak.

Nevertheless above their heads the rain drummed down as relentlessly as ever and they hurried through it to the refuge door.

The dining-room was crowded. Mario, Antonio and Laura Hutchinson had returned. Mario informed the assembly that the road was blocked as he had feared by a rockfall but that it could be easily cleared with the help of willing hands as soon as the weather permitted – which might, he added with a smile, be sooner than they had thought; it looked as though the storm might clear that afternoon.

At these words the pall of gloom that had pervaded the refuge since Oliver Hardcastle's death was instantly lifted. An excited buzz of conversation arose as the diners took their seats and Michou prepared to serve lunch.

Donaghue slipped upstairs to the now empty dormitory and opened his haversack to extract his notebook. A sharp involuntary cry escaped his lips as his hand closed over something hard and sharp and a searing pain shot up his arm.

'What is it, Ulysses?' called Clothilde, who had followed him up the stairs.

Donaghue pulled his hand from the haversack. Embedded in

the palm was the blade of a razor which protruded in turn from a small half-wrapped bar of soap.

'What in God's holy name . . .' he muttered as he gazed, shocked, at the blood that poured from his palm and fell, dripping, to the wooden planks of the dormitory floor. His face had paled, its expression changing rapidly from shock to a kind of determined anger.

'Well,' said Clothilde as she approached him, 'are you going to stand there looking at your hand as if it's a work of art? Here.' She quickly grasped the small bar of soap and pulled the blade from his palm. With an expression of great disgust she placed a handkerchief on the bunk and laid the bloodstained article on to it. She then delved into her rucksack for her traveller's first-aid kit and proceeded to sterilise Donaghue's wound.

'Leave it to bleed until it stops,' she instructed him. 'Don't pat it or dab it. The blood will coagulate rapidly of its own accord. You're lucky you didn't slice the thumb tendon. You could have lost the use of your thumb – or worse, contracted lockjaw.' She half smiled. 'Then where would you have been, Ulysses? Unable to make notes and unable to speak – life wouldn't be worth living for you. What on earth got into you, leaving a bar of soap with a razor blade stuck in it in your bag like that?'

'It's my blade,' said Donaghue as he gazed at the bloody object on the bed, 'but I didn't put it there. Somebody else did. I think perhaps there's a message attached to it.'

Clothilde tentatively picked up the bar and pulled away the paper that was stuck to it. She unfolded the small doubled sheet, read what was written on it then passed it, eyebrows raised, to Donaghue.

A simple message was written in large childlike capitals:

THIS IS A WARNING. IF YOU CARRY ON YOUR
INVESTIGATION YOU WILL DIE.

'That rather clinches it,' said Clothilde grimly. 'Hardcastle was murdered and his killer is getting cold feet.'

'Extraordinary,' said Donaghue as he studied the message. 'I shall have to be very careful. This is a crude and vicious warning. The person who did it is quite capable of killing me in an equally crude and vicious manner.'

'Perhaps you should just cease the investigation,' said Cloth-ilde brusquely. 'After all, the death has not even been officially reported. You can leave the police to deal with it.'

Donaghue looked gravely at his friend. 'It would be very difficult for me to stop now. I know that Hardcastle was killed. I know how he was killed. I am almost but not quite sure of the identity of his killer. I am not sure that my curiosity will allow me to stop at this point. I shall just have to be extremely careful.'

'So Hardcastle was murdered?' said Clothilde. 'How on earth was it done without any visible sign of violence?'

'I know how it was done.'

'But you can't tell me now?'

'I can't put your life in danger.'

'This killer is ruthless then?' said Clothilde. 'He or she is prepared to kill twice?'

Donaghue looked at Clothilde in surprise. 'Ah, but the person who killed Hardcastle is not the one who put the soap in my bag – I'm almost sure of that. But of course, you would assume that that is the case.'

'Now I am hopelessly confused,' said Clothilde. 'Are you telling me that there are two potential murderers in this refuge?'

Donaghue's answer was enigmatic. 'I hope to leave this valley', he said, 'with the knowledge that there was one potential murderer. To succeed in that I shall have to be, as I said, very very careful.'

'I have known you to be secretive,' grumbled Clothilde, 'especially when you are not absolutely sure of your hypotheses, but I've never known you to be *mysterious*.'

'Let me assure you, Clothilde, that there is nothing mysterious in this business.' His tone changed, became uncharacteristically sober. 'The one mystery in life as far as I am concerned is why one man will consider himself justified in taking the life of another. It is an enigma that baffles and saddens me. There is someone here in this refuge desperate enough to threaten my life.'

Clothilde rummaged in her medical box and withdrew a flesh-coloured plaster which she placed over the cut on Donaghue's palm.

'You mustn't let it get infected,' she said in a motherly manner. 'I've plenty of antiseptic cream so there'll be no excuse.' She smiled, her features taken by surprise by the unaccustomed gesture. 'You wouldn't want to die of blood poisoning before you get murdered, would you?'

Donaghue smiled absently at Clothilde's little joke as he fumbled carefully inside his haversack and took out his notebook, this time without injury.

He opened it at the list of names he had written earlier. Rapidly he added a new heading and made a second, more succinct list:

Hardcastle last seen:

Maria Vincente:	2.05.
Michou:	lunch
Browning:	2.05 (heard).
Meryss Jones:	1.50.
Jim Baxter:	1.50.
Nanette Fèvre:	lunch.
Ninette Fèvre:	lunch.
Dr Vincente:	lunch (says wife didn't go to see H – lying).
Sir Hilary:	lunch.

Then he added a further list:

Alibis – between 2.20 and 3.30:

Maria Vincente:	returned to lodge at 2.25.
Michou:	cleaning lodge.
Browning:	back at lodge at 2.15.
Meryss Jones:	2.20–2.40 waiting for guide; from 2.40 on guided visit.
Jim Baxter:	2.15–2.45 on tor; from 2.45 making notes for report in dormitory.
Nanette Fèvre:	stayed in and around refuge.
Ninette Fèvre:	with Meryss and Bridget until 2.40 then on visit.
Dr Vincente:	left tor at 2.30 – returned to lodge.
Sir Hilary:	left tor at 2.20/25 – returned to lodge.

He added the names of those he had not yet spoken to:

Lady Compton:
Mario:

Laura Hutchinson:
Antonio:

Then he looked up satisfied. Clothilde was watching him anxiously.

'I'm worried,' she said. 'A booby trap like that – a razor blade put in a bag – is the act of a madman.'

'Yes,' said Donaghue as he picked up the bar of soap. He carefully wiped the blade free of his blood. Then, having wrapped both blade and soap in the handkerchief, he placed them in the side pocket of his haversack to join the black plastic rectangle that he had found in Michou's dustbin and the fragment of coloured cloth that he had picked from the bush by the lake. He regarded Clothilde thoughtfully.

'You're absolutely right,' he said. 'Such deliberate violence is only ever an act of madness.'

22

As Donaghue followed Clothilde into the dining-room for lunch he heard his name called in a low whisper.

'Mr Donaghue . . .'

It was Mario, who was standing in the doorway to the locker room, removing his outdoor clothes. He beckoned urgently to Donaghue, who followed him into the locker room. Mario quickly shut the door.

'Mr Donaghue,' he said as he put his cape and boots away in their locker, 'I want to speak to you in private.'

Mario looked exceedingly worried. A frown creased his bald forehead and one hand nervously twiddled his moustache.

'There's a lot of talk about the English archaeologist being murdered,' he said. 'Everybody's looking at everybody else, thinking they're a murderer. I know you are looking into it and I know you are a highly respected detective.'

Donaghue smiled modestly.

'Look,' said Mario. He spoke almost imploringly. 'I want you to know that I had nothing to do with it. I had nothing against

Hardcastle.' He stammered. 'N-not enough to kill him anyway. I didn't go anywhere near that lake yesterday.'

Donaghue placed a comforting arm on Mario's shoulder, making the much larger man start.

'I have no reason to suspect you of anything,' he said.

The refuge keeper's face lit up in relief.

'But I would be grateful if you could answer a question or two. You might have seen or heard something that could help me.'

'I didn't see or hear much yesterday,' said Mario. 'I slept most of the afternoon – a siesta.' He grinned. 'It's a Mediterranean custom after a bottle of wine at lunch. I slept longer than usual because I hadn't slept well the night before.'

'Can you remember hearing anyone come into the dining-room?' Donaghue asked. 'Think back, perhaps a sound or a noise – not necessarily anything unusual, just any sound you might have heard.'

Mario's brow creased as he reflected. A look of great sorrow crept into his eyes. 'I heard Petrocelli.' His eyes moistened. 'He was chatting away as usual.'

Then, to Donaghue's great embarrassment, Mario started to cry.

'I miss that parrot,' he sobbed. 'I had him since I was a child.'

Once again Donaghue's stubby arm crept out and patted the Italian comfortingly on the shoulder. 'It's tragic when a beautiful creature dies unnecessarily,' he said.

'Intelligent too,' said Mario tearfully. 'He was an intelligent bird.'

'Was that the last time you heard him speak?' Donaghue asked.

'No, he was talking last night at dinner. Do you remember? He said something about a gun, though where he got that from I don't know – somebody telling a joke, I suppose.' Mario dabbed his eyes. 'He always spoke when people were in the dining-room. He was a sociable bird. He liked company.'

'Can you remember what he was saying yesterday afternoon?'

'I was dozing off but I remember because it was the same thing as in the evening – about a gun.' Mario wiped his eyes again. 'He was a funny bird – took a liking to certain sounds and voices. He liked Antonio's bell and he always liked Sir Hilary's voice. I suppose because it's loud and booming – it must have caught his ear.'

'Did you hear anyone come in?'

'Not that I can remember, but as it was sunny the door would have been open. I wouldn't have heard anyone coming in. I heard Michou getting the stuff ready to clean the lodge. She tends to clatter the bucket around. After that I was out for the count, slept like a log, up on the mezzanine above the kitchen – that's where we sleep.'

He gazed earnestly at Donaghue. 'I promise you, Mr Donaghue, I had nothing to do with Hardcastle dying.'

'I'm sure you didn't,' said Donaghue. He patted Mario's shoulder for the third time. 'Shall we get back to lunch? Whatever it is your wife has cooked, it smells delicious.'

In the dining-room Michou was serving a *ragoût de mouton* from a huge cast-iron pot. The diners tucked in with relish and little was said as they ate the delicious stew and sipped the robust Italian wine that accompanied it.

During the course of the meal the sky outside the refuge became noticeably lighter. As the gloom of the storm started to lift so too did the tension that had hung over the motley gathering ever since they had been forced into an unwelcome confinement.

When the meal had ended and the coffee had been served, Sir Hilary, at the end of the central table, stood up. He was wearing a long-sleeved silk shirt, tie-dyed in flamboyant purples and yellows, over velour jogging pants. His face was jovial as he beamed around at the assembly. His voice boomed out, requesting attention.

'As I know that you are all, experts and amateurs alike, interested in the drawings discovered recently in the valley, I have decided to make my announcement as to their authenticity publicly this afternoon.'

He grinned over at Jim Baxter, who was sitting in the corner with Meryss and the French twins. 'I trust the gentleman of the press has his notebook to hand.'

Jim, somewhat embarrassed, fumbled in his haversack to withdraw paper and pen.

'After much deliberation I have finally reached a decision about the drawings. The decision has taken some time as the execution of the drawings is subtly different from the other existing drawings in the valley, which indicates that they were not made during the same period. At the same time they were accompanied by an inscription the nature of which has never been seen before in Europe. The inscription was executed by the same hand as the drawings and therefore in the same period of time.

'I have come to the conclusion that the drawings and inscription are authentic engravings from the middle to late Bronze Age. I will not suggest a date at this stage – I will leave that to the experts . . .' He nodded, smiling, at Browning and Vincente, '. . . although I would be inclined to date them in the later rather than the earlier period. But I've no doubt that our very capable experts in palaeography will spend the next few years happily researching the exact date of the engravings. Archaeological research is a team effort – it can't be done by one man alone.' He paused, looking gravely around at his audience.

'I have no doubt also that the papers will be reporting at the same time the tragic death of young Oliver Hardcastle who, sadly, will never bear witness to the glory of his discovery. His unfortunate death has, I am sure, left everyone in the refuge in a state of morbid depression – a state not rendered any lighter by the ferocity of the weather which last night very sadly caused another death, that of the refuge parrot, Petrocelli, who will I know be sadly missed.'

Michou dabbed her eyes and Mario placed a comforting arm around her shoulder, his face both sorrowful and grim.

'I can only advise you', Sir Hilary went on, 'to try to remain as cheerful as possible during the time that we are obliged to stay in the valley. Mr Hardcastle's tragic death must not be allowed to dampen our enthusiasm for his extraordinary discovery. I am aware that the uncertainty as to the cause of his death has given rise to the suspicion of foul play – in other words that he was murdered and that there is a murderer among us. Such negative feelings and suspicion, induced I've no doubt by the oppressive weather, should be put from your minds. Your throats are not going to be cut during the night – nor your food poisoned. You have all drunk the excellent refuge wine and eaten Madame Santinelli's delicious *ragoût* – you are all perfectly . . .'

166

Sir Hilary suddenly stopped speaking. His hand flew to his throat. A rasping gurgle issued from his mouth as he fell heavily to the floor.

Lady Compton screamed, a high piercing shriek, and Clothilde precipitated herself across the room towards the fallen figure. Everybody else in the room had stood up and was gazing in stunned silence at the large inert body slumped on the floor.

As Clothilde bent to look at the archaeologist's face one eye opened and winked at her. She recoiled and Sir Hilary, with an astonishing agility, unfurled himself and leapt to his feet. The expression on his large bearded face was one of intense merriment.

He looked around in great amusement at the pale staring faces of his spectators.

'You see how nervous you are?' he said. 'Ready to jump at anything that goes bump in the night!' He put his hands to his throat and gurgled. 'Do you see how ready you are to see murder where there's only play-acting?'

Then, chuckling with merriment, he resumed his place at the end of the table and finished off his after-lunch coffee.

Lady Compton, sitting beside him, stared at her husband in horror. Donaghue, from his nearby table, watched Sir Hilary with great interest for a moment or two then he rose, coughing loudly to gain the attention of the diners. They looked at him apprehensively.

'Don't worry,' he said smiling. 'I'm not going to play any jokes on you like Sir Hilary. I would simply like to announce that I have found a contact lens.' He held up the morsel of tissue that contained the lens. 'Has anybody lost one?'

There was no response.

'I shall leave it then with Madame Santinelli. It must belong to a former tourist.'

He deposited the lens on the counter, then, having, it seemed, come to some kind of decision, he left the dining-room to inspect the brightening sky outside.

Out on the terrace, Mario joined Donaghue in his study of the scudding clouds.

'It's definitely breaking,' he said. 'And the sooner the better.

The sooner the refuge closes down for the winter the better – too many nerves on edge.'

'Sir Hilary thinks the same,' Donaghue commented.

Mario snorted derisively. 'Sir Hilary! A stupid practical joke like that doesn't help matters – only makes them worse!' He looked up at the sky. 'I think we'll be able to start clearing the rockfall this afternoon. If we can find the cable that's down we can get the phone back on and call up help from the village.'

Within a few moments the dining-room was empty and everyone outside. The sun finally appeared from behind a last fleeting cloud and the valley was suddenly marvellously transformed from a bleak craggy landscape to a vista of luminous greens and browns, set off against a brilliant clear blue sky.

Jim Baxter and Meryss moved off towards the map board and sat on an adjoining rock. The French twins followed them and sat nearby, lifting their faces up to the sun as if in worship of it.

Mario announced loudly that he was going to allow his stomach half an hour to digest its lunch then he would be tackling the clearing of the blocked road. He invited all the able-bodied males who felt up to it to lend a hand.

Clothilde whispered to Donaghue that she should perhaps perform the distasteful but necessary task of inspecting Hardcastle's body, and she went off in the direction of the generator shed.

Dr Vincente and his wife, arm in arm, wandered off in a westerly direction and Herman Browning invited Bridget to stretch her legs in a walk up to the tor to see the faked engraving. They set off at a brisk pace, leaving the terrace occupied by Sir Hilary, Lady Compton and Donaghue.

Mario had returned to the dining-room to help Michou clear the tables and Laura Hutchinson had gone up to the dormitory to change into lighter clothing for the task of clearing the rocks. Antonio was nowhere to be seen.

Lady Compton, greatly agitated, stood, twiddling her fingers, at her husband's side.

'I'll have to go for a walk,' she said. 'To get some fresh air into my lungs.'

'Off you go then, dear,' said Sir Hilary, who had settled himself comfortably at the terrace table. He lit a cigar and inhaled with pleasure.

'I'm in need of a walk myself,' Donaghue said to Lady Compton. 'Shall I accompany you?'

Lady Compton looked at Donaghue with what amounted to distress. 'Well,' she said, hesitating. 'Well . . . why not?'

The two set off, Lady Compton walking swiftly but at a pace that was, to Donaghue's relief, much more leisurely than that of his friend, Clothilde.

'Shall we take the path that encircles the refuge?' he suggested. 'It's fairly flat and doesn't go anywhere near a marshy area.'

Lady Compton nodded in silent agreement.

Donaghue glanced surreptitiously at the lady's profile. The pale fraught face was set into tight lines of anxiety.

'It must have been trying for you the last day or so,' he said sympathetically.

'Trying?' said Lady Compton, her tone caustic. 'It's been nightmarish. I suffer from claustrophobia. To have been stuck indoors like this is horrendous. At home I have to leave the house several times a day even if it's just for a short walk with the dogs.'

'I expected you to join us on the guided visit yesterday afternoon,' said Donaghue. 'It was most interesting and a good invigorating walk.'

'Perhaps I should have done,' Lady Compton agreed almost regretfully. 'But I've seen the drawings in the valley hundreds of times. My husband did discover them after all. I preferred to take a walk to the southern end of the valley. It's less arid and I did a bit of bird-spotting.' She hesitated. 'I had been a little upset – something that had happened, something personal – and I needed to think things out quietly on my own.'

'Your husband seems hardly put out by what's happened over the last two days.'

'Hilary is put out by nothing,' said Lady Compton. 'I have to do his worrying for him.'

'I find it an admirable quality to remain calm in a crisis,' said Donaghue. 'I endeavour to cultivate the habit but sadly do not always succeed. Your husband is a man of many admirable qualities, I've noticed.'

Lady Compton glanced curiously at Donaghue. 'Yes, of course. He's a very famous, highly respected man.'

'And yet I feel that you worry about him.'

169

'He's getting old,' said Lady Compton. 'I sometimes worry that he might be getting senile. For instance, since he retired he's become fanatically interested in football. Football! I ask you! Like a common schoolboy – and a man in his position.' She looked distressfully at Donaghue. 'I worry that he's losing his faculties.'

'Naturally,' Donaghue agreed. 'But I do not think you need worry about your husband. I think his faculties are very much intact, more so than many much younger men, I might add.'

'Do you really think so?' Lady Compton looked at Donaghue hopefully. 'It worries me dreadfully that he might do something *foolish*.'

'I think he knows exactly what he's doing. I think you worry about him unnecessarily.' Donaghue spoke reassuringly. 'Your anxiety about him has been magnified out of all proportion by your own anxiety at being confined to a primitive refuge building in a violent storm. It's only natural. You'll see – soon everything will change. The blocked road will be cleared in no time and you will be able to leave.'

Lady Compton stopped walking. She seized Donaghue's arm. 'Is that really so?' she asked, her eyes bright with hope and relief. 'Do you think we'll be able to leave this evening?'

'It's quite possible – if the weather stays clear. Mario seems to think that the rocks can be cleared in an afternoon.'

It was as if a weight had been lifted from Lady Compton's features. Her face brightened and her step quickened as they resumed their walk.

Donaghue, at one point, stooped to pick something up from the path. It was a button, pale pink in colour.

'I think I know whose this is,' he said. 'It belongs to one of the French twins. She said she had walked this way yesterday afternoon.' He popped the button in his pocket then grasped Lady Compton's arm. 'Look,' he said, indicating a spot somewhere to their left. 'I thought I spotted a marmot.'

They watched in silence for several minutes but were disappointed to see no further movement. They finished the walk in animated conversation about the personal habits of marmots. Lady Compton, it turned out, like Donaghue, was an enthusiastic student of wildlife.

*

170

As Donaghue and Lady Compton arrived back at the refuge they saw that a small party had gathered, ready to set out for the rockfall. Now that the sun was shining the temperature had risen sharply and the men of the party were dressed in T-shirts and shorts in preparation for the strenuous work.

The girls, Bridget, Meryss and the French twins, had offered to help but Mario insisted that the initial work would be too dangerous. However, he added, they might be called in to help when the danger of falling rock had been eliminated.

Vincente, Browning, Mario, Sir Hilary, Jim Baxter and Laura Hutchinson were waiting to leave. Donaghue hurried upstairs to the dormitory to change into more suitable clothing.

As he slipped into his oldest shorts and T-shirt he caught a glimpse of something white beneath the pillow of his bunk.

Very carefully he lifted the pillow and pulled out a piece of white notepaper on which a childlike drawing had been crudely sketched.

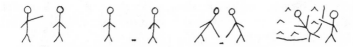

Donaghue studied the drawing for several seconds before slipping the scrap of paper into the pocket of his shorts. As he descended the stairs, his head bent in reflection, Laura Hutchinson entered the hallway. She called to him, 'We're leaving now, Mr Donaghue, if you want to join us.'

'Miss Hutchinson,' said Donaghue as he accompanied her out of the refuge, 'would it be possible to have a word with you in private? Perhaps we could follow at a short distance behind the others.'

She looked at him a little suspiciously but acquiesced. They set off together in the direction of the road. The small group of men had left and were a short distance ahead.

'As you may or may not know, Miss Hutchinson, I am conducting a personal investigation into Oliver Hardcastle's death.'

'You think he was murdered, is that it?' the guide asked sharply.

'I have no opinion on the matter. I am investigating what

appears to be a *mysterious* death. I have no reason to believe he was murdered. Would you mind helping me by answering a few questions?'

Laura hesitated, her angular features knitted into a frown. 'I'm not sure that anything I could say would be of use to you.'

'You would be surprised how much a chance opinion or observation can be of help in a matter like this.'

'Go ahead then,' she said almost reluctantly.

'Can you tell me when you last saw Hardcastle alive?'

Laura hesitated for a few seconds before answering. 'I saw him shortly before I rejoined you after I'd gone back for my walkie-talkie.'

Donaghue looked at her curiously. 'That would have been about what time?' he asked.

She reflected for a moment or so. 'I left you at twenty past two. I remember looking at my watch. It would not have taken me more than fifteen minutes to run back to the refuge, pick up my walkie-talkie and run back. It can't have been more than two thirty-five when I saw him. He was on the path that led to the lake. I . . . I . . .' She hesitated. 'I went to speak to him.'

'Might I ask why?'

The guide averted her eyes from Donaghue's probing gaze.

'I had something to say to him,' she said. 'It was personal.'

'Did you know Oliver Hardcastle well?'

She looked sharply across at Donaghue.

'I didn't know him at all. I met him for the first time this week. I knew him as well as you did.'

'I don't think that's true, Miss Hutchinson,' said Donaghue gently.

The guide's face deepened in colour. 'I might have met him somewhere before,' she said. 'On another site, perhaps, but I didn't remember.'

'I think you did,' said Donaghue. 'But might I be right in saying that he had forgotten you?'

Laura Hutchinson stared furiously ahead of her, her face livid. 'Good God,' she said. 'What are you – some kind of mind reader?'

'May I suggest a hypothesis?' said Donaghue. 'You can simply say whether I am right or wrong?'

Laura nodded, her lips set into a tight angry line.

172

'Some time ago – a year, two years perhaps – you met Oliver Hardcastle and entered into a brief romantic relationship with him. When you met him a few days ago in this valley he failed to recognise you. You had perhaps changed a little in appearance – a new hairstyle, a few kilos lighter, but not enough, you considered, to be unrecognisable. You realised that Oliver Hardcastle was so superficial in his relationships that he actually forgot not only the names of the women he had seduced, but their faces too. It was bad enough not to be recognised but you found it intolerable when he attempted to seduce you again *not realising that he had done so already*. You sternly rejected his advances – I actually saw you do so. I was marmot-spotting and saw Hardcastle approach you. When you saw him on the path to the lake yesterday you could not resist the temptation to finally let him know who you were. Am I right about all that?'

She looked at him in astonishment, then managed a half-smile.

'You are absolutely right,' she said, her voice low. 'I met him four years ago. At that time he was involved with Signora Vincente. What made me absolutely furious when I met him this week was that he obviously hadn't forgotten her!'

'Did your discussion with him at the lake become heated?'

'I suppose you could describe it as heated, yes.' She looked sternly at Donaghue. 'But I didn't push him into the lake, if that's what you're thinking. I didn't hate him enough to kill him. I just wanted him to know who I was and what I thought of him.'

'A perfectly understandable course of action,' commented Donaghue. 'Did you see anyone else in the area close to the lake, either on your way there or back to where you met me?'

There was an almost imperceptible hesitation before she spoke. 'No, I saw no one apart from Sir Hilary on his way down from the top of the tor. But he hadn't yet reached the bottom.'

'Can you tell me, Miss Hutchinson, if, in your opinion, there is anyone at the refuge with a motive strong enough to kill Oliver Hardcastle? You don't have to mention a name – just tell me if you think there could be.'

Again the slightest hesitation before speaking. 'No. I think a lot of people had reason to dislike him, but to kill him – no.'

'There is one other small thing you could tell me. Were you aware that there was a miniature version of the inscription engraved on four rocks on the path leading to the lake?'

Laura looked at him in astonishment. 'If there is, it's been put there by a vandal. There are no genuine engravings in the vicinity of the lake.'

'I am most grateful for your help,' said Donaghue as they reached the site of the rockfall. The others, under Mario's supervision, had already started clearing away the smaller extraneous rubble.

Laura moved off to inspect the perimeters of the fall for any possible further movement and Donaghue joined the men in the strenuous task of removing the fallen rocks.

23

The men worked vigorously for two hours clearing the larger, dangerous rocks, then they were joined by the women. By four o'clock there remained blocking the path only one large boulder which proved impossible to move, even by so many willing hands.

It was agreed that Laura Hutchinson, the most experienced rock climber, should scale the boulder and walk down to the valley to summon the vehicles and equipment necessary to move it. At the same time she could notify the police of Oliver Hardcastle's death.

Within fifteen minutes she was on her way, having climbed the rock with the agility of a cat, and was loping down the track to the village below. She would be able to run down, she had said, in an hour. She was watched with admiration as she left. Her energy and stamina appeared to be inexhaustible.

The sky was still, miraculously, a clear, brilliant blue and with the road almost cleared the tired and perspiring group were in high spirits as they made their way back to the refuge building to shower and change into clean clothing.

Only Antonio remained at the site of the rockfall. He clambered half-way up the remaining boulder and watched Laura Hutchinson until she disappeared from sight. Then, a worried expression on his face, he made his way, not back to the refuge, but westwards towards his hut.

Donaghue, straggling behind the others, stopped suddenly, then turned and followed in the shepherd's wake.

The moustachioed village constable was dozing when, an hour later, Laura entered the rather shabby gendarmerie. He leapt into a frenzy of activity when she explained that a death had occurred in the valley and that the road was blocked at the top of the mountain. The local inspector was called from his afternoon game of *boules*, the doctor summoned and a rescue team organised. Half an hour later Laura was on her way back up the mountain, sitting in the back of an uncomfortable fire service vehicle in the company of several firemen, the police inspector and the village doctor.

Antonio looked up startled as the door to his hut opened and Donaghue peered into its dark interior.

'May I come in?' he enquired. 'I would very much like to speak to you.'

Antonio, apparently in great distress, nodded. The interior of the hut was dark and oppressive, permeated with the odour of stale cheese and wine. Mingled with the rank smell of food was another odour that emanated from a dark corner of the single room. Donaghue could just discern in the dim light a huddled furry shape on the floor that moved weakly every now and again and let out a whimpering bleat.

'The injured lamb?' he enquired gently, nodding in the direction of the dark corner.

Antonio nodded. He had removed his bell, which stood on the crudely built wooden table at which he was sitting. Next to the bell lay a photograph which Antonio had been holding in his hand and which he had hastily dropped as the door had opened. The photograph depicted a young woman in her early twenties smiling cheerfully, her eyes bright, her cheeks healthily pink and rounded. Donaghue was surprised to recognise the features as those of Laura Hutchinson – a much younger Laura, the photo taken perhaps ten years before, and scarcely recognisable but for the same intense intelligence in the grey eyes.

He picked up the photograph.

175

'A beautiful girl,' he commented. 'And very courageous.'

Antonio nodded. He regarded Donaghue almost with fear.

'May I sit down?' Donaghue asked.

The shepherd's matted head nodded again. Donaghue sat on the simple wooden bench that was attached to the table and Antonio pushed towards him a cracked earthenware jug filled with a rather vinegary wine and the cup that accompanied it.

Donaghue declined the offer. After working long and hard, wine would go to his head.

'If you have some water I would gladly accept a glass – or a cup,' he added under his breath as Antonio, his face creased into a sudden gap-toothed smile, leapt up and produced from a curtained cupboard a second jug, this one containing the cool clear water of one of the valley's springs.

Donaghue drank with pleasure.

'Antonio,' he said, 'would you mind very much if I asked you one or two questions?'

The fearful expression quickly resumed its place on the shepherd's youthful but weathered face. He made no gesture – just stared at Donaghue in a kind of animal terror.

'Please don't be afraid, Antonio,' said Donaghue gently. 'I am not here to intimidate you. I would just like to ask you something.'

The expression of terror retreated to be replaced by one of hesitant relief.

'Did you go near to the lakeside yesterday afternoon?' Donaghue asked.

The terror returned. The matted head shook from side to side.

'I think you did,' said Donaghue gently. 'I heard your bell.'

Antonio's head shook wildly from side to side.

'Did you see what happened to Oliver Hardcastle?'

The head shook again frantically.

'Why did you draw this then and leave it under my pillow?'

Donaghue withdrew the crude drawing from his pocket and placed it on the table.

Antonio gazed wildly at the scrap of paper, then at Donaghue, his eyes on the verge of tears.

'You wanted me to know what happened, that's right, isn't it?'

Antonio nodded.

'So you did see what happened to Oliver Hardcastle?'

Antonio shook his head, then, as if changing his mind, started to nod.

'Did you see how he fell into the lake?'

Antonio nodded. His eyes, as he gazed at Donaghue, were filled once again with the terror they had betrayed before.

'In your drawing you show two people in apparent dispute. The one on the left is Oliver Hardcastle, is that right?'

Antonio nodded.

'And the other, is it a woman?'

Antonio's head shook violently from side to side.

'It's a man, then?'

Antonio's head nodded.

'Do you know the identity of the man?'

The head shook again.

'Your drawing indicates that they were arguing over an object – is that right?'

Antonio nodded.

'Do you know what the object was?'

Antonio shook his head.

'And the man accidently pushed Hardcastle into the lake while attempting to retrieve the object.'

Antonio hesitated slightly, then nodded.

'Is that all you know about Hardcastle's death?' Donaghue asked.

Antonio nodded vehemently, his eyes now moist with tears.

The injured lamb in the corner bleated pitifully and the shepherd leapt up and ran to it. He cradled the creature in his arms, tears streaming from his eyes. He dipped a rag into a dirty bowl of milk and pushed the nourishment into the animal's mouth.

'Will the lamb survive?' Donaghue asked.

Antonio nodded his head.

'If it was severely injured would you kill it?'

Antonio nodded again.

'You would stun it and then slit its throat, is that right?'

A further nod confirmed Donaghue's suggestion.

'May I see the stun gun you use?'

Antonio raised an arm and indicated a hook on the wall near the door. Hanging there was a large, cumbersome-looking instrument. Donaghue rose and lifted the heavy object from its hook: a rather old-fashioned battery-operated device that would deliver an electric shock strong enough to stun its victim.

'Could you not simply kill the animal with this?' he asked.

Antonio shook his head.

'If the animal was standing in water, perhaps?' he suggested.

Antonio looked up at him in puzzlement.

'Even a small shock can kill if the victim is standing in water,' Donaghue explained.

Antonio looked blankly at Donaghue. He lifted his shoulders in a gesture that said: So? Why are you telling me what I know already?

He continued feeding the lamb and Donaghue replaced the stun gun on to its hook by the door. He took his leave of the shepherd and walked thoughtfully back to the refuge.

Clothilde sat with Bridget on a rock a short distance from the refuge terrace. They were planning to take a short walk before dinner and were waiting for Donaghue to join them. He was, at that moment, up in the dormitory changing from his working clothes into a track suit suitable for an evening walk.

'I suppose we'll be leaving as soon as the road is clear,' said Bridget a little mournfully. 'It's been such an exciting few days.' She hesitated. 'Not for Mr Hardcastle, of course,' she added.

'One's own death can hardly be considered as exciting,' agreed Clothilde dourly.

'It's been incredibly exciting working on the inscription with Herman,' enthused Bridget. 'He's terribly excited at the prospect of researching it.'

'He might be disappointed,' came Donaghue's voice behind them. He joined them at the rock. He was dressed in a dark green velour track suit and looked rather like an overgrown leprechaun. Bridget made room for him and he sat beside her.

'What do you mean, Mr Donaghue?' she asked. 'Why should he be disappointed?'

'I'll explain later,' said Donaghue absently as he gazed out at the valley in search of a marmot.

'Still being mysterious, Ulysses?' commented Clothilde.

'It's very simple,' said Donaghue. 'I have an idea. If my idea is borne out Mr Browning will be disappointed in his hopes.'

178

'And if your idea is not borne out?' asked Bridget.

Donaghue looked at his beautiful secretary gravely. 'If my idea is not borne out – if I am, God forbid, wrong – then I am placing my own life at risk and probably the lives of others.' He pondered for a few seconds as if considering the possibility of error, then he shook his head. 'No,' he said firmly. 'My idea is not wrong – it cannot be wrong and Antonio has just confirmed it.'

'Antonio?' queried Clothilde and Bridget in unison.

'I spoke to Antonio a short time ago. He informed me by way of a drawing that he had witnessed Hardcastle's death.'

Bridget gasped and Clothilde looked speculatively at Donaghue.

'Do you mean he saw the person who killed Hardcastle?' she asked.

'He saw someone – or he thought he saw someone – push Hardcastle into the lake. But he was not sure of their identity. He watched from a distance and at such an angle that he couldn't be sure. He was on the north side of the lake. But he thought he knew who it was and lied to me as a consequence. But – and this he could not have realised – in his dissimulation he *inadvertently revealed the truth.*'

'Are you saying that you know with certainty what happened to Hardcastle?' asked Clothilde.

'That is what I am saying, yes.'

'Then you will have to tell the police.'

'I will certainly tell the police all that I know.'

'And us?' said Bridget. 'Can you tell us now?'

'I will tell you after I have spoken to the police,' said Donaghue.

'Your discretion can sometimes be utterly exasperating,' Clothilde complained.

'What I don't understand, Mr Donaghue,' said Bridget, 'is what bearing Oliver Hardcastle's death has on Herman's future research into the inscription.'

'Ah,' said Donaghue. 'There you've hit the nail on the head. You've touched the crux of the matter. I cannot explain right at this moment but Hardcastle's death has, I am sure of it, a very strong bearing on the future of the inscription.'

'Do you mean on its authenticity?' asked Bridget. 'But Sir Hilary has already pronounced it authentic – or are you talking about its meaning?'

'Both,' said Donaghue.

Bridget looked at him in puzzlement. 'Do you know something about its meaning that we don't?' she asked.

'What I know was inspired by your efforts – but I cannot say what it is just now.'

Bridget's full lips pursed in exasperation but she asked no further questions. She knew her employer well. It would not be meet to press him for information when he was not ready to give it.

'But you will inform Herman at some point?' she said instead.

'Of course I will tell Herman,' Donaghue reassured her. He patted her affectionately on the knee. 'Don't worry, Bridget. I will tell Herman everything I know, all in good time.'

He looked at his watch. It was five o'clock. 'I would imagine that within the hour the guide will have returned with a doctor and a police officer. Soon after that the matter of Oliver Hardcastle's death will be cleared up to everybody's satisfaction.'

He rose.

'Shall we take a little walk in the meantime?' he suggested cheerfully.

24

The lumbering fire service lorry finally reached the plateau at the top of the mountain. Using the small crane attached to the back, the crew of firemen set to hauling the last boulder from the road. Two electricians went in search of the fallen telephone and electricity cables.

Inspector Baresi, an impressively built local police officer, and Dr Morel, the tall bespectacled village doctor, were greeted by Mario who accompanied them to the generator room to inspect the body.

'I suppose the storm stopped you coming up yesterday morning,' said Mario to Dr Morel.

'Yesterday morning?' queried the doctor.

'A message was left with your secretary to send you up,' said

Mario. 'One of the archaeologists had a bad turn – passed out for no apparent reason.'

The doctor looked at Mario deprecatingly. 'I wasn't called out yesterday morning,' he said. 'No such message was passed to me.' Then he added matter-of-factly, 'Is this person still in need of a doctor's services?'

'Well, no, he seems OK now,' said Mario.

'In that case it's no matter,' said the doctor as he lifted the tarpaulin that covered Hardcastle's body and knelt down to inspect the corpse.

The doctor asked no questions, Laura having explained on the way up the circumstances of Hardcastle's death. Having completed his examination, he replaced the tarpaulin and stood up.

'I would like to speak to the doctor who examined the body,' he stated somewhat curtly.

'And I', said Inspector Baresi importantly, 'would like to talk to the detective who's been investigating the death. Is there anywhere where we can speak in private?'

Mario led the two men to the lodge common room and instructed Michou to find Donaghue and Clothilde.

She found them sitting on the terrace having just returned from their walk. She conveyed her message and Donaghue went first to the dormitory to fetch his haversack and then to the dining-room to retrieve the contact lens which he had left on the counter and which had remained unclaimed. He then inspected himself in the mirror in the shower room.

'Do you think, perhaps, I should change my clothes?' he asked Clothilde. 'Will an Italian police inspector take me seriously in a jogging outfit?'

'He would hardly take you more seriously in your colonial shorts,' said Clothilde disparagingly. 'In any case, Ulysses, you won't be there to impress him with your sartorial elegance – or lack of it,' she added caustically. 'But rather to impress him with the ingenuity of your deductions.'

'Ah,' said Donaghue as they left for the lodge. 'Now that's something I cannot altogether guarantee.'

Mario settled the stocky inspector and the much more elegant doctor into two of the lodge armchairs and offered them an aperitif. The inspector gladly accepted a *vin cuit*, the doctor asked only for a glass of mineral water.

Donaghue and Clothilde arrived, were presented to the visitors and duly installed in two further armchairs, glasses of the same *vin cuit* in their hands. The conversation was conducted in French as Inspector Baresi had no knowledge of English.

Dr Morel succinctly stated the conclusion of his examination of the corpse.

'I can see no immediate evidence as to the cause of death. The young man appeared to have been in general good health. Apart from some minor bruising to the face there appears to be no sign of foul play. Without an autopsy I can only hazard a guess that he suffered a heart attack or stroke of some kind although there is, as I said, no evidence whatsoever to that effect. In short, it is impossible to establish the cause of death without an autopsy, the authorisation for which rests, of course, in the hands of the police.'

He looked gravely at Clothilde. 'Perhaps you would like to state your opinion, Dr Blanche.'

'I have to say that I am in absolute agreement with you, Dr Morel,' she said. 'The origin of the bruising is known to us. It was not directly related to his death, having been the result of one or two disputes with lady friends. He could perhaps have suffered some kind of electric shock but there is no sign of him having been struck by lightning and in any case the time of his death was well before the afternoon storm began. I agree that only an autopsy will solve the mystery.'

'It's in your hands, then, Inspector,' said Dr Morel.

Inspector Baresi nodded in acknowledgement and turned enquiringly to Donaghue.

Both the police inspector and the doctor looked askance at Donaghue's green velour track suit. The doctor appeared to be mentally shaking his neatly coiffured head.

Inspector Baresi spoke.

'The guide, Miss Laura Hutchinson, explained briefly the circumstances of Mr Hardcastle's death and said that you have been conducting a personal investigation into it. Can you let me know the results of that investigation, Mr Donaghue – if you have reached any, of course?'

'Naturally,' said Donaghue. 'I will tell you exactly what I have discovered in the way of information and show you what I have found by way of clues.'

He delved, as he spoke, into the pocket of his haversack and withdrew the small number of articles that he had accumulated. He placed them on the table before the inspector: Hardcastle's diary, open at the list of women's names, the contact lens wrapped in tissue paper, the parsley he had found in the parrot's cage, the piece of brightly coloured fabric found at the lakeside, the black plastic rectangle found in the kitchen dustbin, the bar of soap with a blade stuck into it and lastly the crude drawing executed by Antonio.

Inspector Baresi looked at the collection blankly.

Donaghue then delved into his bag again and produced four sheets of paper. Each contained a neatly written list. The first he handed to the inspector, the other three he placed on the table.

'This is a list of the people present at the refuge at the time of Mr Hardcastle's death. The list is comprehensive and gives the name and profession of each person here. Let me first explain', he said, 'that I investigated the death of Mr Hardcastle because one of the guests, Signora Vincente, asked me to do so. She was a particularly close friend of Mr Hardcastle's and felt sure that he had been murdered. There was no evidence whatsoever that that was the case but I agreed to investigate the possibility. I found myself with a difficult task. As Dr Morel confirmed, there is no evidence at all of foul play of any kind. There was no weapon of any kind found at the place of his death and, more important, there is no apparent motive.'

'Not much of a case,' commented Inspector Baresi. 'Did you find anything in the course of your investigation to cause suspicion?'

'I will tell you, Inspector, what I found and you will have to decide whether there is a case to be made or not. Let me tell you first the significance of the objects that I have found and kept. First the diary: Hardcastle's diary reveals a list of all the women in the refuge, whom he was, it is evident, planning to seduce as a kind of trivial pastime. This activity led, as you can imagine, to considerable tensions and jealousies. As a result he was not a highly popular figure among the people at the refuge.

'The contact lens I found in Hardcastle's room. I believe it belongs to one of the women he attempted to seduce.'

'Do you know whose lens it is?'

'I have a shrewd idea but nobody has claimed it.'

The inspector looked rather disdainfully at the unclaimed lens. He picked up the sprig of limp parsley and looked enquiringly at Donaghue.

'The parsley I found at the bottom of the parrot's cage. Somebody fed it to the refuge parrot. Parsley is a deadly poison to a parrot.'

The inspector looked quizzically at Donaghue. 'Are you saying that the parrot was deliberately killed?'

'Possibly.'

'Why would anyone have killed the parrot?'

'I assumed because the parrot might have repeated something incriminating.'

'Have you any idea what the parrot might have said?'

'The parrot said a lot of things – he had a wide repertoire of words and sounds. Shortly before his death he was heard talking about a gun.'

'A gun? But Hardcastle wasn't shot.'

'No, and no gun was found.'

'Mr Donaghue,' said Inspector Baresi in mild exasperation, 'I'm not sure that the parrot's death has any bearing on the possibility of this Hardcastle being murdered.'

'It's possible that it hasn't,' Donaghue agreed.

Inspector Baresi pushed the parsley to one side and picked up the piece of purple cloth.

'I found this at the lakeside caught on a twig not far from the spot where Hardcastle fell into the lake.'

'And what possible conclusion do you draw from it?'

'That the person who had worn it perhaps witnessed the death.'

'Do you know where the material comes from?'

'I believe it came from a shirt belonging to Sir Hilary Compton.'

'Do you have any proof that it was caught on the twig at the time of Hardcastle's death?'

'None whatsoever. I am only guessing that it might have been.'

Inspector Baresi dropped the piece of fabric alongside the parsley. He said nothing but his manner betrayed his obvious opinion that without proof such trivia were worthless. He picked up the black plastic rectangle and weighed it in his palm. 'What on earth is this?' he asked.

'I'm not sure,' said Donaghue. 'I imagined it must be some kind of sophisticated archaeologist's tool. It belonged to Hardcastle and was found in the kitchen dustbin. It doesn't appear to be functioning in any way and was obviously beyond repair when thrown away. The other archaeologists have never seen such a thing and I am interested in discovering exactly what it is. It might or might not have some bearing on the case.'

The inspector's eyes darted to the bar of soap which he picked up tentatively. Donaghue translated the simple message of warning that accompanied it.

'Now this looks suspicious,' said the inspector. 'Somebody didn't want you to investigate the possibility of murder. Very suspicious, that. Any idea as to who did it?'

'It could have been any number of people but I don't think it was the murderer. This murderer, if there is one, is a sophisticated killer. To kill someone without leaving any sign of foul play takes a great deal of sophistication.'

The inspector nodded his head in agreement.

'I can't believe that such a killer would resort to a crude warning like this. I think rather that it was the work of somebody who was either protecting the murderer or protecting someone who they thought might be suspected.'

'I see,' said the inspector. 'I see your drift.'

He picked up the final piece of evidence, Antonio's drawing, and studied it intently.

'A very childish message,' said Donaghue. 'Designed, I believe, to put me off the track.'

'Do you think it was done by the murderer?'

'No. Again I think it is too crude. I think, like the warning, it was used to protect another person. You see, Inspector, in this enquiry, as I will explain to you, everybody is suspect – everybody here could have been guilty. Shall I tell you the progress of my investigation and the conclusions I came to?'

'Go ahead,' said Inspector Baresi hesitantly. He appeared very slightly dubious. The doctor next to him appeared extremely bored.

'Starting with the assumption that Hardcastle had been murdered, I attempted to discover the identity of the person who last spoke to him alive. I personally overheard him talking to someone in the vicinity of the lake shortly before his death and through my questioning of the others have deduced that the person he conversed with could have been either a woman or a man.'

The eyebrows of both Inspector Baresi and Dr Morel rose a fraction in speculation.

'Is it not obvious that it would be a man or a woman,' said Inspector Baresi with a hint of sarcasm, 'as there are no children, to my knowledge, in the valley?'

'What I meant to say,' said Donaghue, 'is that I have been unable to conclude definitively as to whether it was a man or a woman he was talking to. It seems that he spoke to more than one person in the thirty minutes or so before he died.'

He indicated the list headed: *Hardcastle last seen*. Inspector Baresi picked it up and scrutinised it.

'There you will find the times that each person said they last saw Hardcastle alive. Obviously if one of these people is a murderer he or she will be lying.'

'That goes without saying,' said the inspector a little sardonically as he studied the list.

'On the third sheet,' said Donaghue, 'you will find a list of names and alibis – where each person was and what they were doing at the time Hardcastle died, which Dr Blanche calculated as between two thirty and three thirty. The curious thing, as you can see, is that *nobody at the time had a watertight alibi*. If Hardcastle had been killed absolutely anybody could have done it. Which brings me next to motive – if anybody could have done it, we must narrow it down to who would have been motivated to do so. And here we find again that everyone at the refuge had a reason to feel antipathy towards Hardcastle. On the fourth sheet is a list of the people at the refuge and their possible motives for killing Oliver Hardcastle.

Motives

Sir Hilary Compton: Professional jealousy – believed possibly that Hardcastle had faked drawings.

Lady Compton: Humiliated by Hardcastle who attempted to seduce her.

186

Dr Vincente: Jealous of Hardcastle's interest in his wife. Knew that the two had had an affair. Professional reasons: is having a book published in October which could be rendered out of date by Hardcastle's discovery.

Maria Vincente: Jealous of Hardcastle's interest in other women at refuge. Learnt of his game of seduction.

Herman Browning: Professional jealousy. Hardcastle would gain celebrity having discovered drawings. Possibly jealous of Hardcastle's interest in Bridget Kilkenny whom Browning admired.

Jim Baxter: Known to have punched Hardcastle for showing interest in Meryss Jones – expressed open dislike of Hardcastle's type.

Meryss Jones: No apparent motive but could have been humiliated by Hardcastle's attempted seduction.

Nanette Fèvre: Jealous of Hardcastle's greater interest in her sister.

Ninette Fèvre: Jealous of Hardcastle's interest in other women.

Laura Hutchinson: Known to have argued with Hardcastle shortly before his death because he failed to recognise her as a former lover.

Clothilde Blanche: Possibly outraged by Hardcastle's behaviour towards women.

Bridget Kilkenny: A strict Catholic. She may have been outraged by his attempted seduction.

Mario Santinelli: Jealous of his wife's affair with Hardcastle.

Michou Santinelli: Jealous of Hardcastle's interest in other women.

Antonio: Might have witnessed Laura Hutchinson's dispute with Hardcastle and reacted violently. Antonio is in love with Miss Hutchinson.

'As you can see,' said Donaghue, 'the most common motive is jealousy, whether professional or personal. There was a great deal of personal jealousy as Hardcastle had attempted outrageously to flirt with every woman present. But was such jealousy strong enough a motive to kill him? His death does not appear to have been perpetrated in a moment of passion. It would appear rather to have been premeditated. In fact it was so successfully engineered that *he does not appear to have been murdered at all.*

'In conclusion, there is not only insufficient motive, but no weapon and no visible sign of foul play. In the face of the overwhelming lack of evidence I was forced to abandon my investigation and come to the conclusion that his former lover was mistaken in her suspicion that he had been murdered – that he had in fact died of natural causes, as yet unknown.'

Inspector Baresi looked obliquely at Donaghue. Then he picked up the bar of soap with its embedded razor blade.

'Did this influence you perhaps in your conclusion?' he asked.

'Not at all,' said Donaghue indignantly. 'My conclusions are the result of reason not of fear, if that's what you're implying. I have no doubt, as I said, that the warning is nothing more than the action of some frightened person protecting a loved one. Innocent people can get terribly nervous when brought into close proximity with death.'

'And the drawing?'

'The drawing was done, I am sure, by the shepherd, who wished to protect Miss Hutchinson whom he admired and whom he saw talking to Hardcastle shortly before his death. If not, it must have been a prank perpetrated by the two young art students. You know what art students are like.'

Inspector Baresi regarded the pile of objects, the lists and finally Donaghue himself. He scratched his head distractedly.

'I'll need to think about all this,' he said unenthusiastically.

'Keep everything I've given you,' said Donaghue generously. 'I've racked my brains enough but, with all that I've discovered, can come up with no real evidence of murder.'

Inspector Baresi gathered the evidence together, the puzzled expression still crossing his heavy-jowled features.

'Oh, there's one other thing,' said Donaghue. 'It could be meaningful or it could not. You'll have to decide for yourself. When I searched the site of the death for clues a verse from a Shakespeare play came to my mind. It remained persistently as if there was some clue or message within its lines that had escaped me.'

Both Inspector Baresi and Dr Morel looked at Donaghue in astonishment.

'A verse from Shakespeare?' repeated Inspector Baresi. 'What on earth has a verse from Shakespeare to do with anything?'

'I'm not sure,' said Donaghue. 'But I felt it might have some significance. Why else would it have come to mind?'

Neither Inspector Baresi nor Dr Morel appeared to have any idea why a verse from Shakespeare should come to the mind of an Irish detective.

'Would you like to hear it?' Donaghue enquired. 'It might possibly mean something to you.'

Inspector Baresi nodded dubiously.

Donaghue recited the lines that had come to him at the lakeside:

'Sweet are the uses of adversity,
Which, like the toad, ugly and venomous,
Wears yet a precious jewel in his head;
And this our life, exempt from public haunt,
Finds tongues in trees, books in the running brooks,
Sermons in stones, and good in everything.'

Clothilde translated the verse for Inspector Baresi and he in turn looked blankly back at her.

'It's very beautiful,' he said finally, 'but . . .' he hesitated. 'I fail to see any kind of message in it . . . In any case,' he added a little sardonically, 'I'm no great believer in messages from the other side – wouldn't stand up in court.' He said this with a grin. 'Evidence from those who died five hundred years ago is not generally accepted in a contemporary court of law!'

'Ah,' said Donaghue a little wistfully, 'but it's curious how those who lived so long before us can still have something to tell us.'

Inspector Baresi, having, it seemed, dismissed Donaghue as some kind of lunatic charlatan, swept up the articles into an efficient order and said matter-of-factly, 'I thank you, Mr Donaghue, for your help. I'm sure that with what you have given me I can come to a fairly certain conclusion as to whether the circumstances of this death were suspicious or not.'

Donaghue and Clothilde left the common room together. As the door closed behind them Clothilde looked at her friend, suspicion written large over her craggy features.

'I don't know what you're up to, Ulysses,' she said, 'but I'll expect an explanation. Am I to believe that you are deliberately diverting the course of justice?'

'That I would never do,' Donaghue said gravely. 'You know that.' He patted her arm. 'You will get your explanation, my dear

Clothilde, all in good time. Just bear with me a little and . . .'
He smiled mischievously. '. . . in the words of the Moor: "Yet
by your gracious patience, I will a round, unvarnish'd tale
deliver."'

25

Inspector Baresi lost no time in getting the body removed from
the generator room and into the fire service vehicle. He questioned Sir Hilary and Dr Vincente as to Oliver Hardcastle's next
of kin and informed Mario that the body would be kept at the
police morgue in the nearby town of Mende pending the family's
decision as to whether an autopsy was required or not. The
inspector had seen no reason to suspect foul play. Any investigation, he said, would lead, as Mr Donaghue's had, to a negative
conclusion. From his manner of pronouncing Donaghue's name
it was obvious to everyone that Inspector Baresi considered the
Irishman a bumbling amateur.

As soon as the body, officers and doctor had left, Mario
suggested an early supper for those who wanted to leave that
evening. He set to preparing a quiche, humming cheerfully to
himself – the sooner the gathering had gone the sooner he and
Michou could close up the refuge and return to their comfortable
villa in the village below.

While Mario cooked, those who had decided to leave immediately packed their bags. The French twins along with Jim Baxter
and Meryss Jones were packing up in the dormitory. In the lodge
Lady Compton packed in a kind of desperate haste. As she
folded one of her husband's long purple-coloured shirts she
noted a tear in one corner. She hurriedly tucked the shirt into
her own bag to repair later, then continued with her rapid
packing.

'I never want to come back to this place again,' she said to her
husband, who was unhurriedly pairing up his socks. 'It's been
the most unpleasant three days of my life.'

'The most interesting of mine,' said Sir Hilary. 'I may well come back sometime.' He smiled, a broad boyish grin. 'When they discover the meaning of the inscription perhaps. I'll have to be here when that is finally deciphered!'

In the adjoining room Emilio and Maria Vincente sat sipping a glass of mineral water.

'You were wrong, Maria, that's all,' Emilio said. 'He died of natural causes, albeit unknown. There is no evidence of foul play.'

'All that proves is that the killer is incredibly cunning and astute,' said Maria. 'I know he was killed – I just know it.'

'Conviction is meaningless without proof.'

Maria's small pretty face tightened. 'I shall employ a real detective,' she said purposefully. 'One who will find out the truth. That Donaghue is an oaf.'

'I'm sure he did his best.'

'His best was not good enough,' snapped Maria crossly. 'Whatever information he gave to the police was not enough to even interest them! They didn't even consider there was a case to investigate!'

Dr Vincente spoke consolingly to his wife: 'We shall speak to him after dinner. Then we can leave, if you wish.'

The French twins packed hastily. They had decided to leave immediately. They would not wait for the meal and the lift in the jeep that Mario had offered. They wanted to get away as soon as possible from the valley and their memory of Oliver Hardcastle's white face in death.

Their rucksacks strapped to their backs, they bade a hasty goodbye to Jim and Meryss who were packing in a much more leisurely fashion. On their way out of the refuge they popped their blonde heads into the dining-room to say goodbye to Mario and Michou and the other walkers.

Clothilde, Bridget and Herman Browning, seated at the central table, waved in farewell but Donaghue jumped up and pressed something into Ninette's hand.

'Your lens,' he whispered. 'Inspector Baresi inspected it but has no use for it. And this, I believe, is yours.' He handed

Nanette the pink button he had found on the path. 'You must have dropped it when you walked around the refuge yesterday afternoon.'

Ninette gaped at Donaghue in confusion, then blushed hotly. The girls set off in a hushed but animated conversation.

'So it was Ninette's lens,' said Bridget. 'Why on earth didn't she claim it? Lenses are expensive, after all.'

'Because of where it was found,' said Donaghue. 'I found it inside Hardcastle's doorway. She didn't want her sister to know that she'd been to his room wearing her contact lenses.'

'Why should that bother Nanette?' asked Clothilde mystified.

'Because Ninette had already visited him wearing her glasses. When she wore her lenses she pretended to be Nanette. Hardcastle had planned to seduce both sisters. He thought he had. But in fact *he seduced Ninette twice*. That was why Nanette was so distraught at his death. She had not had a chance to get close to or even speak to her idol.'

'Teenage girls are so immature,' said Bridget disdainfully. 'Thankfully one matures after twenty.'

Herman Browning looked long and admiringly at Bridget. He finally dragged his eyes away. 'Are you guys leaving this evening?' he asked. 'There seems to be a general exodus going on.'

'We had planned to leave in the morning,' said Donaghue. 'Neither Bridget nor I like driving at night. And you?' Donaghue asked him in turn. 'What are your plans?'

'Oh . . . er . . . I think I'll set off in the morning too.' He yawned. 'I need a good night's sleep – and I'd like a word with Vincente before he goes. He's not likely to be rushing off.'

'Good,' said Donaghue. 'That's good. We'll have time to talk then. I have something to tell you.'

'Me?' said Herman curiously. 'You've got something to tell me?'

'Perhaps we could talk after dinner. Would that be all right with you?'

'Sure,' said Herman. 'No problem.' He grinned and popped an arm around Bridget's shoulder. 'Sure hope it's good news – like Bridget here's broken off her engagement to her fiancé.' He grinned sheepishly and Bridget, to Donaghue's great surprise, blushed with pleasure. He had never seen his forthright secretary blush before.

After the light dinner of quiche and jacket potatoes Mario took Sir Hilary and Lady Compton down to the village in his jeep. Sir Hilary waved heartily to those who remained. Lady Compton, sitting in the back of the uncomfortable vehicle, looked fraught and wan as she offered a feeble and reluctant wave of the hand.

Jim Baxter and Meryss Jones set off on foot after the jeep, having refused a lift. They would enjoy the walk down, they said.

'Not much of a scoop in the end,' Jim complained as they rounded the first bend. He hesitated, almost stopped in his tracks, his cheeks turning pink above his straggly beard. 'Apart from you, of course,' he said. 'You are the best scoop I've ever had, Meryss.'

'Oh Jim,' said Meryss happily, linking her arm in his. 'That's the nicest thing anyone has ever said to me.' She smiled coyly at him. 'Not only do you have a way with chess pieces, you have a way with words too!'

Jim's sober features were taken by surprise for the second time in two days by a beaming smile. The couple tramped cheerfully down the mountain track.

Up at the refuge Mario and Michou cleared the tables, Mario still humming cheerfully to himself.

Donaghue suggested to the Vincentes and Herman Browning that they join him, Clothilde and Bridget for coffee on the terrace.

The evening was calm and warm. Laura Hutchinson appeared from the shower room. She was ready to leave, her back-pack secured over her shoulders. She shook each hand in turn; wished them good luck, then, calling goodbye to Mario and Michou, loped off at a steady stride down the mountain. The dark eyes of the Vincentes followed her progress. 'You know,' said Maria, 'I was sure that she had killed Oliver. She looked at him sometimes with such bitter hatred.'

'Antonio thought the same,' said Donaghue. 'He saw her talking to Hardcastle just before his death. She was wearing a purple sweater. A few minutes later he saw a purple-clad arm reach out and push Hardcastle into the lake. He assumed it was Laura and lied to me in order to protect her.'

Maria gazed at Donaghue, anger growing in her dark eyes. 'Are you telling me that you know Oliver was killed by somebody? Why are the police not investigating it? Why have they gone away as if nothing had happened?'

'If you will bear with me I will explain after my own fashion,' said Donaghue quietly. He turned to Herman Browning. 'It's important that you in particular hear what I have to say. Your future work will depend on it.'

'Go ahead,' declared Herman. 'I'm all ears.'

Donaghue looked at each person at the table in turn: the handsome, intelligent features of Dr Vincente, the dark intensity of his spirited wife, the rounded freckled features of Herman Browning, Bridget's ingenuous beauty, the green eyes gazing avidly at him, and finally the leathery craggy face of his friend Clothilde.

'I am going to tell you – just you – what happened to Oliver Hardcastle.' He addressed Signora Vincente first. 'You, Signora, should know, not just because you asked me to investigate his death, but because you of all the people here *sensed* the truth. Dr Vincente should know because he is fundamentally rational and objective, a true scientist. He will not be emotionally disturbed by what he hears. Herman Browning should know because, as I have said to him, his future work may depend on it. Clothilde and Bridget may know as I trust them implicitly not to divulge what they learn.

'What you are about to learn is no secret – anyone could have discovered it. In fact I gave all the information I had obtained and discovered to Inspector Baresi. I concealed nothing from him. But it is unlikely, if not impossible, that he will come to the conclusion I have come to. Inspector Baresi is not a man who would let his unconscious guide him. He will, as a result, rarely see the truth of what goes on around him.'

Donaghue lifted his cup and sipped his coffee. He poured a little cognac into the bottom of the cup.

'If you will be patient,' he said, 'I will start at the beginning.'

26

'Let me show you first a few objects that have helped me in my investigation.'

Donaghue took from his pocket a small string bag from which he spilled out on to the table the articles that he had shown to Inspector Baresi. There were six in all.

'There should have been seven,' said Donaghue. 'The seventh, the contact lens, I returned just now to the French girl, Ninette Fèvre. It was no longer of any consequence. It might have been significant had one of the twins proved to be a killer, but that is not the case so the lens can be forgotten. I will explain the significance or otherwise of the various articles as we go along.

'When Hardcastle died I felt, as Maria Vincente had, that he could not have died of natural causes. I felt sure, as she did, that he had been killed.

'My belief was confirmed when I found the instrument of his death.'

He picked up the black plastic rectangle and held it out to Herman Browning.

'Do you recognise this?' he asked. 'Do you know what it is?'

'No idea,' said Browning. 'I'd guess it's some kind of remote control device.'

'It belonged to Hardcastle,' said Donaghue. 'I thought at first that it must have been a rock-dating instrument, or something like that, but having examined it I discovered that it is a highly sophisticated electrical stun gun – a small, innocent-looking piece of technology that could stun a grown man into insensibility. It was that that knocked you out, Browning, in the corridor. You said it was like a bolt from the blue. What you received was exactly that – a bolt of electricity that knocked you off your feet for enough time for Hardcastle to go off and attempt to seduce Bridget.'

Bridget's face reddened in fury.

'The . . . the blackguard!' she spluttered.

Browning's sandy eyebrows rose a millimetre as he tentatively turned the instrument in his hands.

'It's all right – it won't give any shocks now. The batteries have been removed.'

'Why in God's name would he keep a thing like this? Self-defence? Who did he think was going to attack him?'

'I think I can explain why,' said Donaghue. 'But it certainly wasn't to commit suicide with. He was killed by a shock from the gun but the gun was found in the dustbin of the refuge kitchen. That someone had killed him using the gun was confirmed by the death of the parrot during the night. On the evening of Hardcastle's death the parrot was heard to talk about hiding a gun. The following morning he was dead, having been poisoned with parsley. The person who killed him was knowledgeable about wildlife. They left the window nearest the cage open to make sure that the parrot died. Tropical birds cannot survive icy winds.

'I was sure now that Hardcastle had been killed but I wasn't sure that it was a case of murder. During the course of my questioning of the people present I discovered that several lied: Dr Vincente, his wife, Sir Hilary, Lady Compton, Ninette Fèvre and Antonio the shepherd all lied about their own or their loved ones' activities yesterday afternoon. If these people lied I concluded that they were doing so in order to protect themselves or their partners *because they believed a murder had taken place*. I then concluded that if a murder had taken place there must have been a reason – a motive.

'I considered each of the people present and their possible motives.'

He held up the list that he had shown to Inspector Baresi.

'As you can see, almost everyone at the refuge had a reason to dislike or even hate Oliver Hardcastle, but did any of them have a reason to kill him? As far as I could see only three people had motives remotely strong enough to justify murder: Dr Vincente, his wife Maria, and Antonio, the shepherd.'

Dr Vincente said nothing; he regarded Donaghue intently, his dark handsome face impassive. Maria bristled and shifted angrily in her chair.

'And these in turn', Donaghue went on, 'were three of the people who had lied to me when I questioned them, Maria about the time her husband returned from the tor, Dr Vincente about his wife leaving the refuge and Antonio about the person he saw at the lakeside with Oliver Hardcastle.

'Dr Vincente's wife was a long-time lover of Hardcastle's. By anybody else's standards her husband should have been insanely jealous. But from what I can see Dr Vincente is simply not the jealous type. He is profoundly rational and objective, a scientist in all things – even in matters of love. He lied in order to protect his wife whom he suspected of having killed Hardcastle.

'I too strongly suspected Maria Vincente. She displayed great jealousy and anger over Hardcastle's interest in other women. I had overheard them in heated conversation in the lodge and then heard a similar conversation between Hardcastle and another person at the lakeside just before he died. I assumed naturally that the other person was Maria and indeed she admitted speaking to him at the same spot – but I discovered later that more than one person had spoken to Hardcastle beside the lake early yesterday afternoon. Laura Hutchinson, for example, admitted arguing with him close to the lake. That could well have been the conversation I overheard.

'And then I asked myself, would Maria Vincente, after killing Hardcastle, have thrown the gun into the kitchen dustbin? The answer had to be no. Signora Vincente is a very *ordered* woman, both in her thinking and her personal habits. She would, I am sure, have done as I would have done and placed the gun back in Hardcastle's room.'

Donaghue smiled across at Maria. 'Maria Vincente's thinking is very much like my own. Throwing the gun in a dustbin was the action of a much more undisciplined character.

'The only other person who felt a passionate hatred for Hardcastle was Antonio, the shepherd. Antonio was in love with Laura Hutchinson. He adores her in much the same way a teenage boy is infatuated with a cinema star. He was, I am sure, aware of Laura's hatred of Hardcastle, who had profoundly insulted her by failing to recognise her as a former lover. It occurred to me that Antonio might have killed him in a moment of fury. He himself had used a stun gun on animals and would know that such an instrument could kill if the victim was standing in water, as Hardcastle had been that afternoon. The earth at the lake's edge is soft and marshy and almost completely waterlogged.

'But I had to discount Antonio for the same reason I finally discounted Dr Vincente and his wife. Although these three had the strongest motives for killing Oliver Hardcastle they were, of all the people present at the refuge, the most *compassionate* in their natures. Dr Vincente's tolerant understanding of his wife's infidelity shows a profoundly compassionate nature. Maria, when she spoke to me, claimed to be as dispassionate as Hardcastle was himself but her tone when she spoke was unconsciously filled with the compassion of one who loves unwittingly. Antonio, in his care of living creatures, proves himself to be a person who protects life not takes it. In my long experience I have never come across a *compassionate* murderer. The person who killed Hardcastle was as dispassionate as his victim, of that I became certain.'

Donaghue sipped his coffee then resumed his monologue.

'Still not sure whether Hardcastle had been murdered, I tried to keep my investigation and questioning as discreet as possible. I did not want to rouse any possible murderer to wrath. The parrot could have been killed by the murderer or, as I was inclined to believe, by somebody protecting the killer. My belief was confirmed when I received a rather crude and vicious threat to my life.'

Donaghue indicated the soap with its blade and menacing message.

'When I found this I was almost sure that the person who had placed it in my bag was the same person who had killed the parrot – both actions spoke of a desperate and frightened individual. But, curiously, I did not see Hardcastle's killer as such a person. I saw two people: the killer, cool, calm, almost indifferent, and the person protecting the killer, frantic and fearful.

'The problem was at this point that my reason was battling with my intuition. My intuition told me that Hardcastle had not in fact been murdered – killed, perhaps, but not murdered. Words spoken by Sir Hilary Compton came to my mind: "Who would be bothered to kill Oliver Hardcastle?" Sir Hilary had pooh-poohed the idea and I could not help but agree with him. There was simply no motive strong enough: there was jealousy and dislike, but nothing strong enough to justify a cold-blooded murder. But if he had not been murdered, why had he died, and why was somebody desperately trying to stop the investigation? The obvious answer was that whoever had threatened me *thought that the person they were protecting had murdered Hardcastle.*

'Then I received a curious message.' Donaghue held up the stick-figure drawing. 'The message came from Antonio. He gave it to me in order to put me off my track but in doing so inadvertently showed me the truth. Antonio believed that Laura Hutchinson had killed Hardcastle. He heard her arguing with him. He drew a scenario which shows a *man* in dispute with Hardcastle over an unidentified object and Hardcastle accidentally falling into the lake. The man in the drawing appears to be attempting to save Hardcastle from falling. *Antonio depicts an accident involving two men.* In doing so he lies because he believed he had witnessed a murder perpetrated by his beloved Laura. But what Antonio does not know is that what he saw was an illusion and that what he drew was in fact exactly what happened. This, I believe, is what took place: Antonio was on the north side of the lake tending his sheep. He saw Laura approach the lakeside wearing a purple sweater. He hid behind a rock and from his vantage point saw Hardcastle clearly but not his interlocutor. At one point she disappeared. A few minutes later he heard Hardcastle's voice again in dispute and a purple-clad arm attempt to wrest something from his hand. He saw the object fall, both figures attempt to retrieve it, then the arm reach out again and Hardcastle fall backwards into the lake.'

Donaghue held up the shepherd's drawing for all at the table to see.

'Hardcastle reaches out to the other person. He has something in his hand – the stun gun. The other person attempts to take the gun from him. The gun falls to the ground.

'Both Hardcastle and his adversary attempt to retrieve the gun.

'Hardcastle picks it up. He is standing in waterlogged ground and receives a fatal shock. He falls backwards into the lake. His adversary reaches forward in an attempt to stop him falling.

'Antonio failed to recognise the small plastic object as a stun gun. His own is a much older, more cumbersome instrument. He saw what appeared to be a fight and a deliberate murder. What he didn't see was what followed. He didn't see the other person retrieve the gun, return to the refuge and dispose of it by throwing it into the kitchen dustbin.'

'So Hardcastle wasn't murdered?' said Bridget.

'No, he was not murdered – but the curious thing was that most of the people at the refuge felt sure that he had been. People became frightened and cautious, convinced that a murder had been committed and that there was a murderer among them. And, strangely enough, they were, in a sense, right. *A murder had been planned and a murderer had come to the valley.*'

'What on earth do you mean?' asked Clothilde. 'Who was this murderer, then?'

'The murderer was Hardcastle himself.'

'But he died,' said Bridget.

'Yes, he was killed by the person he had planned to kill himself.'

He held up the shepherd's sketch again. 'Look at the first drawing. Hardcastle's arm is reaching out to the other person, the gun in his hand. It is obvious to me that he was trying to kill his adversary with it. Why, otherwise, would he have taken it with him? *He had taken it with him because he had planned to kill somebody with it.*'

Everyone at the table regarded Donaghue in a perplexed silence.

'Are you going to tell us who his adversary was?' Clothilde asked quietly.

'It was Sir Hilary Compton,' said Donaghue. 'Two things convinced me that it was Sir Hilary who last saw Hardcastle alive. One: the fact that of all the people who had been up to the tor he was the only one to return with wet shoes, which meant that he was the only one to speak to Hardcastle at the lake's edge. Two: Sir Hilary, of all the people who lied, was the only one who lied to protect himself. All the others lied to protect another person.'

'But why on earth did Hardcastle want to kill Sir Hilary?' asked Browning in incredulity. 'Because he might have pronounced the drawings fake?'

'It is my belief', said Donaghue, 'that Hardcastle planned to kill Sir Hilary whether he pronounced the drawings fakes or not. The older man, as long as he remained alive, would steal Oliver Hardcastle's glory. Hardcastle was too far gone in his egiosm to tolerate any kind of competition. He was arrogant enough to believe that with the little piece of technology that he had discovered he could commit an undetectable crime. He didn't count on Sir Hilary Compton's quite extraordinary physical agility and strength. When he attempted to stun Sir Hilary the older man's reflexes would have been too fast. He didn't expect Sir Hilary to knock the gun from his hand.'

'And it didn't occur to Hardcastle either that his crime might be witnessed,' Browning commented. He grinned. 'He didn't expect to be seen by a dumb shepherd.'

'Not only by the shepherd,' said Donaghue. 'There was a second witness. Another person saw what took place and, like Antonio, misinterpreted what they saw. The person was hidden in the bushes to one side of the clearing wearing a brightly coloured shirt. The shirt caught on a twig and I found the torn piece of fabric.' He held up the tiny scrap of violet silk.

'Who was it?' Bridget asked eagerly.

'I can tell you now that she's gone. It was Lady Compton, Sir Hilary's wife. She had put on one of his brightly coloured shirts, perhaps in response to his criticism of her rather dowdy choice of dress, and had perhaps planned to join him up at the tor.'

'So it was Lady Compton I saw leaving the lodge, not Sir Hilary,' exclaimed Browning. 'I thought my eyes were playing tricks on me!'

'She must have spotted Sir Hilary approaching the lake and wondered what he was doing there. She saw what took place from behind the two men. She saw her husband reach out

201

towards Hardcastle and, not knowing that he had received a shock, thought that her husband pushed him into the lake. She would not, of course, have recognised the gun for what it was. She must have followed him back, heard him muttering about hiding the gun, then, in her desperate attempt to protect him, killed the parrot after hearing it repeat her husband's words and threatened me in a childishly crude manner. I had to quickly reassure her before she tried to carry out her threat!'

'Boy!' said Herman Browning, gazing at Donaghue in admiration. 'That's one helluva piece of deduction. What I don't understand, though, is why Sir Hilary didn't report exactly what had happened if it was nothing more than an accident.'

'It was more than an accident – it was an attempted murder. I think Sir Hilary had an idea why Hardcastle wanted to kill him and I am sure that Sir Hilary would not have wanted any adverse publicity to interfere with his own purpose in the valley. Had he reported what had actually happened, it would have appeared as a highly suspicious accident. Sir Hilary reacted as I would have expected him to. He was, in his own way, as dispassionate a character as Oliver Hardcastle was – but where Hardcastle took himself seriously Sir Hilary took nothing seriously. He would, I am sure, have seen no reason to make a fuss *and no reason either to discredit Hardcastle now that he was dead*. As far as he was concerned, Hardcastle had got his just deserts. Having ascertained that the man was indeed dead he would have left things as they were – an accident to be discovered all in good time, as accidents usually are. He did not know, of course, that his wife had seen him and would do all she could to protect him.'

Browning looked at Donaghue enquiringly, a puzzled expression on his face.

'But what has all this to do with my future work?'

Donaghue smiled. 'It is inextricably linked,' he said. 'I think that if Hardcastle had not died Sir Hilary would have pronounced the drawings fakes.'

'Why on earth do you say that?' asked Dr Vincente.

'Let me explain,' said Donaghue. 'I have a theory about the drawings that is, I must admit, based only on conjecture. My theory is this: I believe Sir Hilary faked the drawings himself with the intention of perpetrating on the dull academic world of palaeography a huge practical joke. His plan was thwarted by Oliver Hardcastle's inadvertent discovery of the drawings. Sir Hilary had planned to "discover" the drawings himself. I believe he came to the valley with the express plan of denying their authenticity. He had no desire to see an arrogant upstart like Oliver Hardcastle steal his thunder. While alone at the tor he faked a further series of drawings, adding a circle to a figure on the rock and a further inscription in tiny symbols close to the lakeside. These obvious fakes would confirm the falseness of the others. He would say that the execution was the same and that therefore all were fake. I can imagine him chuckling as he engraved the circle next to a figure with outstretched arms – to give the perfect image of a goalkeeper saving a goal! Sir Hilary has, in his retirement, become passionate about the game of football.

'When Hardcastle accidentally died he found himself unexpectedly in his original position. He denounced the circle as a prank, assumed that nobody would find the tiny inscription by the lake and declared the drawings authentic. His practical joke could still stand. The world would believe that the drawings were genuine and the inscription would give rise to a phenomenal debate. Researchers like you, Browning, would spend years investigating its meaning.'

'And the joke?' asked Browning glumly.

'The joke, I believe, will be that in, perhaps, a year or two from now Sir Hilary will announce to the world that it had been tricked and that he had faked the engravings. The true significance of the mysterious inscription will then be revealed. And I have a shrewd idea what that significance will be.'

Dr Vincente and Herman Browning regarded Donaghue with great gravity.

'Well, sir,' said Browning finally, 'what can I say? The idea's fantastic but, as you say, it is based on conjecture. How am I to know that it is all no more than a figment of your fertile imagination?'

'One small thing confirmed my idea. When I asked her about it the guide, Laura Hutchinson, knew nothing about the tiny inscription on the rocks by the lakeside. Sir Hilary had lied to me when he said that their presence was common knowledge. But,' said Donaghue resignedly, 'it's true – one cannot be certain. I can only ask you to give me the benefit of the doubt and wait before you start your research.'

He picked up one of the sheets of notepaper. 'But first let me remind you of the last symbol of the inscription.'

He sketched the last, unknown symbol, the open square:

'Wouldn't you say that it looks remarkably like a goalpost?' he said. 'I think you will find, when Sir Hilary finally reveals the truth, that the message pertains to the game of football.'

Browning smiled rather wryly at Donaghue.

'You've just shattered all my hopes for a pleasant few years' research, with Bridget here popping over every now and again to help me.'

He turned to Bridget, whose face registered an almost equal degree of disappointment. 'If your employer is proved wrong – which I know from what you've told me rarely happens – will you come over from time to time to work with me?'

'Of course I will,' said Bridget affectionately. 'Of course I will, Herman.'

27

In the first-class cabin of the trans-Channel aircraft a stewardess served Sir Hilary and Lady Compton with a refreshing glass of champagne. She glanced curiously at his brilliantly coloured T-shirt with its strange abstract markings, then at the very similar symbols on the notebook that lay on his lap.

'Are those prehistoric drawings, sir?' she asked pleasantly.

'Not at all, my dear,' replied Sir Hilary in amusement. He chuckled to himself. 'You could call them contemporary graffiti, I suppose.'

He sipped the excellent champagne and began writing under the symbols. The stewardess refilled his glass then left the couple, thinking that it took all sorts to make a world.

Sir Hilary finished writing, then handed the notebook over to his wife.

'I've just been working out an interpretation for the inscription,' he said. 'What do you think, Bea?'

Beatrice regarded what her husband had written with mild apprehension. She was suspicious now of everything he did and said.

$$\Diamond \, \mathbb{A} \, \Diamond \, \ast \qquad \text{Ч} \, \mathbb{A} \, \Diamond \ast \qquad \sqrt{\mathbb{A}} \, \sqcap \ast$$

From the mouth of man comes the vision of God.
From the hand of man comes the word of God.
From the foot of man comes the goal of God!

She looked up at her husband, a glint of extreme suspicion in her eye.

'Hilary,' she said. 'Hilary . . . is this some kind of joke?'

'Yes,' he said, chuckling. 'Yes, Beatrice, that's exactly what it is – a joke!'

He laughed heartily, great loud booms of laughter. Every head in the cabin turned towards him.

The ancient 2CV that Donaghue and Bridget had hired in Nice and left at the bottom of the mountain failed to start so they were forced to accept Clothilde's offer of a lift to the airport in her Ferrari.

Bridget, as terrified by high-speed vehicles as her employer, sat apprehensively on the narrow back seat that had, it seemed, been designed for children or adults under four feet in height. She curled up her long legs and hugged her knees nervously.

'Really, you two,' grumbled Clothilde. 'You should have been born in the nineteenth century. Travelling at speed is no more dangerous than any other activity that doesn't involve absolute immobility. All modern cars above a certain price range are equipped front and rear with air bags that expand on the slightest impact. There is absolutely no risk of either of you being impaled on anything sharp or metallic.'

'They've got it the wrong way round,' said Donaghue grumpily. 'One should drive with exactly that – the risk of being impaled on something sharp and metallic. If I had my way every car built would be equipped with a sharp spike just here . . .' He indicated a spot on the windscreen approximately level with Clothilde's forehead. 'It would project to within five centimetres of the head. You'd see – there would be *no* high-speed impacts, let alone safer ones.'

Clothilde chuckled with merriment as Donaghue clicked his seat belt shut and the car leapt off, apparently, it seemed to him, without any contact between wheels and road. He resorted to the childhood haven that he had always resorted to in moments of fear, and prayed.

'You have the strangest ideas, Ulysses,' Clothilde said, patting his knee. 'The strangest ideas.'

POSTSCRIPT

A year later. Extract from The Palaeographical Gazette.
Report by Jim Baxter.

One year after the late Oliver Hardcastle's discovery of Bronze Age engravings in the Vallée des Prêtres on the Franco-Italian border, the academic world has been rocked by an announcement by Sir Hilary Compton, the celebrated archaeologist who had confirmed the authenticity of the drawings, that he himself had faked them along with their accompanying inscription.

The enigmatic inscription which has aroused intense debate and research during the year since its discovery proves to be nothing more than a cryptic 'play on symbols' with a facetious reference at the end to the game of football!

Sir Hilary, it seems, has played a huge, rather schoolboyish joke on the academic world from which he retired only a few years ago.

Sir Hilary's only comment was, 'We take ourselves and our so-called erudition rather too seriously.'

There are some in the academic world who might agree with him!

....

....

....

———

West Bend Community Memorial Library
West Bend, Wisconsin 53095

DEMCO